A KNIGHT THERE WAS

A KNIGHT THERE WAS

THE KNIGHTS OF ENGLAND SERIES, BOOK TWO

MARY ELLEN JOHNSON

Book and cover design by eBook Prep

www.ebookprep.com

February 2020

ISBN: 978-1-64457-018-0

ePublishing Works!
644 Shrewsbury Commons Ave
Ste 249
Shrewsbury PA 17361
United States of America

www.epublishingworks.com

Phone: 866-846-5123

FOREWORD

In *The Lion and The Leopard*, the first in my five part *Knights of England* series, I introduced readers to Maria Rendell, she of the tragically romantic or romantically tragic nature, and the Rendell family. I also shared my version of the doomed reign of Edward II.

In *A Knight There Was*, we meet Margery Watson, illegitimate daughter of Maria Rendell's son and a peasant woman. Caught between two worlds, that of the nobility and that of the commoner, Margery falls in love with someone who is antithetical to everything she believes in—a callow, naïve and endearing (at least to me) knight named Matthew Hart.

In the age of that most magnificent of medieval kings, Edward III, England is at the height of her power. Edward III, likened to a second Arthur, is a warrior king (the very opposite of his unfortunate father, Edward II) and well beloved. He and his son, the Black Prince, preside over a series of stunning wins against France in the beginnings of what history refers to as The Hundred Years' War.

But this is also the time of the Black Death, which plants the seeds for the Peasant's Revolt of 1381 (detailed in Book Four, *A Child Upon the Throne*).

Some notes about the real characters you will meet in *A Knight*

There Was. Edward of Woodstock, our fabled Black Prince, was never called The Black Prince until many years after his death. But since Edward is universally known by that moniker—and there are so darned many Edwards floating about—it made sense to differentiate him thus. Neither was his wife, Joan, contemporaneously referred to as "the Fair Maid of Kent," though all agreed she was a beautiful woman. I very much admire Edward III, the king who lived too long, and of course his fabled sons, the Black Prince and John of Gaunt. As ever, I am protective of them and mislike some less flattering portrayals. We all have access to the same facts; we just interpret them differently.

I know I've inadvertently made mistakes in my historical research, which will be pointed out by sharp-eyed readers, but there are times I deliberately stretched boundaries. For example the oldest reference to a *danse macabre* fresco is some fifty years after the rebel, Thurold Watson, mentions it (*Within a Forest Dark*, Book Three). However, given the number of churches that have been obliterated in the last six hundred plus years, frescoes whitewashed away, and the psychic wound of the Black Death upon the European populace from 1348 onward, I'm comfortable with my educated guess.

Having said that, I hope you enjoy *A Knight There Was* and will follow Margery, Matthew, her step-brother, Thurold, the Mad Priest John Ball, and all the rest to the end of my *Knights of England* series.

Mary Ellen Johnson

A KNIGHT THERE WAS, and what a gentleman,
  Who, from the moment that he first began
  To ride about the world, loved honor, chivalry,
  The spirit of giving, truth and courtesy.
  He was a valiant warrior for his lord...

— ~GEOFFREY CHAUCER, *THE CANTERBURY TALES*, THE KNIGHT

PROLOGUE

*S*ome called him Pestilence, others called him Second Coming, but Death was his name.

Across the steppes of China he crept, through ancient palaces and peasants' hovels, aboard caravans bound for ports in the Tatar region —cities like Baghdad and Constantinople.

When sailors loaded silks and spices aboard their ships, Death stowed away. South, along the Bay of Bengal, he sailed toward India.

His arrival was heralded by frogs, serpents, and lizards which rained from the sky, congruent with thunder, lightning and sheets of fire. Wrapped in a heavy stinking smoke, Death himself descended, and Indians died by the thousands.

Donning a sorcerer's cap, he caused mountains to vanish and, in their place, lakes to rise. The earth fissured, then spewed forth blood or balls of fire. Skies exploded with comets. In Venice the bells of St. Mark's rang by his hand and Plague Maidens rode the whirlwind.

At sunset Death fashioned a pillar of fire above the Palace of the Popes in Avignon. There, people died in such numbers that Pope Clement blessed the River Rhone and allowed corpses to be dumped in waters which soon turned red with blood.

Death passed through Greece and Italy in the guise of a miasma so noxious it caused wine to spoil, crops to wilt and fruit to rot. The sun was obliterated, as were the moon and stars, and only a gray creeping fog showed on the horizon.

Again taking to the sea, Death sailed for Venice and Genoa, where he was driven off by volleys of burning arrows. Thwarted, he turned against those on shipboard. Like a prostitute plying her trade, he lay with each sailor, cabin boy and captain. Soon galleys, manned by spectral crews, haunted the European shorelines, wandering hither and yon at the whim of the changing tides.

Pausing at Calais, Death gazed across the Channel toward England. England, arrogant and seemingly invincible, as sweet to look upon as Satan before his fall. England, protected by turbulent waters and sweeping winds. Proud, impregnable England, with her white cliffs and prosperous towns, sharp-eyed yeomen and bright-cheeked maids.

On the Feast of St. Peter ad Vincula, Death docked at the port of Melcombe, and it soon became apparent that the English would succumb as easily as the Chinese, Italians and French—as easily as any man. Through Southampton, Dorset, Bristol, Devon, Somerset and other sea counties, Death passed, smiting all he touched. Bells tolled ceaselessly and graveyards became so full that bell-ringers had to dump the overflow in communal pits.

Rather than administer last rites, priests fled for the countryside, as did every city dweller strong enough to travel. Aristocratic ladies, seated inside swaying coaches, shared the roads with merchants, knights on palfreys, villeins carrying their babes in panniers slung across their backs—and Death.

On All Saints Day, 1348, Death reached London.

With nearly seventy thousand people, London's crowded conditions made it as vulnerable as rotten fruit clinging to a branch. Death shook the tree and London fell. People began to die. Scattered cases were reported among the whores of Southwark, the criminals in Newgate, the skinners along Peltry Street, and the grocers and apothecaries of Bucklersbury.

Citing the increase in plague, King Edward III prorogued parliament and soon the nobility began deserting London.

But not soon enough.

CHAPTER 1

London, 1349

A dense mantle of fog hung over London as Matthew Hart and his family made their way along Fleet Street.

Matthew eyed his mother, who rode several yards ahead, her scarlet cloak spilling over her palfrey's rump like a pool of blood.

Nay, not blood, Matthew corrected himself. *'Tis simply a red cloth.*

But logic did little to soothe his anxiety. He peered off to his right, where the sprawling Convent of White Friars struggled through the mist. The convent, which housed the royal and ecclesiastical councils, was normally overflowing with clerks and petitioners and His Grace's retainers. This morning, however, a single Carmelite, pulling his cowl closer around his face as if it might somehow protect him from contamination, scurried, crab-like, past the limestone cloisters.

Matthew found the stillness even more discomforting than the lack of people. London usually reverberated with ringing church bells and mongers hawking their second-hand clothing. Merchants begged business from their stalls; vendors peddled their homemade medicines, soaps, perfumes, nuts, quinces and pears. But not today.

Today Matthew heard the jangling of bridle bits, the sucking of horses' hooves in the spongy dirt, and the ragged breath of his nine-year-old brother. He shot a quick glance at Harry, whose face appeared shrunken and pinched as a monkey's.

Matthew silently cursed his mother's incessant piety. If Sosanna had not insisted on worshipping one last time at the tombs of Thomas Becket's parents, the Harts would already be headed north for his sister's wedding. In a kingdom that possessed nearly as many churches and relics as it contained sheaves of grain, why must his mother obsess upon one particular shrine?

"Matt? Matt, I…"

Harry's unnaturally wide blue eyes, focused on Matthew, added to his stricken expression. He licked his lips as if trying to speak, but no further sound emerged.

"Do not look so timid." With a quick jerk of his thumb, Matthew gestured toward William Hart, riding so tall and straight and commanding, alongside their mother. "With Father protecting us, we have naught to fear."

Which was true enough. From earliest memory, Matthew had always likened their father to a lion: watchful, dangerous and proud. Should Death himself spring from the mist, William would glower fiercely and Death would slink away.

Harry's mouth gaped open and he looked at Matthew, his expression pleading. If William could be likened to a lion, Harry, God protect him, was more reminiscent of the delicate hart that graced the family crest. Or right now, a feeding fish.

"We'll soon be finished at St. Paul's," Matthew said. "Just cease worrying and everything will be fine."

Nay, it will not, Harry countered, though he didn't dare express his feelings until he was sure their father wasn't eavesdropping. William Hart's back had been straight as a sword blade, but now he swiveled in his saddle and said something to his wife.

Good, Harry thought with relief. *If they are talking to each other, they'll not be looking to me. Unless, of course, Father is telling Mother what a mewling pup she has for a son.* He shifted his reins from one hand to the other and repeatedly wiped his sweaty palms on his tunic.

Or that I'm a useless piece of baggage and Matt is worth a hundred of me.

"God's bones, brother, do not roll your eyes so. Someone will mistake you for a dullard."

"I do not like this weather, Matt. Don't you wish we were already with Elizabeth and her fiancé? Edmundsbury's walls are very stout, are they not? Nothing could penetrate them."

Matthew stifled a sigh. He knew full well that Harry was referring to the plague, since his every conversation inevitably came round to that subject. Pretending to misunderstand, he said, "London's weather is always miserable in winter."

"But 'tis mid-March, and yet everything still looks..." Harry's voice trailed away. It was so difficult to give utterance to the thoughts that clouded his head—thoughts all connected with his nightmares, the reason why he had spent these past weeks on his knees to Saints Sebastian, Giles, Christopher and Adrian.

He tried again. "I am just so...everything smells so..."

Harry silently implored Matt to understand, so he wouldn't have to vocalize some form of that awful word—Plague, Pestilence, Death. Ever since its arrival, Harry had locked away all relevant scraps of information, hoping to later discuss them with his older brother. Matthew was so good at turning aside his fears with a laugh or a shrug or a comforting explanation, yet when Harry attempted to communicate his racing thoughts, sometimes his tongue seemed to thicken in his mouth, leaving him mute. At those times he was left alone with his imagination, which conjured up such frightful possibilities that his entire body would tremble as if suffering from St. Vitus' dance.

"...Odors from Fleet Prison and the tanneries and the latrines," Matthew was explaining. "They dump their waste into the city ditch. It makes the air noxious, but 'tis not harmful."

"I do not care about the air. I care about what is *in* the air."

"There is naught in it at all!" Matthew knew he sounded snappish, but he hoped to end the matter. Once Harry launched into the Death, there would be no surcease. First Harry would detail each one of the plague's symptoms. Then he would report, as if nobody save himself

7

knew, that the plague preferred women and children to men. Then he would elaborate upon its origins. It had started, Harry would say, when the sun went to war with the Indian Ocean and had drawn up all the sea water in a vapor befouled by millions of dead fish. It was this vapor that was currently drifting across the world, destroying everything in its wake.

Learned men asserted otherwise, that the pestilence had been caused by earthquakes that had vomited forth corpses and fiery rains. Matthew didn't know which theory was correct; nor did he care. So long as the pestilence left him and his loved ones alone, why clutter one's mind with useless speculation?

"I feel poor." Harry pressed his hand against his stomach. "'Tis a peculiar sensation." The fog seemed to push against him like an enormous smothering coverlet and the scenery swam before his vision.

Matthew rolled his eyes. Harry had complained of feeling peculiar since they'd first learned of the Death.

"Stick out your tongue," he commanded. A swollen, furry tongue was one of the first plague symptoms. Harry's looked the same it had last hour and yestermorn and last week, though one could never be too careful.

"There is naught wrong with you. Now stop your mewling before Father hears you."

But Harry, certain he was about to faint, gulped mouthfuls of sodden air. Then he noticed a donkey sprawled alongside the road with maggots, white like plague boils, feeding upon its belly. Something between a cough and a gag scratched at his throat.

Matthew threw him a disgusted glare, kicked his horse, and bolted ahead.

Even Matt has forsaken me. Harry blinked back hot tears. *No one loves me. No one cares if I live or die. Because I am a coward and a nuisance.*

He raised his eyes to the squat structure of Fleet Prison, located directly inside the city gates. The Fleet was a brutal, forbidding place. It reminded Harry of William. *What sort of building would Matt be? A castle, surely, and Mother would be a pretty cottage. And Elizabeth*

8

would be something out of one of her romances. A round table, mayhap. He suppressed a nervous giggle. *What would I be?*

They neared Ludgate, where beggars huddled beneath the painted statues flanking the entrance. Usually the beggars scrabbled and cried for alms, but today they appeared nearly as lifeless as the piles of waste flanking the road. One ragged figure, wearing the shroud of a leper, staggered to his feet and tottered forward, clacking a pair of castanets.

Harry's glance skittered to the man's right cheek, which was rotted away. He did indeed look like a leper, but perhaps this was merely a new plague symptom. Perhaps the pestilence rotted people before it killed them. Harry's hand crept over his heart until he encountered his Agathes, a special plague-preventing stone which had been sewn to his tunic.

The leper held out his begging bowl.

"Off with you!" barked William Hart.

The leper made a garbled sound and slunk back to his companions.

Not a plague monster at all, just one of God's poor children.

Fingering the smooth black-veined surface of his Agathes, Harry's anxiety faded. Didn't he have a bevy of saints protecting him? And hadn't Mother plied the whole family with protective potions that contained everything from irises to the bark of an oak tree?

By the time they reached Bowyers Row, the fog had descended to the tile roofs and clay chimney pots. Everything was gray and bleak and desolate, exactly the way Harry pictured purgatory. Only in purgatory the wisps of fog would be souls, drifting around until those on earth prayed them up to heaven.

But purgatory would never smell so incredibly foul.

The lane upon which they traveled was fetlock deep with food leavings and the overflow from chamber pots. Yet a noxious odor was also a symptom of plague, Harry reminded himself, his precarious sense of security evaporating. He pinched his nostrils, fearful that even now he was inhaling the sickness.

I am going to die.

Then he would be faced with Judgment Day. St. Michael the Archangel would be awaiting him, holding out the scales of justice. As would Lucifer, who would be weighting down his bowl of sins in order to tip the balance in favor of damnation. But Harry dreaded meeting God, who he always pictured as a larger version of William, even more than he dreaded meeting Satan. Aye, Harry knew without a doubt that he was doomed.

Gripping the bridle reins so tightly his nails dug into his palms, he told himself and any saints who might be listening that he simply could not die now. He wasn't ready. When they reached St. Paul's, he could hide in one of the chantries. Surely the plague wouldn't follow him onto sacred ground.

Yet he had heard rumors of entire congregations being felled in the midst of hearing mass.

St. Paul's Jesus Bells boomed. Harry nearly plummeted from his saddle. Even Matthew jumped.

"St. Valentine protect me," Harry squeaked, crossing himself.

Matt laughed to cover his own nervousness. "'Tis only the bell ringers announcing tierce." Leaning forward, he patted the neck of his palfrey, as if *he* had been the startled one.

Moments later they reached Carter Lane, which adjoined the cathedral precincts. Save for a scattering of abandoned vegetable carts and the black rats whose carcasses bloated beside the dung and lay stalls, the area was vacant. After dismounting, William turned to Sosanna, wrapped his arms around her waist and helped her dismount. Matthew did the same for Harry. As they entered the courtyard, Harry slipped his hand through Matthew's.

William glanced over his shoulder and his rugged features hardened. "Stand tall, Harry. Quit clinging to your brother. If you canna show more spine, I'll pack you off to a monastery where cowardliness is considered an asset."

Harry dropped Matthew's hand.

As soon as their father's back was turned, Matt whispered, "He did not mean it about the monastery," and touched his brother's arm in a comforting gesture.

They entered the churchyard proper where a group of perhaps

thirty men and woman, naked save for a linen sheet encircling each waist, shuffled round Paul's Cross.

"By the rood," Matthew breathed, watching them. He had heard of saints like Thomas Becket, who wore hair shirts beneath their clothes, and others who denied their bodies all material comfort. He had seen knights missing an arm or a leg or an eye, and pilgrims who were afflicted with wasting diseases or stomach-turning skin rots. But never had he seen anything like these strangers circling the cross. Their torsos were a mass of pus-ridden lesions and raw, ribbon-like wounds; their bodies so swollen and discolored that, save for the length of their hair, 'twould be impossible to determine their sex.

"Have you ever...I cannot...dreadful." Harry clutched at his stomach, then doubled over and vomited upon the paving stones.

Matthew wanted to cover his ears and eyes, but he merely stepped in front of Harry in order to protect him from their father's gaze. "Hurry," he urged, reluctant to get too far away from William's protective presence.

Harry moaned and shook his head.

Matthew grabbed his arm and dragged him after their parents, who had reached the outskirts of a small crowd.

"Who are those people?" William Hart asked one of the spectators. His arm was wrapped around his wife, who looked little bigger than a child next to him.

"Brethren of the Cross, m'lord. Here to stop the plague."

"The Flagellants?"

The man nodded.

Harry wiped his mouth with the hem of his tunic. "What are flagellants?" he whispered.

"Some sort of peculiar sect," replied Matthew. "They are convinced that only they can avert the end of the world. Europe is aswarm with them. Some say they can heal the sick, drive out devils, and raise the dead, but Prince Edward says they belong at St. Bartholomew's with the rest of the madmen."

While Harry digested this latest disturbing piece of information, his hand returned to his protective stone. He wished he had worn a whole casket full of amulets. Or at the very least, an Opthithalminus, which had the power to render its wearer invisible. "You do not believe they are right about the end of the world, do you?"

Matthew was beginning to believe anything was possible but he merely shook his head before squeezing next to William.

A trio of men had gathered in the middle of the flagellants. At a signal from one, the others began to chant. The mournful sound shivered through Matthew's soul. He turned toward his father to gauge his reaction, but William's face betrayed nothing—and Matthew knew why.

An ancient memory stirred. He was five, chasing after his leather football, which had taken an unexpected detour into the family chapel. Spotting the ball near the altar, he had scurried over to pick it up, only to be confronted by a hideous creature, dark as a shadow and no more than two feet tall, with a face resembling a gargoyle's. As Matthew stared at the creature, its lips drew back in a hideous grin.

Matthew had run screaming from the nave, but when he howled his terror to his father, William would have none of it. "Most likely 'twas a strange play of light. Or perhaps a church grim, for they sometimes live in bell towers. But whatever it was, we shall go back and face it square."

They had searched the entire chapel and found nary a trace of anything untoward, let alone monstrous. Hunkering in front of Matthew, William had tilted his son's chin so that their eyes were on the same level. "Throughout your life you will encounter things that will frighten you. But a true knight never shows fear. And he never runs. Understand?"

Now, watching his father's expressionless face, Matthew did indeed understand. William might be angry or experiencing the same anxiety as his sons, but no one would ever guess. *That is what it means to be a knight,* Matthew told himself. If one must experience fear, he must also adopt a courageous facade as an example to others. If one could act the part long enough, someday he would come to believe it. As William obviously had. As Matthew would.

Inside the circle, the Master Brethren had retrieved an iron-tipped scourge from a large pile. When he raised his arms over his head the other flagellants dropped to the ground and lay with their arms outstretched in the shape of a cross. The Master walked among them, the thongs of his scourge flicking like a viper's tongue. Some flagellants moaned while others quivered or rolled around, waving their arms and legs.

After the Master had finished, the Brethren struggled up from the paving stones. Arming themselves individually with scourges, they began beating their own backs.

Horrified, Matthew watched iron knots rip into the Brethrens' ravaged bodies. Pus and bits of flesh exploded outward. Blood splashed upon the steps of Paul's Cross and its carved walls, upon the paving stones, upon the faces of the bystanders.

Matthew's breath came in hot gasps. Every fiber of his being screamed for him to flee, but he did not. On the battlefield he would see far more blood and carnage. He would have to chop off arms and legs, even heads, without a qualm. He was twelve years old and a page in the household of Edward the Black Prince. He was not allowed to be afraid. He would *not* be afraid.

The Master climbed to Paul's Pulpit. "Almighty God, have mercy on us, your sinful children!" he shouted. "Repent and turn to the Lord, for our time be short!" He raised his arms as if to embrace the mist slipping from the clouds.

Hearing a sob, Matthew looked over at Harry, who had stuffed a fistful of knuckles into his mouth.

"There is no need to fear the Brethren," Matthew soothed. "They canna harm us. 'Tis just something to watch, like a juggling act or a puppet show."

The scourging reached a frenetic crescendo. Some Londoners groaned and cried in sympathy. Others trembled or hid their eyes. The mist increased to a drizzle, sweeping onto upturned faces. One woman fell to the stones in a fit. Another ran to the blood brightening the steps of Paul's Cross, wiped it up and applied it to her sores.

Abruptly, the crowd parted, making way for a man carrying a young girl. The man placed his daughter atop the flagellants' pile of discarded white and red robes. Her face was covered with black spots; a trail of blood snaked from her open mouth. Beneath her armpits nested a cluster of buboes.

"Plague!" Sosanna Hart shouted, pointing.

Harry screamed and collapsed against Matthew's chest.

William wheeled about, pushing his wife before him. Sweeping an arm around each of his sons, he raced toward the courtyard and the waiting horses. Others ran past, echoing Sosanna's cry.

Releasing Matthew and Harry, William lifted Sosanna onto her mare, then vaulted into his own saddle. Despite his trembling legs, Matthew also managed to seat himself. But Harry merely clutched one of his jennet's stirrups, and sobbed helplessly against its barrel. In passing, William hooked his youngest son around the waist and deposited him atop his mount.

Matthew followed their parents out of Carter's Lane. "Make haste," he urged Harry, who lagged behind.

"Wait," Harry wailed. "Matt, wait for me."

But Matthew pretended not to hear. A knight must be prudent as well as brave.

The family reached Aldergate without further incident, and by the time he had passed through the city, Matthew's natural confidence had returned. Now that he was headed to Edmundsbury Castle, he had naught to fear. In his latest dispatch, Matthew's soon-to-be brother-in-law, Lawrence Ravenne, had written that East Anglia was one of the safest places in all of England.

And so the Hart family retreated from one danger and rode directly toward another.

CHAPTER 2

East Anglia

Margery Watson awakened with an enormous yawn. Overhead, drying strips of eel stretched across the wooden platforms. Beside her, three-year-old Giddy stirred and sighed before settling deeper into the coverlet of dogswain. Usually her half-sister thrashed in every direction, but now she pressed against Margery's back.

If I move, Giddy might wake and cry. Sometimes she wished God had never sent her a little sister, especially one so whiny and bothersome. *Whitefoot is far more agreeable.*

Honker strutted through the front door of the Watson cottage, trailed by her goslings. Even that cantankerous old goose had been blessed with a sweeter nature than Giddy's. Margery tried to ignore her half-sister's breath, blowing hot and cold against her spine. Snail-like, she edged away.

The sounds of an awakening Ravennesfield drifted in from the open window. Cocks crowed, Whitefoot barked, shutters slammed, a swinegelder blasted his horn. Margery had heard similar sounds every day of her nine years. They made her feel safe, and nearly as happy as when her mother, Alice, held her and stroked her hair. Which was not at all the way she felt when Lord Lawrence Ravenne intruded upon them. She hoped their lord would soon leave Ravenne Manor, never to return. But he might stay a long time, because of the Terrible Thing. Margery wasn't certain what the Terrible Thing was, since grown-ups always lowered their voices whenever she or the other children came near.

Margery watched her mother arrange turves inside the hearthstone. As she struck flint against steel to start the fire, Alice sang a familiar lullaby. Listening, Margery felt even better than when she contemplated their new cottage, which was the finest in all of Ravennesfield, and topped with real wooden shingles. Before, rain would work through the thatch and stream down the walls, making such a mess that Alice would spend days cleaning.

Happily, her mother no longer had to fret over leaking roofs. *Because of me,* Margery thought. *Because of my father. My* real *father.* She mouthed his name. Thomas Rendell. Lord Thomas Rendell. It was lofty sounding, with none of the coarseness of the names she usually heard—Alf Watson, Will Brakest, John Bune. And while Lord Rendell oft seemed as unapproachable as his title, Margery had to admit he was always nice to her. Thomas had given Alice the silver coins she kept hidden in the storeroom loft—coins that had built their cottage and provided their cow, Crop Tail. They had also bought Margery's soft feather mattresses and all the other amenities that Father Egbert said caused Alice to commit the sin of pride.

"Good morrow, Stick-Legs."

Thurold Watson plopped down upon the scarred clothing chest at the foot of the bed and put on his knobbed shoes. Her stepbrother was much nicer than Giddy. Thurold never tattled, and he only complained about their lords—never her. While at thirteen years of age he liked to pretend that he was fully grown, he could still be persuaded to play Hide-the-Thimble or Hoodman's Blind. Thurold's mind was as quick as his manner of moving and talking, though Father Egbert, who'd taught him and a handful of other village boys the rudiments of reading and writing, lamented that a passable mind should not be cluttered with heretical thoughts. Whatever that meant.

"Come along, boy," Alf Watson called. "We've the harrowing to do, and ye be slower than a cart bogged in mud."

Rising from the chest, Thurold shrugged his thin shoulders into his old coat of cary cloth. "I can work ye into the earth, old man," he muttered, but Alf didn't hear, and the tension Margery often felt around Thurold and Alf evaporated. When they two argued, her belly would churn and her head would pound, though she couldn't blame Thurold for snapping at Alf, who, was a man of few words—a few sullen, sarcastic words.

Thurold swiveled to face her. "Time to get up, Stick-Legs. Alice says ye've dyeing to do."

Margery rolled off the mattresses onto her feet and stumbled across the floor into her mother's outstretched arms.

Alice kissed the crown of Margery's tousled head. "Good morrow, angel."

Seated at the trestle table, Alf grunted his disapproval. When he was drunk, he sometimes taunted Margery for being spoiled and worthless and presuming high above her station, another puzzling turn of phrase.

Since Alf's opinion was of no importance, Margery ignored him. He was merely a husband-of-convenience, after all. Alice had married Alf Watson four summers past, after his entire family—save for him and Thurold—had perished during an outbreak of the scarlet sickness. Thurold said the disease caused those afflicted to burn with a heat as fierce as the flames of hell. Margery often thought about hell and wondered how painful it would feel when flames licked at her body for all eternity. She imagined horrible welts popping out on her skin and her hair blazing like a torch. She did not want to go to hell, which was too bad, because Father Egbert warned that most everyone was going to end up there.

"Is it not time ye be about the milkin', girl?" Alf mumbled through a mouthful of buttered black bread. "The sun be already 'alfway cross the sky."

Margery made a face against the folds of Alice's gown.

Alf tossed the dregs from his ale into the fire, retrieved his wide-brimmed hat from a peg, and stalked out the door, followed by Thurold.

Once they were alone, Margery washed and dressed and sat down on a stool so Alice could comb her hair. She looked forward to this moment, when Giddy was still asleep and the others had left the cottage. Sometimes her mother schooled her on her grammar, which she said must match Margery's favored position in life. Sometimes Alice discussed plant lore, including wondrous techniques such as drawing down the moon in order to charge seedlings with its special power. Sometimes she explained how to keep creatures from the other world at bay, creatures such as Night-Elves which caused nightmares by riding their victims like mares, and which could be thwarted by hanging verbena or St. John's wort throughout the cottage.

And sometimes Alice talked about Thomas Rendell. A powerful lord far to the south, whose family was famous for, among things that Alice did not elaborate upon, an event called the Cherry Fair. While her mother was not sure she'd ever even seen an actual cherry tree, she still described it and the legendary fair in great, if inaccurate, detail.

Today, easing a comb through Margery's chestnut-colored tangles, she said, "Your father has such grand hair."

People oft remarked on Alice's own flaxen mane, which when braided fell thick as a man's arm to her waist. Unlike the other village women, she seldom covered her head.

"Father's hair is black, is it not?" Margery asked, knowing full well it was.

"Sometimes it looks black and sometimes more the deepest brown. And 'tis so thick. And soft as down, just like yours."

Margery was pleased at the lilt that warmed her mother's voice. Yet when she herself dwelt upon her father, she felt more confused than happy. She saw Lord Thomas Rendell yearly at Sturbridge Fair, and he seemed a kind man. But like all members of the nobility, he was as alien as the will-o'-the-wisps inhabiting East Anglia's marshes. In his presence, Margery would think how different he smelled and how odd his voice—soft and quick like stream water racing over rocks. And Thomas Rendell was tall, not stooped and stocky and weathered like the men she daily saw.

He was also a knight.

Margery was *very* confused about knights. Thurold held them responsible for all the world's ills, but Father Egbert said they must be respected since they defended Englishmen and women from the French.

Knights also played a very loud game called "tournament."

The tournament Margery had attended last spring at Edmundsbury Castle had been more frightening than the earthquake which had shaken the ground at Michaelmas. The lists had been filled with monsters, and the jousting had been noisy and bloody. Father Egbert might liken knights to St. George the Dragonslayer but they seemed more akin to the Terrible Thing.

"Tell me how you and Father met at Sturbridge Fair," Margery urged her mother, as Alice plaited her hair. Margery knew the story of her parents' introduction by heart, but Alice enjoyed the re-telling. The basic facts were simple enough. Thomas Rendell's family lived days away, near Thomas Becket's shrine in a place called Canterbury, but Sturbridge Fair attracted visitors from across the kingdom. Silks from Italy, iron from Spain and timber from the Baltic all found their way to Cambridge and the fair. During the fall of 1338, Thomas Rendell had found his way there, too, and Margery had been the result.

By the time Alice finished her task, the bells of St. George's Chapel had begun tolling prime and Giddy was stirring.

"The milking awaits, angel. Mayhap this afternoon, after we've finished the dyeing, I will show you how to cast a love spell. Someday, when you be grown, you might have need of one."

Margery had no use for either boys or such spells, but to please her mother she nodded and smiled, as if nothing in all the world would please her more.

ALICE FED a length of newly woven wool into a cauldron of purple water. Margery hated dyeing. The wet wool was heavy and stank while the blueberry dye stained her hands and gown. Besides, the final product was so mottled it hardly seemed worth the trouble. The one thing Margery envied her lords was the vivid, crisp shades of their clothing. When they congregated together, they reminded her of brightly-plumaged birds.

"Take Godiva and wait for me at the river," said Alice, reaching for a long pole to stir the fabric.

Giddy shook her copper-colored curls, so Margery grabbed her arm, pulled her out the door, and dragged her past the family garden, which had sprouted feeble-looking cabbages, onions and garlic. Ignoring her half-sister's wails, she hauled her through the apple orchard, where the trees still bristled with spiky buds rather than blossoms.

Margery's stomach began to feel the same way it did when Alf and Thurold quarreled. Something wasn't right. She felt it at some primal level. *'Tis the rain. It has ruined everything.*

Her gaze swept the horizon, where only Ely Cathedral's distant spire thrust above the surrounding pastureland. Father Egbert said that because of its flatness, East Anglia possessed the widest expanse of sky in England. Once the sky had changed colors but now it was always gray, scarred by yellow-edged clouds. And the air felt thick with gathering rain; a harsh rain that would neither freshen the earth nor brighten the sky.

Margery scowled. It seemed such a long time since the sun had dazzled and warmed her, or since she'd heard birds sing. Father Egbert preached that nature was misbehaving throughout England, that a wrathful God was sending winds and storms. And unless man mended his sinful ways, harsher retribution was imminent. Was this the Terrible Thing? Margery couldn't be sure, but the prospect of an enraged God frightened her.

"Hurry," she said to Giddy, who was dawdling over a trio of pigs huddled in their sty.

Upon reaching the River Ouse, Margery handed her stepsister a stick. "Make pictures in the mud. See if you can draw the corn mill over there."

Giddy stuck out her lower lip. "No!"

"Then Whitefoot or Crop Tail. Just draw *something*. And stay away from the water."

Margery hunkered down among the corn cockles foaming along the river bank. When in full bloom they reminded her of bright purple clouds, but this morning the few with open blossoms looked dull and beaten, as did the river reeds.

Breaking off a reed, she stripped it and began plaiting the white pith beneath it. Giddy poked a dozing Whitefoot.

"Stop that!"

Giddy glared at her and whacked Whitefoot between his ears. Margery yanked away the stick and tossed it toward the sluggish current.

"Hate you!" Giddy yelled, collapsing against Whitefoot's ribs. The dog grunted before returning to his nap.

Margery removed her clogs and dipped her toes in the river. Upstream, ducks and swans circled the wheelrace below the corn mill. She could hear the faint creaking of the mill's gears. What was keeping her mother? By now they should be rinsing their length of cloth.

Giddy rose and tottered toward the water's edge. "Look," she said, pointing to a silver flash in its depths.

"'Tis a fish. Like what we ate yester eve."

Or it might be a River Woman. Alice said River Women were like mermaids, except mermaids were even more beautiful because of their hair, which changed from dark green to a blinding yellow in the sunlight.

Yellow hair like Mama's. Margery swiveled her head toward the cottage. Alice should have been here by now.

"Come along, pest. Let's see what's keeping Mama."

Giddy shook her head vigorously and stomped into the water.

"If you don't obey this very instant, I'll tell one of the dracs who live in the fens to snatch you from your bed. After he carries you off, he will eat you down to your toes. Then you'll wish you'd not been such a trial."

Subdued by her threat, Giddy docilely followed. But when they rounded the path to the front of the cottage and Margery saw the tethered black stallion, she immediately knew what had happened to Alice.

Lord Lawrence Ravenne.

Uncertain, Margery hesitated. She had naught to fear from Ravenne, for he always treated her well enough. In fact, he liked to pat her head, as if she were Whitefoot, and he gave Giddy all manner of cunningly constructed animals which he bragged that he himself had carved. Still, Margery hated him for one simple reason. Because Alice did.

Her mother was careful to hide her feelings, but when she returned from their rides she would be strangely quiet, or snap at Giddy, or hug Margery and cry into her hair. And Alice gave away or burned every one of Ravenne's presents, including the wooden geese, chickens, cows and dogs he fashioned for Giddy.

"In," Giddy said, pulling Margery toward the front door. Reluctantly, she allowed herself to be led. Once inside, her sister tottered over to Whitefoot, who had headed for his favorite spot beside the bed.

Spying Margery, Ravenne boomed, "Good morrow, little one!"

Margery winced, for his voice was as loud as St. George's bells. She curtsied before him. "Good morrow, m'lord."

He beckoned her forward; her stomach began to ache.

Lawrence Ravenne was of medium height, with piercing green eyes, flowing red hair and a beard to match. When Margery reached him, he patted her head and chuckled. Rather than look him in the eye, she focused on his beard.

The color of blood, she thought suddenly, suppressing a shiver. *Father has a neatly clipped beard, black as night. God be thanked you are not my father.*

Margery studied the thick cloud of steam rising from the bubbling cauldron to the cottage's smoke-blackened ceiling.

I wish I could turn myself into steam and float away.

"Have you been helping your mama this morning?"

Margery had some difficulty understanding Lord Ravenne's words, for English was his second language and he possessed a thick accent. He repeated the question even more loudly.

Margery nodded. Did he think her deaf?

"Good girl." He patted her head again and waggled his fingers at Giddy, who was watching from her perch near Whitefoot. She giggled and hid her face.

"The wedding shall take place at Edmundsbury Castle in a fortnight," he said, resuming his conversation with Alice. "My betrothed already awaits me. I am leaving today. Naturally, I will expect you, as I expect all of Ravennesfield, to attend."

"Aye, m'lord." Alice stirred the cloth, seemingly unaware of the waves spilling over the cauldron and hissing upon the flames.

"Afterward, we shall return to the manor house. This part of England is the safest place to be, for the Death cannot traverse the fens."

Alice crossed herself.

Margery's eyes widened. What did Ravenne mean? She knew what death was, but what was *the* Death?

"Is it true what they say, that London is a city peopled by ghosts?" Alice asked.

Ghosts? According to Father Egbert, London was a huge place, the largest in the world. Margery imagined thousands of misty figures peering through hundreds of window openings.

I would die of fright. This truly is a Terrible Thing.

"...relatives in the city and they have sent word that the plague has barely made its presence felt. I myself was in London last Christmas, and the city looked no dirtier than usual."

Plague? Margery wondered what that meant. A disease like the scarlet sickness? She could already feel her body burning. But the scarlet sickness did not wipe out entire cities, and Lord Ravenne's assurances made no sense. What did dirt have to do with something called plague? Unless it was a plague of dirt, which made no sense either. How could someone die from dirt?

The cottage door flew open, slamming against the wall. Margery jumped. Two knights, wearing chain mail and brandishing swords, charged into the room. One, whom Margery recognized as Ravenne's bailiff, Gerard, shouted, "We found your poacher, my lord!"

Ravenne stepped away from Alice. "Caught in the act?"

Gerard nodded. "He tried to hide the carcass."

Frightened by the chaos, Giddy scampered toward Alice. Margery wished she could hide behind her mother's skirts too, or concoct some spell that would make these intruders vanish. She tried to understand what was happening, but they were conversing so rapidly in Norman French she could only decipher an occasional phrase.

Ravenne abruptly departed, trailed by his men.

"What is wrong?" Margery cried. "Will Lord Ravenne hurt us?"

"Nay, angel. This has naught to do with us." Alice moved to the wall opposite the open door, where she could watch without being seen. "Holy Mother! 'Tis Peter Baker."

Gathering her courage, Margery tiptoed toward a window opening and peered through. Peter, his face sickly white beneath streaks of grime, was bound around the waist and wrists and held captive between a pair of Ravenne's mounted retainers.

She watched as Peter sobbed his innocence and Ravenne slammed him in the stomach, causing him to collapse on his knees.

Alice pulled her back by the shoulders. "You must not watch, sweeting."

Margery had heard talk of Peter, how he cheated his customers, how he was a drunk and a gambler, but she had never heard him called a poacher.

"What will they do to him?" Her mother's hands trembled atop her shoulders.

"Thank God 'tis not a royal forest but only our lord's," Alice said as if to herself. "At least he will not die for his foolishness."

"But what will happen to him, Mama?"

"Never fear, angel. We have laws to protect Peter until he is proven guilty."

Margery did not think that Lord Ravenne cared about laws, even when Alice further elaborated, "By the time Peter is tried, Lord

Ravenne and his bride will be somewhere far away. He'll na give a thought to any of us. We must believe that."

"Why should I believe it if it is not true?"

Shaking off her mother's grip, Margery crept forward again.

Peter was still on his knees, his bound hands folded before him as if in prayer. "Please, good lord. I crave your mercy. I've a wife and five children."

"A poacher is like a rabid dog. Both must be destroyed."

Alice disentangled Giddy from her skirts and pulled Margery's arm. "'Tis time for Godiva's nap. Take her over to the bed and stay with her until she falls asleep."

"But what are they going to do to Peter?"

"Obey me, Margery."

As she grabbed Giddy, Margery heard Peter scream.

Alice shut the door firmly behind her and steadied herself against it.

Margery heard thuds, another scream, the pounding of horses' hooves. She imagined Ravenne hacking Peter to pieces and then feeding his flesh to the hawks.

Alice crossed to the cauldron and jammed her stick into the water.

Giddy had curled up on the bed and was clutching her wigged hempen doll.

Margery stood as if rooted to the floor.

Murder. Our lords can kill whomever they please, whenever they please. And there is naught we can do about it.

AT SUNDOWN THUROLD raced into the cottage. "Did ye hear what 'appened to Peter?"

Alice compressed her lips but laid out the table without comment.

Alf poured a bowl of ale. "Peter should na been poachin'. And 'tis the end of any talk." He slurped his ale, poured a second portion, and sat down to sup.

Thurold's bright brown eyes narrowed, but before he could vent his temper, Margery hurried over and slipped her hand through his. One word from Thurold and the room would explode like a parched meadow in a lightning storm. "Please," she whispered. "Let us eat in peace."

Thurold squeezed her hand and slumped down on a nearby chest. He sighed heavily, his unfocused gaze on the far wall. Then he shuddered the same way Whitefoot did when emerging from the river, and sat down at the table.

Afterward, Thurold said, "Let us go for a walk, Stick-Legs."

"Stay away from the oak," Alice warned, her voice sharp.

Thurold nodded.

They began strolling along Cottage Lane, heading toward the Crown and Sceptre Inn.

"What was Mama talking about?" Margery asked. "What oak?"

"The big one by the mill."

"What is wrong with it?"

Thurold merely looked angry.

They passed the Crown and Sceptre, which was unusually quiet, as was all of Ravennesfield. Peering into various un-shuttered windows, Margery remembered her mother's mention of ghosts.

The Death is here. 'Tis lurking near the oak, waiting to snatch us.

"Where is everyone, Thurold?"

"They be afraid, so they cower behind their doors and pray their bastard lords will leave 'em be."

"But I saw Lord Ravenne ride past, along the highway, toward Bury St. Edmunds."

"His henchmen still be around. 'Tis a question whether they be done with their bloodletting."

"What bloodletting? They canna do as they please. Father Egbert says England is a kingdom of laws, not men. He says—"

"Just because a silly old priest says something does na make it so."

Margery walked alongside her stepbrother in silence, all the while imagining various ways to drain blood from a man. Had they slit Peter's throat the way Alf slit a pig's?

"What did they do to Peter? Please tell me."

"I will show ye, but only if ye promise not to tell."

Margery nodded, though her heart raced in her chest. If Thurold wanted her to keep a secret something very bad must have happened.

Twilight had suffused their surroundings, including the corn mill, which, next to Ravennesfield's church was its largest building. A buttery patch of light leaked from the mill's lower window. Usually of an evening Walt the Miller's seven children would be playing near it, but tonight the area was deserted. Save for a pair of birds fluttering around what looked to be a sack of grain hanging from the limbs of a nearby oak.

Margery's steps slowed. She peered more closely at the sack. Father Egbert oft said, "Day belongs to man, but night belongs to the devil."

I do not like scary things. I wish I had not mentioned dracs to Giddy. God will punish me for my meanness.

Margery did not need Thurold to tell her that the sack of grain was actually Peter Baker.

They halted beneath the corpse. Thurold's grip was so tight it hurt. Margery was unable to discern much beyond Peter's shape, but 'twas an unnerving sight. Not that she was any stranger to death. Every winter, vagrants could be found frozen along the highway. Last winter she'd even seen Lettice Tomsdoughter's father crumple to the ground, as if cut down by an invisible sword. But such deaths were acceptable. This death was a deliberate act of cruelty.

"I hate 'em all," Thurold blurted, his voice loud enough to cause the circling birds to take flight. "They rule our entire lives. When we've corn to grind or bread to bake, we must pay to use their mills and ovens. We canna cut wood to warm ourselves without paying a wood penny. We canna fatten our pigs on their acorns until after we pay a meat penny. We be forbidden to kill pigeons or hares, even if they destroy our crops. We canna shoo away the rams or boars that trample our fields."

Dropping Margery's hand, he clenched his fists. "And should a man who suffers from an empty belly think to fill it with a tender piece of venison such as *they* enjoy every day, he be hanged."

Margery didn't know what to say. Thurold was right, at least about

Lord Ravenne, but all members of the nobility were not like him. It was contrary to scripture, contrary to her knowledge of her true father.

"And now that Peter be dead," Thurold continued, "his wife will 'ave to pay her best beast to the manor as heriot. Know ye what that means?"

Margery was having a hard time following her stepbrother's logic. "That we're only worth as much as a cow?"

I am half Norman. I am not like you and Giddy and Alf, or even Mama. What am I worth?

"It means that Kate must pay for the privilege of 'aving her 'usband murdered. We be the spawn of a defeated nation and must always bear that burden. The law decrees that the descendants of anyone who fought with King Harold at Hastings must forever remain serfs."

"None of our ancestors fought William the Conq—"

"'Tis not the point! I hope 'tis true, what they say. That King Harold and Arthur be not dead but sleeping, and someday they will awaken to lead us against our invaders."

"Father Egbert says we canna consider the Normans invaders since they've been here three hundred—"

"I hope Ravenne is struck down with the pestilence! I pray he dies a foul, lingering death!"

Margery's fingers curled; she suppressed the urge to make a protective sign of the cross. Half expecting Death to leap out of the gloom, like one of Father Egbert's demons, she thought, *How I do wish I had not threatened Giddy with Dracs.*

As she wished God would not let any more bad things come their way.

CHAPTER 3

Ravennesfield

"*N*ay, Godiva, do not put the broom in the fire. And leave the hen alone. Broody canna sit on her eggs if you poke her." Alice retrieved the birch broom from Giddy, who promptly started screaming.

Margery distracted her sister with her doll.

"'Tis glad I am to have your help," said Alice, stroking Margery's cheek.

Alice's palm felt over-warm and her eyes were red-rimmed, as if she'd been too long in a smoky room. During Sunday mass, earlier this morning, Alice had sat on the floor instead of standing, something she'd never done before.

"Do you have a fever, Mama? Would you like me to tie violets round your wrist and see if they wilt?"

Alice shook her head. "The day is a bit close, 'tis all."

Their neighbor, Joan Tomsdoughter, poked her face through the doorway. Possessed of a snaggle-toothed smile and a merry laugh, today she was neither smiling nor laughing. "Have ye 'eard the plague's appeared in Bury St. Edmunds?"

"That canna be," Alice cried. "We were at Edmundsbury Castle a week ago for our lord's wedding and everything was fine."

Apprehension settled in Margery's belly like sour milk. Adults no longer whispered about the Terrible Thing, which was a terrible thing in itself.

"Me daughter talked to one of our lord's own men," Joan said, entering the cottage. "Why think ye so many lords be packing up to leave the manor? So many 'ave already died in Bury St. Edmunds and even Cambridge that the plague pits canna hold them all."

"St. Jude protect us!" Alice eyed the stalks of wheat molded in the shape of a cross mounted above the door, one of many plague protectors scattered about the cottage interior.

Joan inspected Alice. "Feel ye well? Your cheeks be red as raspberries."

The corners of Alice's mouth lifted in a smile that did not reach her eyes. "I feel fine." She made a great show of gaining Giddy's attention by clacking together various spoons carved from cattle horn.

After a final worried appraisal, Joan left.

Immediately Alice released Giddy and turned to Margery. "I am fearful for your father. I pray he is healthy, wherever he might be."

"I am certain he is, Mama." They'd no more than glimpsed Lord Rendell, who was married to Lord Ravenne's sister, at the Ravenne-Hart wedding. But surely her father was safely south again. Besides, wouldn't they have heard, somehow, had he been struck down? Yet Father Egbert said The Death came and went as quietly as the fog.

"Always remember you are the daughter of a great lord." Alice's voice was curiously slow and thick. "You will grow up to a fine life. My lord Thomas promised me. Pray very hard for him. I could not bear it..." She closed her eyes for a long moment before retreating to the bed. Sinking onto the coverlet, she buried her face in her hands. Then she raised her head. "Would you lay forth the midday meal, angel?"

Alf and Thurold returned from the fields and sat down to their cheese and bread. No one commented on Alice's absence, least of all Alf, who gulped his ale and chewed his food as if his wife sat beside him. Margery found it impossible to eat, for her throat had tightened until she could scarcely breathe and her gaze kept returning to her mother.

Alice struggled upright, staggered, steadied herself against the chest at the foot of the mattresses, and crossed carefully to her loom. Easing onto the stool, she folded her hands in her lap and stared at the hempen homespun.

After dinner, Alf plaited reeds into weeles for catching fish, just as he did every Sunday. Thurold rubbed goose grease into his boots and sang to Giddy, who played with a mortar and pestle. Margery cleared the table.

Giddy abruptly squealed, dropped her makeshift toy and headed for Honker, who had wandered in through the open door. Honker honked. Alice winced.

Mama's ears hurt. "Do you need something?" she asked. "Would you like me to send Giddy and the goose outside?"

"Thirsty," Alice said in that peculiar voice. "Ale, please."

Margery poured her a bowl. After drinking it, Alice folded her hands again and sat motionless, staring into space, until afternoon shadows crept across the cottage floor.

Alf put aside his baskets and stretched. "'Tis time," he said, referring to the dancing which took place every Sunday on the green.

"Go along," his wife said. "We'll follow later."

By the time they left the cottage, the sun had slunk below an overcast horizon. Margery's skin felt sticky, and the air smelled like clothes beginning to mildew. She turned and looked back at their cottage, whose lime white walls set it proudly apart from the dull yellow of the older homes.

Pipe music wafted from the green, but the hour was so late they would miss most of the festivities. Not that Margery cared, but Alice usually delighted in dancing.

Giddy clung to a cat she'd scooped up along the way, and repeatedly stopped to gather the tall slender foxglove she called "Thimble Flowers." Margery reached out to hold her mother's hand and tiptoed in order to avoid stepping on the last remnants of sunset, which spattered like drops of blood across the rutted road.

31

Someone headed toward them, still several houses away. Margery saw with relief that it was Thurold. No doubt he'd returned to check on Alice.

Margery waved to him.

Alice stumbled to a halt. Gazing up at the steeple of St. George's Chapel, she whispered, "Do you smell it, angel?"

A clammy wind fingered her cheeks and coiled round her heart. "Smell what, Mama?"

"Death? Death in the air?"

Near the junction of High and Queen Street, beside the Crown and Sceptre, Alice clutched her arms across her stomach. An animal wail of pain emerged from her lips, just before she vomited up a viscous mess, black as the converging darkness.

Thurold had reached them. "By the Cross! Mama has the plague!"

"Nay," breathed Margery. Helpless, she watched her mother vomit again. And again. Finally edging straight, Alice staggered to the inn's wall and leaned against it. Her face was lost in the darkness—all save her eyes which were bright with fever.

Thurold reached for her. "We must get her home."

"My head," Alice moaned, clasping her hands over her ears. "Pounds and pounds."

Margery swiveled around, facing the crossroads. She heard the pounding too, for it was coming from along Queen Street. Horses, probably several. 'Twould not be villagers who went everywhere afoot. Lord Ravenne? She turned to Thurold, but he was bent over Alice and didn't seem to hear. Margery's palms were slick with sweat. What if it was Lord Ravenne and he hanged Alice for vomiting on his street?

"Hurry," she begged, as Thurold tried to wrap Alice's arms around his shoulders and raise her to her feet.

One of the knights carried a torchlight which jumped and sputtered. Margery counted six riders—and Lawrence Ravenne.

Margery stared, paralyzed with fear. What would Ravenne and his men do to them?

The party rode closer. The knights seemed to fill the narrow street, their shadows shooting up against the surrounding cottage walls, melding into darkness.

Thurold had managed to get Alice upright and leaning against him. "Get on her other side so we can help her walk." When Margery continued gawking, Thurold yelled, "Move! And Giddy, leave that cat be. Walk over here, behind us."

Margery's legs finally obeyed her command to move. After reaching Thurold and her mother, she slipped her shoulder beneath Alice's armpit, and turned her face away with a grimace. Alice smelled bad, not like herself at all.

The knights rode a cart's length away.

Alice tried to twist around to face them.

"Ye be going home!" shouted Thurold, as if she were hard of hearing. "Ye'll feel better then!"

Alice made an unintelligible sound and halted in the roadway. Despite Margery's grip on her waist, she thrashed like a speared fish until she had freed herself. Bolting away from them both, she darted in front of the knights.

"Mama, no!" Terrified, held back by Thurold, Margery watched as the cursing knights drew rein.

"What is happening here?" Lawrence Ravenne's right hand rested upon the hilt of his sword.

Alice stumbled toward him. Clutching his boot and spur, she peered into his face. "My Lord Thomas?"

Loud voices, speaking in French. Then the torchbearer, who bore the badge of a hart, which Margery recognized from their lord's wedding, addressed Alice in English.

"Leave go of your lord, woman. Are you mad?"

Lawrence Ravenne tried to shake off her hand. 'Twas obvious he did not recognize Alice in the wild-eyed woman who clung to him.

"The plague," a second knight exclaimed. "Jesu, Larry, I'll wager the creature has the plague."

"Leave go!" Ravenne kicked at her, but Alice held tight. The other knights, fearful of contamination, made no attempt to pull her off.

"Do not hurt her!" Margery shrieked.

Darting between the horses, Thurold reached for Alice just as Ravenne struck her across the neck with the flat of his sword. Alice began to fall, flailed out, and frantically gripped his leg.

Ravenne began beating against her back. "Leave go, you filthy peasant! Do not touch me!"

"Stop," shouted the most commanding of the knights, who also wore the hart badge. "Leave her alone and let us be gone."

Ravenne ignored his new father-in-law, William Hart, and slammed Alice again.

Thurold yelled. The knights yelled. Giddy wailed. Margery stood motionless. This new Alice, this disheveled creature with her unkempt hair, appeared frozen in the torchlight. Stubbornly, she clung to Ravenne's leg.

Lawrence Ravenne raised his sword.

The blade descended, arcing across Alice's back, cleaving through her as easily as Alf halved a cabbage. Margery screamed. Her mother crumpled, blood spurting from the juncture where the sword had sliced her spinal cord.

"Damn you, Lawrence!" shouted William Hart. "What have you done?"

Movement returned to Margery's limbs. Rushing forward, she knelt on the ground, searching her mother's face for some sign of life.

"So 'tis you, Margery Watson," Ravenne roared. "You all had best get that thing off the streets where she cannot spread her foulness."

Margery cried, "That thing is my mother!"

"I do not care who it is. Get her out of here. And be forewarned. If I am afflicted with plague, I will return and hang the lot of you."

Ravenne kicked his horse and bolted away. The other knights followed; only William Hart cast a final backward glance. With the men went their torch, its smoking trail curling about Margery and the rest before fading into the darkness.

Thurold stepped to Margery and pulled her to her feet. Both stood looking down at the shape on the road, of no more form than the ruts or garbage. No need to hurry in order to get Alice Watson home. Or to do anything else. Save bury her.

ALICE WAS NOT BURIED in the churchyard. Hearing she had plague, Father Egbert refused to allow her there, or even to administer last rites.

"'Tis typical of priests," said Thurold. "When you need them they slink away, their tails between their legs."

Margery's torment now took a new turn. Without last rites God would never allow Alice into heaven, and without the benefit of consecrated ground she would become a spectre, wandering between earth and the hereafter, forever seeking entrance. This possibility caused Margery to cry harder than anything else, but when she told Thurold, he reassured her.

"Our mother will get a proper burial. I will see to that."

He and Alf dug a hole in the far corner of the curtilage and placed a pinch of earth, rather than the host, in Alice's mouth, after the manner of the old days. They fashioned a rough cross for the head of the grave, wrapped a blanket around her, lowered her into the ground and then Thurold muttered the *Pater Noster* and a handful of prayers for the dead.

Afterward, Alf jammed the cross in the ground, said, "'Tis done," and retreated to their cottage. Thurold smoothed the grave mound with his shovel.

Slowly, Margery, with Whitefoot padding faithfully beside her, retreated to the cottage. Every morning she had traveled this path, secure in the knowledge that nothing would ever change. Oh, seasons would come and go, and the amount of available food might alter, or the weight of the taxes levied. The number of Honker's goslings could change, as could the number of Walt the Miller's children. Even the king of England could change. But important things, like her mother, would always stay the same.

How could this have happened?

Whitefoot nuzzled Margery's hand. She knelt and hugged him.

The world will never be right again, she thought, burying her face against the mongrel's fur.

The impossible had happened. Plague had arrived at Ravennesfield. Not winds, nor amulets, nor bathing with pig urine, nor fires of green wood and herbs had kept it away. Death walked among them. Who would he touch next?

"DIG GIDDY'S grave next to her mother's," Alf said. "I will help after a time."

Watching her stepfather from across the room, Margery knew he wouldn't be helping anyone. Alf had the plague. Already he was staggering, just like Giddy, just like Mama. But Giddy had died so quickly. Would it take Alf long to die?

How long will it take me to die?

Giddy had not suffered much, and Margery was glad of that. Thurold said sometimes boils appeared, and then the death was long and agonizing. Margery didn't know if Giddy had boils, for no one had washed her. Alf had forbidden them. In death, Giddy seemed no bigger than her hempen doll.

By the following morning, Alf had slipped into delirium. However, he wasn't going to die as quickly as Mama and Giddy. He babbled and cursed and vomited until the cottage stank with him.

"He will be gone 'ere the day's out," Thurold said, "and 'tis dangerous to linger. We should leave the old man...let him die in peace."

"Leave? But where will we go?"

Thurold pushed her toward the door. "The fens."

CHAPTER 4

The Fens
 The fenland was a forbidding area, treacherous to cross. Animals that strayed from the higher pastures sank without a trace, captured by the boggy peat. In winter, after the water froze, fenmen traveled on skates made from bones.

Thurold planned to live there until the plague had passed. Food was no problem. An abundance of birds thrived among the alders, willows, reeds and sedges, and the muddy waters teemed with fish.

"The winds be so fierce," Thurold told Margery, "they will blow away the Death."

Much of the fen's grassland still remained under water, so they retreated to Ravenne Forest, a private deer park. Villagers were generally forbidden inside the forty acres but Thurold fretted less over Lord Ravenne's wrath than the plague. In the past, Margery and her mother had often hunted among the beech and oak trees for plants used in the making of household products and remedies. With their lord's permission, of course.

Thurold built a hut, buttressed against a fallen tree, large enough so that they could lay down inside. When he left to fish or hunt, Margery gathered the few plants that were in season. Fearful of meeting Lord

Ravenne or contracting the plague, she never ventured far from their shelter. If she scrambled onto the fallen tree, she could see beyond the forest to the edge of the fens. She could watch Thurold until he was but a speck and glimpse his return from miles away.

In the evening, they curled up with their backs against each other. The forest, so still during the day, stirred awake at night, like a snake warmed by the sun. Crickets sawed, frogs croaked, owls skimmed from treetops on whispering wings. Margery expected some horrible fen monster to come creeping through the brush, sniff out their shelter, and snatch her away from Thurold.

When she spoke of her fears, he laughed. "I've been over every inch of the fens, Stick-Legs, and I've ne'er seen monsters. I'll wager they do na even exist."

While Margery couldn't quite believe him, her worries transferred to more mundane animals, such as wolves. She imagined them circling their makeshift hut, waiting for Thurold to fall asleep. Then they would rush in, drag her away, and tear her to pieces.

"Wolves were driven out of England years ago," Thurold soothed. "They only return in bedtime tales to frighten babies, which you are not, so go to sleep."

On the afternoon of the fourth day, Thurold returned with a swallow kite. Wrapping it in leaves, he buried it deep in the coals from a small fire. While the bird cooked, he repeatedly surveyed the surrounding countryside.

"What is wrong?" Margery asked.

"I mislike fire. The smoke is too easily seen."

"But you built one yesterday. And charcoal burners are all about. Their smoke can be seen from forever."

Thurold smiled and mussed her hair. "Pay me no mind, Stick-Legs." But earlier he'd glimpsed Lawrence Ravenne and three others out riding. It looked to be his new wife and most likely her brothers, for they appeared young.

As Margery finished the last of their meal, Thurold suddenly bolted to his feet. She felt the color drain from her face. "What is it? Do you hear something?"

"Hush!" He pointed to their hut, which could not be seen by anyone entering the forest. "Go! Hide!"

Now Margery heard it--hoofbeats. She scurried toward the shelter while Thurold kicked dirt over the fire and spun around to follow her.

"Halt!" Margery recognized Lord Ravenne's voice, calling out first in French, then English. "What are you doing in my forest?"

Heart slamming against her ribs, Margery peered over a tree trunk in front of the hut at four riders and Thurold, who was moving away from Margery toward them.

"No," she breathed.

Now she knew all too well. Plague would not take her and Thurold, but Lord Ravenne would—cut them down and leave them bleeding on the forest floor.

Ravenne drew rein and looked down with eyes as chill as the fen waters. "I asked you, villein, what are you doing in my forest?"

Mindful of Margery's safety, Thurold strove for a respectful manner. "I was fishing in the fens, m'lord."

Ravenne stared toward the lingering coil of smoke. "Were you burning my wood? 'Tis against the law, though what do you care?" He glanced at his companions, who watched with mild curiosity. "Just use as you please, and be damned with what is yours."

Anger edged Thurold's words "I used peat. I took naught of yours."

"Do not be so harsh with him, husband," said his new bride. While the former Elizabeth Hart was large and almost mannish in her appearance, she possessed a pleasing, melodious voice and a gentle—some would say dreamy—nature. With a glance at one of her brothers, she added, "He looks little older than Harry."

Ravenne leaned forward in his saddle and crossed his arms over the pommel. "If left alone, children will grow to full-fledged criminals."

"'Tis a chivalrous thing to show mercy," she persisted, "even toward your villeins."

"This is not one of your romances, wife," he said, cutting her off.

Matthew Hart cast his new brother-in-law a baleful glance before returning his attention to Thurold Watson and the surrounding area.

"Let us be off," said Harry, shifting nervously. "Now that the plague is in your village, 'twould be folly to linger overlong in the open air. Who knows what foulness might be borne on the wind?"

Considering his next move Lawrence Ravenne craned his head toward the sky. Harry was right about lingering, but his wife should not publicly gainsay him and this serf's manner was too arrogant for his liking.

"I think you not only took my wood," he said to Thurold. "I think you poached something. A deer mayhap? I have hanged thieves for poaching."

"See ye a deer about, m'lord? I've done naught wrong."

Matthew spoke up. "Elizabeth is right. Leave him go."

"Aye," echoed Harry. "'I fear the wind is picking up."

Ignoring them, Ravenne swung a leg over the saddle and dismounted. "You are lying," he said to Thurold. He planted himself in front of him. "Tell me what you've stolen."

Thurold felt his temper slipping away. Unconsciously, he balled his fists. "Look at me closely. Do ye na know me?"

"Why should I? Have you stolen from me in the past?"

"I should na be surprised, not when ye treat me and mine as if we be invisible. You ride through our fields and trample our crops. You demand week-works and boon works and give naught in return."

"Oh, dear," Elizabeth breathed. If a peasant should intrude in one of her epic tales—though she couldn't remember one ever having done so—he would never speak so disrespectfully.

"Swine!" Ravenne bellowed. "I'll cut your heart out and feed it to my dogs!" He grabbed for Thurold but he jerked away.

"Just like you killed me mother? Do ye not remember? You came sniffing around 'er often enough until ye sliced 'er through with your sword, ye bloody bastard!"

Thurold kicked him hard in the groin. Ravenne doubled over with a pained yelp.

Darting past the others, Thurold raced for the safety of the fens.

From her hiding place Margery saw Ravenne stagger to his horse, struggle into the saddle and race after him. Before they disappeared from sight, Margery saw their lord lean down and scoop Thurold off his feet.

In the ensuing silence, Elizabeth Hart sighed dramatically. She already suspected her marriage was not going to follow the trajectory of Lancelot and Guinevere or Tristan and Iseult or some other passionate—however doomed—relationship from one of her Arthurian romances. Which meant she had to look to practicalities, such as maintaining good relationships with their villeins.

"I think, Matt, that we'd best catch up with my lord husband before he harms that lad, no matter how justified."

"You two go along," said Matthew. "I'll follow presently."

Harry frowned. "You are not that familiar with this area. What if you get lost? 'Tis foolish to tempt fate."

"I do not get lost. And I'll be but a moment."

Matthew watched his brother and sister ride away before turning his gaze to the spot where Margery Watson was hiding. He called out in English, "You can come out now."

Margery pressed against the earth as if she might somehow meld into it and become invisible. But no place was safe from Lawrence Ravenne and his kind.

Beyond her heart drumming in her ears, she heard the creak of saddle leather, heard the stirring of undergrowth as Matthew Hart approached her.

"Come out, little one. I'll not hurt you."

Margery felt like a trapped hare. Well aware of the target her exposed back provided, she could almost feel the bite of sword as the blade cut her in two…

A hand bunched the neck of her gown, pulling her up.

She screamed and pummeled Matthew, trying to scratch out his eyes, kick him in the groin, do anything that would make him loose her. Though three year's younger and one-quarter his strength, terror caused Margery to fight like a demon.

Finally, Matthew pinioned her arms behind her. Following the curve of her back with his body, he said against her ear, "Stop. I have no thought to harm you."

Margery's arms felt as if they were being ripped from their sockets. Finally, she ceased struggling and crumpled to her knees, awaiting this young lord's vengeance.

"I just wanted to see who you were, what you were doing here." Matt loosened his grip. "If you agree not to flee, I'll release you."

Margery nodded. Once freed, she turned to face him. Her mind flashed back to Alice's murder, to William Hart shouting, "What have you done?" Lord Hart was Ravenne's father-in-law.

"'Twas a bad thing your companion did to his lord," said Matthew. "Though I cannot completely blame him. My brother-in-law's temper matches his hair."

Margery was too frightened to make sense of his words. "I must save my brother! Lord Ravenne will kill him and I canna let him die. I'll have no one left to care for me."

Matthew frowned. The girl's words made no sense, but her agitation was real enough. "Why do you mistrust your lord? Your brother will not die for his act, no matter how dishonorable. This is the England of His Grace, Edward III, after all. Most likely your kin will escape with a fine of some sort." Seeing that words meant to placate made no difference, Matt added, "I will ask my sister to soothe his temper. Women have their ways."

Margery did not believe him. Ravenne had probably already murdered Thurold.

Matthew's gaze swept the deepening horizon. "You should not be out in the forest after dark. You live in Ravennesfield, do you not?"

Margery nodded.

"Has your house been struck by the Death?" Even with the plague roaming about, Matthew personally felt little fear that he or his loved ones would be harmed.

When her head bobbed up and down, Matt said gently, "You are very young to be alone."

I wasn't alone until your relative killed my mother.

Most likely this creature even knew about Alice's murder. Had Lord William Hart later made light of the incident to his sons, jesting

42

about mad peasant women, or using Alice as a warning about the closeness of the plague?

"I…I also have the Death," Margery blurted, desperate to make him leave. "I have been vomiting for days and my arms have swelled. You had best be away. If you come near me again, you will surely catch it and die most horribly."

Matt inspected her more closely. "You do not look sickly. Dirty, mayhap. But not ill."

"I am though. I should be dead ere morning."

Matthew considered this. The girl obviously wanted to be rid of him and was making up tales. However, only a fool would risk the Death. Nor did he really relish travelling unfamiliar territory after sundown.

"I will try to ease things with your brother," he said, by way of leaving. "'Tis a shame that, with you dying, you will not be around to know."

CHAPTER 5

The Fens

"*T*hurold?" Margery jerked awake. What had startled her? She looked out at the lightening sky. Nothing at all but morning, blessed morning.

She whispered, "I am fine. I am still here." The words sank like rocks dropped in a well. She might still be alive, but she was alone.

Finally, as a rheumy-eyed sun struggled through a bank of clouds, Margery left the immediate area. Following the path along which Thurold had disappeared, she searched for some sign of him. Hidden in every shadow, beside every bush she expected to find his body. While walking through a small meadow thick with silvery ladies smocks, which were sacred to faeries, she remembered Giddy with her fist full of Thimble Flowers.

"Please," Margery whispered to no one. "No more bodies."

All the while calling Thurold's name, she zigzagged through the forest until she reached the area of the fens. Fearing its treacherous nature as well as its openness, she merely stood at the clearing, her eyes probing for Thurold's crumpled corpse.

By late afternoon Margery left off seeking her brother and began hunting for food among the lilies-of-the-valley and cowslips carpeting the forest floor. Nestled amid fallen leaves she spied a spread of scarlet fungi and plucked several. She'd eaten similar mushrooms before but her mother had gathered them. Hadn't Alice cautioned that the wrong type sowed strange dreams? Margery looked longingly at them, but finally tossed them aside and settled for a handful of beechnuts. Immediately, her empty stomach rebelled and she bent over, retching.

Do I have the Death? If so, she would die here with no one to care for her.

By sunset, with no more plague symptoms, she was wearied of searching for someone she knew would never return, and pondered retreating to Ravennesfield. At least at the cottage there would be food and turves for fuel. Better not to think of Alf, who must be long dead.

She retraced her steps until Ravennesfield spread before her, half a mile away. The tower of St. George was outlined against a sky the color of cooled pottage edged in a skim of grease, and from a handful of houses a yellow-tinged smoke curled outward, hovering above their thatched roofs. A gray mist seemed to rise from the road and cling to the lime-washed cottages. Even from this distance, Margery smelled sulphur.

Apprehensively, she approached the village. At sunset men usually returned from the fields, cows bawled to be milked, and mothers called to their children while readying oatcakes for the even meal. But not tonight.

Skirting the garbage-strewn kennel in the middle of the street, Margery tiptoed between the silent cottages. An occasional hen or pig rooted in the dung heaps flanking each door. Garden patches appeared untended. Roses and gillyflowers and scarlet-edged Sops-in-Wine drooped toward the earth.

Margery ran toward High Street and her house on Cottage Lane. Tripping, she sprawled, landing amidst decomposing filth. A black rat lay inches away, motionless, just like the sheep dotting various meadows. She struggled to her feet and careened onward, passing the

Wytbreads, the Weavers, and Walt the Miller, all with red crosses painted on their doors. The paint ran like blood. Alice's blood. Giddy's blood. Alf's blood. Thurold's blood.

Along the narrow street, her footsteps rattled like clacking bones. The heavy air caught in her lungs. A light flickered from behind a shuttered window. She heard a continuous moan. It sounded like Whitefoot when he smelled a bitch in heat, only this moan was human. She turned on Cottage Lane, toward her house. The black tar on its outside timbers glistened like a forehead wet with fever. A red cross marked its door.

Through her ragged breathing, Margery became aware of new sounds. The creaking of a cart. The ringing of a bell. Not the comfortingly noisy bell of St. George's, calling villagers to mass, but a lonely jangle. She hid inside a doorway.

"Come out, one and all," someone called. "Bring me your dead."

Peering beyond the doorway, Margery recognized the old man who cared for Ravennesfield's graveyard, walking behind a cart drawn by a bony ox. In one hand he carried a hand bell, in the other a rushlight. The light illuminated the back of the open cart, the gleaming arms and legs and bodies which had been tossed inside like seeds in a hopper. Margery saw dried blood caked at the corners of grinning mouths. She saw staring eyes and faces black with the mask of plague. She saw golden hair, cascading over a creaking wheel. Hair like Alice's. Margery squeezed her eyes shut until the cart had passed.

Soon it will be me in the cart, my hair trailing upon the ground, my eyes fixed on nothing.

She crossed the street to her cottage.

What will it be like to be dead, without a body to walk around in?

She knew. Death would be black, and her thoughts would be trapped among the stars, and she would be alone in the darkness, searching for her mother.

As she laid her ear against the door, she thought she heard something.

Broody? Honker? Whitefoot? Or one other?

Margery pushed back visions of Death seated at the trestle table.

Heart in her throat, she shoved open the door. Someone stood in the middle of the room by the cold hearth—a shadowy figure, staring at her. Margery swallowed hard and blinked several times until the figure came into focus.

"Alf?" she whispered.

CHAPTER 6

Ravennesfield, 1350-1351

$\mathcal{H}$arvest time arrived, though few fields were harvested. Only a handful of laborers remained to tend the crops or thrash grain. The entire countryside possessed a mournful look, with sagging fences, untrimmed hedges, rotting fruit, and fields marred by the remains of diseased sheep, oxen and horses.

East Anglia itself suffered more than most of England. The city of Norwich lost half its population. In Cambridge, only enough people remained to fill one of the city's seventeen churches. More than two thousand clergymen died. Since priests maintained that the plague was God's punishment for sinners, ordinary people wondered why the Almighty had chosen to so ravage the ranks of his earthly emissaries. Monasteries were particularly decimated, with so many stricken that few inside remained well enough to tend their brethren. Most East Anglians kept their wonderings locked inside, however, and seldom spoke of them. Plague memories remained too fresh to assimilate, too frightful to dwell upon.

Ravennesfield mirrored the surrounding devastation. Death had not spared any family and half the cottages were vacant. Much of the garden produce had been lost to weeds or various blights. Occasionally, a few men sowed the fallow fields, but most neglected their strips. The majority of villagers seemed inclined to spend their days sitting in their doorways, staring at nothing.

Ravennesfield's priest, Father Egbert, succumbed early on. "Say penance to avert the plague!" thundered the priest who followed him. Church members obeyed, only to have the pestilence become more virulent.

A third priest, sent to replace Father Egbert's dead successor, ordered townspeople to form a barefoot procession and march around the village, hefting crosses and singing psalms. "That will appease God's wrath," he said. A week later, the third priest's corpse had been tossed into the common pit.

Villagers took note of these and other happenings, but seldom spoke of them.

For now, winter was coming.

For now, it was safer not to think of anything at all.

MARGERY HUNCHED her shoulders against a sharp wind. She pulled Thurold's cary coat closer, but the wind nipped her exposed ankles. More than two years had passed since the pestilence and in that time she had grown so much her clothes no longer fit. She'd cut and re-fashioned one of her mother's gowns as best she could, though sewing was just another of the puzzling and impossibly difficult things she now had to do.

Last week, after Alf had killed their lone remaining pig, she had cut and salted its carcass, stored the salted joints in a barrel, and hung one of its haunches above the fire to make smoked ham. Her stepfather had always helped Alice, but he'd allowed Margery to struggle while he sat in front of the hearth fire, drinking and staring into the flames.

Margery did her best to master her mother's daily chores, and even attempted beer brewing, though Alf termed the final product undrinkable. Far simpler for him to retrieve a coin from Alice's store of money and send Margery to the Crown and Sceptre.

No wonder their coin purse was nearly empty. Whenever Margery pondered their dwindling money supply, she fought down a rush of panic. She wished Alf would provide. She wished that she, like he, could sit in front of the fire and stare into space.

But if she did, they'd freeze or starve to death. So she cut turves for fuel, caught fish and salted it, made rushlights for the long winter evenings, and what small repairs to the cottage that she could.

Lord Thomas Rendell had oft promised to provide for her, but that had been when Alice was alive. Would he do so now?

Margery would soon find out. For her father and his wife, the lady Beatrice, sister of the killer Lawrence Ravenne, had stopped at Ravenne Manor on their way south. After the plague's end, the nobility had resumed their routines, which included frequent traveling to various demesnes as well as visits with relatives. After spending time with Lord Ravenne and his wife, the former Elizabeth Hart, who'd just been blessed with their first son, the Rendells were headed for Thomas's main family holding, Fordwich Castle, in Kent.

Tomorrow I will seek you out, Lord Father. And see if you truly are a man of your word.

MARGERY and her fellow villagers used Ravenne Manor's bakehouse to cook their coarse rye bread. Today was baking day. While Margery awaited her loaves, she watched the surrounding activity. The bailey was much shabbier than before the Death, though there were signs of rebuilding. And members of the Rendell household, with the blue jupon of the wolf upon their clothing, bustled about, grooming horses, surveying hawks on their perches in front of Ravenne Manor's mews, unloading supplies from wagons, playing dice, sharpening their weapons or just gossiping.

She prayed that Lord Rendell would put in an appearance for she did not have the courage to ask after him. She had no idea how to even approach his retainers, who barely glanced at her and the other villeins gathered around the bakehouse.

Finally, just as she'd retrieved her loaves from the oven and placed them in a basket, Margery saw him. Thomas Rendell was walking with his head down, his air preoccupied, away from the manor house toward the stables.

"My lord Father," Margery called, though she didn't know whether that was an appropriate title. "My lord," she repeated more uncertainly.

At first Thomas was happy to see her. He scooped her up into his strong arms and hugged her so tightly she was breathless.

"I feared you were dead of the plague," he said, after releasing her.

He could have found out easily enough. 'Twas a short walk from Ravenne Manor to Ravennesfield, wasn't it? Margery drew back to gaze into her father's face, noting new lines around his eyes and mouth. Lord Thomas Rendell, so big and handsome, who according to Alice's stories, was associated with cherry trees and crumbling kingdoms and scandals involving murdered saints. Who'd always seemed like a character out of a fable. Now looking worn and tired and all too human.

"Mama died," Margery blurted, though her throat seemed stopped shut when she tried to relay the circumstances.

Thomas did not appear surprised. Had he known already? Had Lawrence Ravenne, or Ravenne's sister, discussed Alice's murder during a relaxed dinner conversation after which they'd clucked their tongues and changed the subject?

"So many are gone." Thomas's voice was gruff with emotion. "I'd hoped God would spare more."

"Life has been hard," Margery said. "We've little money and Alf does naught save drink and I fear without help more bad things will happen."

Thomas said, "I canna take you to Fordwich with me."

Margery blinked in surprise. She had not thought to ask him. Fordwich might as well be across the world as however far away it actually was.

"Things are not well with us. My son, who was but two weeks old, died at Eastertime. My wife..." he shrugged, leaving the rest of the sentence unfinished. "Lady Beatrice also had the pestilence, but she

51

survived, though…with problems. She is with child again. I cannot upset her, and she is easily upset."

Margery tried to decipher her father's words. Why would anything pertaining to her upset Lady Rendell?

"I need heirs. I am twenty-seven years old. My wife grieves… differently. I fear you would be a reminder of what she has lost. I am sorry for that. I would have it otherwise…"

Thomas tipped Margery's chin with rough fingers. "I see Alice in your eyes, in the set of your mouth. She must have had noble blood somewhere, for I've seldom seen a comelier woman." His expression softened. "I suspect she looked very like you when she was small." He placed his hand atop the crown of Margery's head. "Save for the color of your hair, of course."

"My lord husband!"

Both turned toward a petite woman standing near the front of the manor house, some twenty feet away.

"I am going to rest," she said, absently stroking a tiny white dog in her arms. Her hair, the color of firelight, was caught in a net on either side of her ears. Hair the color of her brother's. Margery could see the resemblance in their facial features, though Beatrice Rendell's eyes appeared almost black when contrasted to her whey-tinted complexion. "I have a loathsome headache. Come play for me."

"The only time my lady wife can sleep is when I play the lute," explained Thomas in a soft voice.

Spotting Margery, Beatrice approached them, her eyes narrowed suspiciously.

"Who is this?"

"A lass from the village," Thomas said, his manner placating.

"Another of your bastards, husband? Fornication seems to run in your family, does it not?"

Thomas turned away from Margery and hurried to his wife, who clutched the now squirming fluff in her arms while simultaneously upbraiding her husband in an indecipherable torrent of French.

Margery shifted uncertainly from one foot to the other. *We must have money…*

"My lord, we will soon be starving," she persisted, loudly enough that he must hear. "Can you not help me?"

Thomas turned his back, and with his arm around his wife, retreated to the manor house. Margery could only stare after him, her face as hot as if she'd been standing flush to the bakehouse. He'd ignored her. Her own father did not care if she starved or froze to death.

She blinked back tears. *Thurold was right. Lords are kind and fair only when it suits them.* The lone difference between Thomas Rendell and Lawrence Ravenne was that Thomas possessed a sweeter surface. *But a maggot dipped in honey is still a maggot. Never again will I expect anything from a lord.*

On her way back to Ravennesfield, someone called, "Hey, you, little one. Wait."

Margery turned.

A short, stocky man wearing the Rendell badge caught up to her. "My lord said I am to give this to you." The man stretched out a coin purse, fatter than any Alice had ever received. "He said 'tis all he can spare, and you are not to try to see him again while he is here." Seeing her posture stiffen, he added, "Lord Rendell is concerned for his wife's safety. He has lost much. We all have. He does not mean to hurt you. He was most distressed when we spoke."

Margery contemplated the outstretched purse. Its contents meant they could survive for years. But Thomas Rendell was only giving her money to buy her silence, to shoo her away so she would not cause trouble. Thomas had wanted Alice because she was beautiful, and he had met his obligation to Margery only because it provided a convenient opportunity to see his leman.

"I do not want his money," she whispered, feeling as if she were sinking into one of the sucking holes in the fens.

The man frowned at her. "'Tis a great sum, more than most ever see. Here, take it."

Margery shook her head.

He studied her intently. An odd expression crossed his face before he shrugged, as if dealing with a matter of no importance.

"All right then."

Thomas's retainer turned and strode back toward the manor, tossing the coin purse in the air and catching it as he did so.

Eyes blurry with unshed tears, Margery continued to the Watson cottage. She thought of her father, strumming his lute and singing to his wife, who would cry and clutch at her growing belly. She remembered the way Thomas had looked at Alice, remembered his promises to care for the both of them. Margery stumbled in the rutted road. What had Father Egbert said? That God had ordained separate duties for all his children, and life would remain fine so long as everyone kept to their proper roles.

"We are the eyes which show men to safety," he'd said, likening the various classes to a body. "Knights are the hands and arms. They are obligated to protect Mother Church and the weak, and promote peace and justice."

Such foolishness. What had Father Egbert said about peasants? "You are the lower part of the body and 'tis you who are duty-bound to nourish the eyes and limbs."

What body part am I? Will I ever belong anywhere?

Margery knew one thing well enough. "I am glad my hair is brown," she said to the silent cottages on either side of Ravennesfield's narrow lane. "When I grow up I shall look nothing at all like Mama. I will be so sour and ugly that no man, either noble or villein, will ever dare approach me. Because if he does, I will cut out his heart."

CHAPTER 7

Ravennesfield, 1355

 hen Margery Watson looked back upon her life from the fullness of years, she chose one seemingly insignificant event as the moment that changed *everything*. Before, when she'd pondered her future—in the manner of a soothsayer rather than the fifteen-year-old maid she was—her path seemed tidily arrayed before her. Marry a fellow villager, have children, work, expire. Whether she would or not, and when it came to marrying one of the handful of possible suitors in Ravennesfield, she most definitely would not.

God has not created the man who'd ever interest me, she'd told herself many times.

As if she'd known that to be truth, as well.

On this day, this very special day, Ravennesfield's villagers were going "a-ganging," a rite meant to re-affirm the traditional boundaries of gardens and hedges and roadway, reinforcing who lay legal claim to what. 'Twas an ancient ceremony, one Margery found comforting since it harkened back to a time before the Death. But she felt no need to join in and lagged behind the crowd, which included Father Oswald carrying a full-sized cross and muttering arcane prayers at seemingly random intervals while celebrants enthusiastically flogged the surrounding vegetation.

Margery had removed her clogs and was enjoying the feel of the packed earth, the breeze lifting her unbound hair and carrying to her the pungent scents of peat and manure; the warmth of the waning sun. She suddenly thought of that long ago time when her life had been moored around Alice, yet she could actually remember so very little. Giddy and Thurold had faded until only the sense of loss remained, and, though she clung to her mother's memory as tenaciously as Giddy had clung to her cat, in truth Alice was beginning to resemble the wooden virgin in St. George's Chapel.

Perhaps such reminisces had been brought on by the re-appearance of Lord Lawrence Ravenne, who'd returned to Ravenne Manor for one of the few times since those dreadful days. When Margery and his other villeins had brought him the customary Easter offering of eggs, Ravenne had remarked on her resemblance to her mother in such a casual way, as if he'd forgotten that he had murdered Alice. Then he'd pinched Margery's cheek and patted her bottom through her skirts and she'd felt such a terror that she'd nearly bolted the hall.

For the past six years, she'd fantasized how she would someday dispatch Lawrence Ravenne—with an arrow from Alf's longbow, which in reality she could scarce bend; with poison somehow slipped into ale or soup or some such. Or perhaps she would use a knife when her lord's back was turned, or when he was asleep—though how she would find herself in such intimate proximity she hadn't quite worked out. But after that Easter meeting she'd known she'd not the courage for revenge. Rather she would pray that God in his righteous wrath would ordain Lawrence Ravenne to be killed during England's forthcoming campaign against the French.

It was then Margery heard the blast of a hunting horn and the barking of dogs, and spotted peregrines and sakers circling above the fens, obviously searching for heron or other water fowl. Shading her eyes, she spied several riders. Some, trailed by their dogs, rode toward Ravenne Manor, while a trio headed in her direction. One was riding double, with a female in front.

"Lettice Tomsdoughter," she breathed, recognizing her neighbor. Then she knew Lettice must be perched upon Lawrence Ravenne's stallion for the fourteen-year-old had bragged at the Easter assemblage that she meant to have her lord's bastard child.

"So he will provide for me," Lettice had explained.

Which meant her wits were as addled as her morals.

Margery lifted her skirts and increased her stride in order to catch up with Father Oswald and the others, now nearing Ravennesfield's outskirts. The hoofbeats grew louder.

"Margery Watson!" called Lawrence Ravenne.

Margery pretended she didn't hear but when he ordered her to halt, she knew she must obey. With limbs that suddenly felt incapable of support, she forced herself to stop, managed to turn and readied to curtsy. And found herself face to face, not with her nemesis, but with the man she would love forevermore.

Initially, she could only vaguely place Matthew and Harry Hart— not at all from Lord Ravenne's wedding when they'd all three been in attendance, but later from that terrible incident in the fens.

Both young men had sun-streaked blond hair and both wore harts on their cote-hardies. If Margery were judging objectively, she would have said that Harry Hart had grown to be the more conventionally handsome, with perfectly sculpted features and vulnerable, long-lashed eyes that made one long to soothe away his cares.

But it was Matthew who immediately commanded her attention. Big and broad-shouldered, with a restlessness that was evident even when he seemed outwardly in repose. As if he could never be tethered to one spot but would ever be bounding off to some adventure, each more exciting than the last.

I knew even then, she would later tell him, as they lay encircled in each other's arms, though of course that could not be true.

Aware of Margery's interest, Matthew returned her gaze in a direct and curious, faintly amused—and impersonal—manner.

"Margery Watson, what are you doing out here by yourself?" Ravenne reined in his black stallion. "Why are you not enjoying the celebration?"

Margery suppressed the urge to wipe her suddenly sweaty palms on her gown. Instead, she shook her head, as if mute. Fortunately, Lettice Tomsdoughter broke the silence, babbling about hawking and having the grandest day and how her lord had let her wear his hawking glove —covered with diamonds and rubies it was—and hold one of his birds.

"'Tis not meet that you should be alone," Ravenne said, interrupting Lettice. His gaze swept Margery, weighing, appraising. "Times are lawless. A pretty maiden needs protection."

Matthew Hart turned to his brother. "Larry is right," he told Harry, speaking French. "She *is* very pretty, is she not?" He had been searching his memory, trying unsuccessfully to remember why the girl seemed familiar.

"Hush, Matt. What if she can understand you?"

"They only know English." Matthew absently stroked the hooded lanner perched upon his hawking glove. "Though *her* voice is musical and refined. 'Tis unusual among her kind…" It was then that he too remembered their encounter in the fens. All saints be praised that Margery Watson had survived and survived nicely, from the look of her. He then smiled at her, a smile that went unnoticed as Margery's gaze was fastened upon the ruts at her feet.

"God has blessed her with the most remarkable hair," he continued. "Look how it shines, like sunlight glancing off a stream."

Margery, who was self-schooled enough to understand most of what Matthew and Harry were saying, found her fear of Lawrence Ravenne temporarily replaced by annoyance. Speaking about her as if she were a witless ewe!

"'Tis blessed you'll be a knight and not a poet, brother," Harry said, with a roll of the eyes. "And what are we going to do about Larry? Surely, he should at least pretend to be a gentle-man around us rather than pawing everything in skirts. I've a mind to tell Elizabeth. Or Father even."

Intent on the interaction between Ravenne and Margery, Matthew did not respond. He had become uneased by the hungry expression in his brother-in-law's eyes and though 'twas hard to read the girl's reaction, he sensed Ravenne's crudity repelled her.

"...as ripe as your mother," Ravenne was saying to Margery, who stood still as one of the wooden carvings for which he was famous. Then, as if reaching a decision, he looped his reins around his pommel and growled to Lettice, "Off with you."

"But...my lord?" Lettice reluctantly dismounted. Ravenne emphasized his command by pushing her away with a stirruped leg.

"He aims to trade one girl for another," Harry whispered to Matthew. "He should have a care to his immortal soul—and to our sister!"

While Matthew wasn't concerned with damnation and knew few husbands kept their marriage vows, Margery's stricken look caused him to shift uneasily in his saddle.

Ravenne beckoned to Margery, as if expecting her to obey like a well-trained dog. "Come! 'Tis long past time you and I became better acquainted."

Not one to give up so easily, Lettice whined, "M'lord, ye promised—"

Ravenne gave her a more forceful shove with his knee. "We are done, you and I."

Hand over her mouth to muffle her weeping, Lettice stumbled off. Margery remained rooted to the spot. She parted her lips, as if she might actually gainsay her lord, but managed only another mute shake of the head.

Ravenne's eyes narrowed. "Would you deny me, Margery Watson?"

Thinking he might have to intervene in some fashion, Matthew guided his mount closer while Harry addressed Ravenne in a quavering voice. "'Twill soon be sunset and Elizabeth said you were to help Tristan and Arthur finish sanding their rocking horses—"

Ignoring him, Lawrence Ravenne extended his hand to Margery. "Come, girl! Now!"

Matthew wasn't quite sure how it happened, but he found himself dismounted and standing at her side, one arm looped possessively around her shoulder. "Nay, Larry. If she seems reluctant to go with you, 'tis for good reason."

Ravenne drew back his hand with a scowl. "And what might that be?"

Matt smiled and drew Margery closer to him. "She has promised herself to me!"

"'Tis so," Harry agreed, his relief evident. "He told me all about it yester…whenever."

Sensing his brother-in-law's skepticism, Matthew gave Margery a quick, hard kiss on the lips. "Is that not so, Margery Watson?"

Too shocked to reply, she could only stare dumbly from one to the other.

Ravenne's gaze swung from Matthew to Margery, considering. Then he laughed. "Bed her then, and I'll envy you your prize."

"Elizabeth will be—" Harry managed before Ravenne interrupted with a "'Tis back to the manor house for us, lad," and a spur to his horse.

After one last worried look over his shoulder, Harry followed, leaving Matthew and Margery alone.

THE HORIZON WAS a panorama of scarlet, orange and pink. Behind them, Matthew's stallion, worn by the hunt, followed, docile as a dog.

"Do you mind if I call you Meg?" Matthew asked politely.

He might call her "Rooster" or "Cow Dung" or any name he so decided, Margery thought, so why was he pretending to seek her permission? "Whatever pleases you, sir."

She felt little gratitude toward this strange creature. If Matthew Hart had rescued her, it was only because he wrongly fancied himself a hero or expected something despicable in return.

"'Twill soon be dark," Matthew observed. "Are you not glad I am beside you to act as protector?"

Margery eyed him from the corner of her eyes. Was he teasing? "I am not afraid of the dark, sir. Ravennesfield is too isolated to attract robbers and cutthroats, and I've never seen the witches and goblins and vampires that are said to lay in wait through the night."

"You would be a difficult person to defend, Meg," Matt said mildly.

Margery grimaced at his nickname but could think of no appropriate response. Her nerves were strung taut. Throughout their walk, she had been inspecting Matthew Hart as methodically, if surreptitiously, as she inspected her garden for weeds. No doubt that he was an intimidating presence with a body that made one think of wrestling and sword play and feats of physical prowess. And there was that intriguing energy that made her want to reach out and touch him, as if whatever magic he possessed might somehow transfer. Her survival had long depended on correctly weighing and measuring people and situations, but, now, as she would find so often in the future, he simply confused her.

"So you tell me that you do not fear the dark when I've always thought 'twas man's natural state, to mislike what he cannot see," Matthew said. "You are rare indeed. Is there anything that frightens you?"

Margery was taken aback by the question. *Everything. Hunger, being alone forever without love. Change. The Death. Knights. Lord Ravenne. You, she thought glancing at him, though mayhap for different reasons.*

"I doubt, sir, that you would fear the dark either."

Matthew grinned. "That makes me either very brave or very stupid. My brother tells me I am stupid. What say you?"

"I would not venture an opinion."

They reached the edge of Ravennesfield. Matthew halted and faced her. Though her instinct was to step back from him, she forced herself to maintain her ground.

"Would you like to pet my hawk?" He stretched out his gloved hand, and while she hesitated, rearranged his lanner's gold-embroidered, pearl-encrusted hood. The price of the hood alone would have kept her and Alf in necessities for years.

"Nay." Hawks were another of their lords' possessions it was best to leave alone. Fines were imposed on peasants who failed to return a missing bird, and the gallows for anyone stupid enough to steal one outright.

"You need not fear Thunderbolt," he said, mistaking her hesitation. "She won't hurt you." He brought his arm and his bird closer. "Females are most often used for hunting since they are larger than males. Go ahead. Touch her."

Margery gingerly thumbed the silver bells resting atop Thunderbolt's talons, which were engraved with letters she could not decipher. "Your bird's claws are long and sharp, sire. They must hurt."

"Nay, Meg. Hawks kill their prey so quickly they do not have time to feel anything."

Margery doubted that a hawk's victim would feel no pain and resented his certainty. Was Matthew Hart so confident about everything? "I prefer robins."

"I'll grant you robins are also fine. Do you know why they have red breasts?"

Margery told herself that she disliked his intimate manner, behaving as if they were companions. Having to admit that she did not know the answer was a concession she misliked giving. "Nay, sir."

"At the crucifixion, a robin tried to ease our Savior's pain by lifting His crown of thorns. A thorn pierced the robin's breast. Ever after, its red breast has symbolized its love for Christ."

"Did the robin die?"

"Of course."

"Then 'tis a sad tale."

"It is merely a legend, Meg. I do not have much faith in legends."

"Now I'll not be able to look at a robin without remembering."

"I would not have told you had I known it would distress you." Matt lashed Thunderbolt to his saddle, removed his hawking glove, and flexed his fingers, which were thick and powerful, brutal-looking. "I do not like to dwell on distressing matters, either. Life is too filled with pleasure to ponder pain."

She was not surprised that someone in his position would find it so, but she kept her own counsel. They continued their walk in silence save for the clip-clop of the stallion's hooves and singing from the Crown and Sceptre.

They reached Cottage Lane. "I thank you for your escort, sir." Margery gestured vaguely toward her house, barely visible in the twilight. "I can continue the rest of the way myself."

"Do you fear my brother-in-law?" Matthew asked suddenly. "Has he harmed you in the past?"

Margery stiffened. "I do not fear Lord Ravenne or anyone."

And then it occurred to her. King Edward's campaign. If she must suffer this person's presence, she might at least extract some useful information. "Will Lord...will all of you soon be bound for France?"

"Aye," Matt said, and she felt that crackle of energy, that restlessness, that had first drawn her to him. "Twill be my first campaign and I will be up to my knees in French blood. I shall kill a hundred Frenchmen and ransom dozens of prisoners. I shall be knighted on the battlefield, the same way my lord the Black Prince was knighted following Crecy."

Margery grimaced, but Matt's words seemed spoken more in innocence, as if he were a boy imagining fantastical tales.

"I plan to perform so many acts of bravery that the minstrels will sing my praises in the same breath as Arthur's and Roland's."

Was he mocking himself and all those stories he and his kind devoured for entertainment? Or was he serious? *What strange dreams lords have!*

"Will many Englishmen die in France, sire?"

"Aye."

"What about Lord Ravenne? He could be killed, could he not?"

Matthew laughed, as if such a fate was too ludicrous to imagine. "My brother-in-law may not be one of England's finest, but remember, we are fighting the French."

Perhaps so, but England's churches were filled with the tomb chests of knights, accomplished or otherwise. In battle anything could happen. The possibility lifted her spirits.

"I hope the battles are very bloody," she said.

"Aye!" Matthew was surprised and pleased that Margery Watson understood the joys of combat. He gazed at her with deepening interest.

Her stomach flipped, as if she'd ingested something peculiar. "I crave your leave, sire," she said quickly. "My stepfather will be awaiting me." A lie, of course. Alf would be slumped over some table at the Crown and Sceptre.

Matt hesitated, and for a moment she feared he might kiss her again. "I will see you before I leave, Margery Watson," he said, swinging up on his stallion.

"I pray not," she breathed, watching him ride away. Turning back, Margery straightened her shoulders and continued her walk along Cottage Lane, toward the Watson cottage. Leaks from its dilapidated roof had exacerbated a structural flaw causing it to lean sideways, as if seeking companionship from its neighbors. The walls, inside and out, were badly stained, and the interior always smelled vaguely of death. Or at least its accouterments; the accouterments of plague.

She heard a low-pitched moan and gauged its direction. Most likely Walt the Miller, having another one of his attacks. Walt's entire family had been wiped out by the Death, driving him to madness. Before Sunday mass, Father Oswald would tie him to the rood screen, hoping unsuccessfully that God's word might cure his condition.

Margery found Walt slumped beside the entrance to an abandoned house. Reaching down, she gently rested her hand on top of the cross that had been cut into his hair—a remedy against his mental condition. "'Tis Margery, Walt. Let me take you home."

Turning anguished eyes toward her, he rolled his head from side to side. "I've no home," he wailed. "No home. No home."

Margery looked around at all the buildings that were gutted or in disrepair, providing shelter for little more than pigeons. She thought of Alf, who drowned the past in drink, and Lettice, who rutted with Ravenne in the vain hope of securing some favor. She thought of Matthew Hart, who depicted his future in terms of carnage. She thought of her mother, who had died within footsteps of this spot.

"You are right, Walt," she whispered, helping the miller to his feet. "None of us has any home now."

CHAPTER 8

Ravennesfield, London bound

Over the next three days, Matthew Hart was often in Margery's thoughts, though not in a happy fashion. Rather she dwelled exclusively on his imperfections, which were nearly countless. One of the precepts priests taught was: "As above, so below." This meant that heaven and earth mirrored each other, and astrologers used the saying to explain why a man's fate was cast in the stars. Margery told herself that any physical imperfections Matthew Hart possessed mirrored the imperfections of his soul.

And she would root out every one.

She started with the color of his eyes. Their changeability, sometimes green, sometimes blue, bespoke an erratic disposition. His nose and jaw line was not strong and determined but rather insolent and cruel. She found his full mouth distasteful, for it implied sensuality. No doubt he enjoyed success with the ladies, but sensuality was a sin. Well, not sensuality exactly. Priests used other words, like fornication and gluttony and sloth, which meant the same thing.

Since his hair was more sun-streaked than blond, he must spend his life largely outdoors, hawking and hunting and practicing war games, which meant he possessed a depraved temperament, for he obviously enjoyed seeing creatures killed or killing them himself.

When Margery could not sleep, she found herself reliving their encounter and endlessly recounting Matthew Hart's flaws. By the time she drifted off, she'd once more convince herself that the young squire possessed so many faults it was a wonder God had allowed him to be born.

On the fourth day, upon opening her window shutters, Margery saw the object of her opprobrium riding up the lane toward her cottage.

"Jesu!" She had thought about Matthew Hart so often she could almost believe he was a chimera, until he dismounted in front of her door. Suppressing the urge to run her fingers through her hair and smooth her gown, Margery met him outside and after a curtsy, bluntly asked, "What are you doing here, sir?"

She was surprised at how breathless was her speech, how light-headed she felt. *Hands,* she thought. *Arrogant.*

"I wanted to see you before we left, Meg. Ravennesfield is not so very far from Cumbria. Well, at least it is on the way. And when the campaign is over, I shall visit again."

She had spent so much time transforming Matthew Hart into a lecherous swine, he now looked almost achingly young. He could have been a grinning lad of twelve, standing outside her cottage, asking if she wanted him to teach her how to juggle. She felt a moment's tenderness toward him, but only a moment's.

"Ravennesfield is a dying village," she said. "There's naught here to interest the likes of you."

"I believe there is."

Reaching out, Matt cradled her face. His fingers curled in her tousled hair—blunt, brutal fingers. She felt his callused palms against her cheeks and her stomach did that curious thing again. Then he drew back.

"I shall bring you a present from France. What would you like? Just tell me, and it will be yours."

"I want nothing, sir."

"Come along, Meg. Would you have an emerald necklace or a diamond brooch? Cloth of velvet or brocade?"

"What would I do with such finery?"

"You must want something. All women like pretty things."

Not daring to meet his gaze again, she looked down at the ground and shook her head.

Matt laughed and stepped away, to his horse. "Nevertheless, I shall bring you a present. And now I must be off. Our men are gathering even as we speak."

Watching the young squire ride away, Margery felt the oddest sensation, something akin to sadness or longing, though of course that could not be the case. She hastened toward Alice's grave, where she could see the highway. There, she waited until Matthew Hart joined a group of knights who were headed south.

"I hate you," she whispered fiercely, watching him disappear amidst the waving banners. "I hope both you and Lawrence Ravenne die in France."

AS MATTHEW RODE beside his younger brother, he tried to count the line of knights stretched out in front of them. Three days of arduous riding had done nothing to dampen his enthusiasm for the forthcoming campaign. From across the kingdom, two thousand six hundred men-at-arms were even now converging on Southampton, where they would set sail for Bordeaux under the command of Edward the Black Prince. Once in France, they would inflict total destruction upon their enemy and Matthew Hart would be in the forefront. Of that, he had no doubt.

If only I could transport us all across the channel upon command, he thought, squirming in his saddle.

When he wasn't up front with his father and brother-in-law, listening to them reminisce about past battles, Matthew dutifully dropped to the rear. There, he tried unsuccessfully to engage Harry in conversation. Since his brother appeared to have lost the art of speech, Matthew passed the time drinking in the surrounding sights and sounds. Never had he seen so much color—in the caparisons of the high-stepping palfreys, in the shields tied to their saddles, the jupons the knights wore over their armor, the standards trembling in the breeze.

Wave after wave of color. Brown highway winding through miles of green countryside; white lilies-of-the-valley boiling out from the woods and rushing down hillsides. Untilled fields, riotous with purple foxglove, yellow daffodils and buttercups, red primrose and red campion. Blue and white blankets of periwinkles clotting the road-sides; hawthorn hedges, bristling with fragrant white and pink flowers, enclosing sleek brown cattle and sheep the color of cream.

Someone started singing a ribald song about a tavern wench and a randy squire. Matthew joined in, ignoring the silent waves of disap-proval emanating from beside him. As he sang the chorus, he glanced sideways, wondering at the troubled look on Harry's face.

It cannot be my singing; he's worn the same look for days.

Perhaps Harry was unhappy because he was going to miss the current campaign. But at fifteen, he still had plenty of time. Perhaps he did not like serving in John of Gaunt's household. Or perhaps the other knights yet teased him.

Harry had shed some of his timidity, but he would always be more a talker than a fighter. Matthew sometimes worried that Father might make good his threat to pack Harry off to a monastery—a threat which had been hurled with alarming regularity throughout their childhood.

"Do not cringe so in front of the horses, lad," William would say.

"Stand up to the other boys."

"Look me in the eye when I speak to you."

"Do not turn to your brother for help."

"Do not cry."

A thousand commands, all ending with that dreaded threat.

Even if Harry had been acceptable to William, the church was always a possibility for a second son. Matthew would inherit every-thing, and if Harry failed to carve for himself a proper place in the world, he might have no other option save some gloomy monastery. There, he would have naught to do save recite the monastic hours and weed the monastic gardens and quarrel with other monks over who could most skillfully illumine a manuscript, or who was most diligent at fasting, or who currently enjoyed the abbot's favor. God's bones, what a life!

Fortunately, Matthew had taken care of Harry's future, just as he had taken care of Harry's bullies and Harry's hawks. He had groomed his brother's pony when Harry forgot. He had lied to William about the amount of time his brother spent in the solar being petted and pampered by their mother and her maids. Now that they were squires in separate households, it was harder to protect him, but Matthew was also certain that Harry was toughened and would be as good a knight as any. How could he not with the Hart blood in his veins?

On his thirteenth birthday, he had guaranteed Harry's future by announcing that he would never marry. His parents had met his declaration with indulgent smiles, for a lifelong bachelor, especially one from a wealthy family, was rare as an eclipse of the sun. Matthew, however, had meant what he said.

He intended to spend his life on the battlefield. Marriage would only complicate matters, and Matt didn't like complicated things. More importantly, his bachelorhood would keep Harry out of the clutches of the church and guarantee him a prosperous life.

In fact if not in theory, Matthew had handed Harry the mantle of first born, with holdings stretching from Cumbria in the north to Sussex in the south. Which was fine.

I shall obtain all the wealth I need from ransomed knights and war booty, and all the fame I desire from fawning minstrels.

They passed one of a multitude of villages with thatched roofs and a wooden church spire that contrasted pleasantly with the soft blue sky and occasional wisp of cloud.

"Just think, Harry. In no time at all, 'twill be French skies I'm looking upon, French towns I'm burning. If God is good, I may even be knighted on the battlefield."

Confronted by his brother's perpetual state of ecstasy, Harry's spirits plummeted even further. Matt seemed so eager to grasp his future, so unconcerned with the prospect of dying, so unaware that he'd have to soon endure dreadful hardships that were so much a part of any *chevauchee*. Not for the first time, Harry wondered whether he himself might be a changeling.

He had been praying that Matt secretly shared his fears, that his brother's bravado was merely an accomplished act. And yet Harry would have wagered the kingdom—if it had been his to wager—'twas not so. By contrast, what did that make Harry? A half man? A coward?

Harry slid a sideways glance at Matt, who gaped all about him with unrestrained delight. Sometimes Harry wondered at his older brother's wits. He sighed deeply, dramatically, as if Matthew might hear him above the surrounding noise and question what was wrong. A matter had been weighing heavily on Harry's mind. Soon they would reach London, where Matthew would join his liege, Edward the Black Prince, and he would lose all opportunity to broach it.

He must speak now.

Harry tried easing into the subject. "'Tis true what they say about the Death. England will never be the same. Remember last Christmas when we visited York Minster? Six years have passed and no work has been done on the west front or the nave. 'Tis strange to walk inside and see scaffolding still in place."

Matthew was pleased his brother had finally broken his silence, though not at his choice of topic. "I never give a thought to that time. 'Tis the future that beckons, not the past.

"The plague never touched our family," he continued, hoping his words might smooth Harry's troubled countenance. "It preyed more on the clergy than true knights. Not one member of His Grace's Order of the Garter was stricken. Is that not reason enough to believe God loves us?"

Harry suppressed another sigh. Matt was missing his point; he often did. Death could come swiftly, unexpectedly, invisibly. Death could come riding upon the wind, or screaming on the blade of a sword.

"Remember before the plague, Matt? All the portents? The freak twins joined at the chest who were born in Kingston-upon-Hull? The flooding in York? I have been having dreams filled with burning windmills and rivers of blood. I fear they bode ill for the future."

Expecting a reaction, Harry glanced across at his brother, but Matt was preoccupied with a brace of swallows, soaring upwards to catch in the clouds.

Will there be swallows in France? he wondered. *Does it rain there as much as it does here? Will it be flat like the fens, or mountainous like Cumbria?*

Harry had wanted to steer Matthew gently but his brother had never been one for subtlety. "What if something bad happens to you in France?" he asked bluntly.

Matthew looked at him, surprised. "What could happen?"

"You forget you are going off to war, not a joust. There might be glory in war, but there is also death."

"Not mine. I have no intention of spilling my life's blood on enemy soil."

"You have not had any portentous dreams? Troubling omens?"

"Of course not. We are knights, Harry. We dream of fine horses and magnificent battles. We dream of being feted by ladies with golden hair and rosebud lips."

Matthew suddenly remembered Margery Watson, who was neither a lady nor in possession of golden hair. Nor would he describe her lips as rosebud, whatever that meant. But she had been intriguing all the same.

"I am pleased your dreams are peaceful." Not that Harry could imagine anything *bad* happening to Matt, in sleep or otherwise. Like their father, Matthew was indestructible, akin to the forces of nature. Harry cleared his throat, his fingers unconsciously tightening upon the reins in his hand. "Promise me something, Matt."

"If I can."

"Prince Edward and his squires were knighted following Crecy, were they not?"

"Aye, Harry. Everyone knows that."

"And the prince plans to totally crush Jean le Bon this time, does he not?"

"How can he fail?"

"I know you would like to be knighted on the battlefield, but if

71

Prince Edward moves to do so, would you wait until you and I might be knighted together?"

Matthew turned to his brother in amazement, barely suppressing his first impulse, which was to box Harry between the ears. "Jesu! Do you realize what you ask? To be knighted on the battlefield means a thousand times more than some formal church ceremony. Why would you think to deprive me of something so important?"

"Remember when you were seven and you left Cumbria to serve as a page in Prince Edward's household? Remember how I cried and begged you not to leave me?"

Matthew nodded warily. "What has that to do with anything? We were children."

"I remember it well. You said I mustn't fear, that someday we would serve together. You said, 'I will wait for you. We will be knighted together and fight wars together and we will never be separated again.' Those were your very words."

"You will not trap me with ancient promises, Harry. You were so upset then not even Father's threats could silence you."

"All those months you were gone, I would say 'Matt will soon be back. And when we are grown, we shall do everything together, just as he promised.' It was the only thing that made life bearable.'"

Matthew ran his fingers distractedly through his hair. "I do not even remember exactly what I said. I merely thought to calm you. Please do not hold me to words so thoughtlessly given."

"If you are knighted on the battlefield, Father will hold that up to me until the day I die. 'Look at Matt,' he'll say. 'Now there is a real man, and what are you? Just a back-door knight.'"

"Father was knighted in the customary manner."

"But no one doubts his courage, or his skill. I shall never be knighted on the battlefield, but I can be as good a fighter as most. I just canna be as good as you. I beg of you. Do not make life more difficult for me."

Voices from their childhood welled up in Matthew's memory. "Do not let them hit me, Matt."

"Can you do it for me? 'Tis so much easier for you."

"Do not tell Father I forget to feed my hawks."

"Do not tell Father I was in the garden."

"Do not tell Father I fell off my horse."

"Do not tell Father…"

Harry leaned across his saddle to place a hand on Matthew's arm. "Please?"

Around them riders chattered about mundane things. Ahead snaked the endless train undulating toward London–and beyond that to Matt's glorious future.

"You ask too much!"

Harry's eyes filled with tears. "Father will never let me live it down. I want him to be proud of both of us, and I can prove myself to him, I know I can."

Undone by Harry's tears, Matthew stared at his stallion's mane. When Harry was upset, it was hard to deny him anything. Mayhap he was right. When he became a knight, William might change his demeanor. And if they were knighted together, a measure of Father's good will could very well transfer itself to Harry. Still, to be knighted on the battlefield—

His fist clenched on his thigh. They might not even engage the French. A truce could be negotiated while the English were still in Bordeaux. The Black Prince might not knight anybody. But he might, and Matthew wanted to be one of the men chosen. His gaze swept the line of knights, the green hillside and the brown rope of highway. The colors no longer seemed so bright, the day no longer bursting with such promise.

Matthew inhaled deeply. He felt something slip inside him, but this was his brother after all…

"All right," he said, finally, "I shall wait. But I will not like it."

CHAPTER 9

Poitiers, 1356

uch of the 1355 campaign had been a blur to Matthew Hart, yielding only scattered impressions. Through chroniclers wrote that the plundered land, which had not known "war of a long season," had been bountiful before the English arrival, Matthew could think of nothing complimentary to say about France. Compared to England, it was an ugly country. Beyond Bordeaux, with its miles of vineyards, rolling hills stretched seemingly forever toward the jagged Pyrennes Mountains. Matthew remembered the scattered forests only for the villagers he'd flushed out of their huts and caves; he remembered the *plat pays*, typical of so much of France, for the peasants he'd chased across their bleakness.

Matthew's most vivid memories were of fire. Fire and rain. He recalled countless windmills, their revolving vanes ablaze with flames, standing above the surrounding destruction like flailing skeletons, crumbling to ignite the grasses below. He had helped torch innumerable villages, wheat fields, even monasteries.

And the rains, how could he ever forget them? December's skies had been as relentless as a biblical deluge, soaking bones, transforming discomfort into sickness, turning roads into dangerous morasses.

He remembered endless river crossings with overloaded pack horses slipping on muddy banks, urged like squeamish maidens into treacherous currents swollen by the rains. Dwindling supplies. Empty bellies. When the horses could not find drinking water, they had been given wine.

Drunk horses. Exhausted men.

By Christmas, 1355, the English were safe and warm in Bordeaux. According to the standards of *Maximum Damnum*—total destruction— Edward of Woodstock's campaign had been a success. But measured by Matthew's criterion, it had not. They had not fought another Crecy. They had engaged peasants and the bourgeoisie, not true knights. The campaign had yielded much booty, but Matthew had come to fight a war, not loot and pillage.

After setting out on their second campaign in the summer of 1356, Matthew had high hopes. So far, however, it had been a mirror of their first with booty laden baggage trains and only marginal skirmishes.

Circumstances changed with the waning summer. Finally, the French King, Jean le Bon, decided to engage. Possessing a much smaller army, Prince Edward had hoped to combine forces with Henry, Duke of Lancaster, but when that failed, retreated toward Bordeaux. With the French fast upon them, Edward allowed no rest, no matter how rocky the terrain or dense the forest. The pace was grueling. The English traveled four hundred miles in little more than forty days. No one complained for all knew they must outflank the French.

In mid-September the English approached Chauvigny, near the town of Poitiers, or "Peyters," as Prince Edward called it. Scouts galloped into camp with word that Jean le Bon had blocked their exodus southward to Angouleme.

"We must fight now," Matthew Hart told his father, who, as a member of the war council, was privy to all decision making.

"We cannot fight," William responded grimly. "We do not have enough men and those we have are exhausted. Somehow, we shall have to slip through their lines."

But even as Prince Edward raced to outmaneuver the French, even as Matthew spent another rigorous day and night in the saddle, he prayed they would not evade Jean le Bon's grasp. No matter how great the odds, Matthew was certain the English would triumph.

BY SUNDAY, September 18, 1356, Prince Edward knew he had no other choice. Five miles out of Poitiers, he called a halt and readied his men to make a stand.

Cardinal Talleyrand of Perigord begged both sides to avoid bloodshed on God's most holy day. While the Cardinal attempted to mediate a permanent truce, Edward ordered his men to dig trenches and fashion stake-filled pits along the line of hedges that would shield the archers.

Matthew decided the fortifications strengthened an already near perfect defense. The English were encamped on the crest of a wooded slope and the surrounding terrain was hilly. In addition to the copious undergrowth, marshy patches bordered on the River Miausson, at the foot of the hill. The slope opened onto a wide field, dissected by one narrow road—the only route by which the French could attack. In fact, the English were protected on all sides—left and right by steep drop-offs, at their back by woods so densely treed that a man on horseback could not effectively maneuver.

Cardinal Talleyrand's mediation failed. Believing the Black Prince could not successfully resist the overwhelming odds against him, Jean le Bon demanded the impossible. "I will accept only unconditional surrender from Edward of Woodstock, as well as a hundred of his knights."

Keeping his expression appropriately sober, Matthew Hart inwardly rejoiced. *On the morrow we will face the French. And my life will never be the same.*

ASSEMBLED with the rest of Edward's troops, Matthew waited for their prince to speak. When he thought about the inevitability of combat, his heart raced, yet he tried to etch every moment, every impression, in his memory.

A cloudless cerulean sky intensified the colors of nearby vineyards, which were beginning to brighten to gold and rust. The slightest breeze brought to Matthew's nostrils the scent of leather and animals, the morning cook fires, and the musty, almost indefinable odor that marked fall's arrival. Above the wooded hill behind which Jean le Bon's troops were encamped, one sparrow hawk struggled upward before soaring toward the sun.

The green and white of the archers' tunics, the crimson and gold of Edward's banner, the beasts and animals and plants upon the knights' shields, all seemed almost unbearably vivid.

Prince Edward strode to the center of his men, dressed in the black armor that was his hallmark. "God has decreed that on this day we will fight the French," he began. "Just as you know we are outnumbered, you also know our cause is just. Your king, my father, has an inherent right to the French throne, to the very ground upon which we stand, and by the Grace of God, after this day his claim will be more secure."

Bareheaded, Edward moved among his troops. A breeze lifted a strand of golden hair and a corner of his jewel-encrusted jupon.

Matthew thought, *I will tell Harry that our prince looked as fine as the saints illustrated in a Book of Hours, and we knew we could not fail with Edward of Woodstock to lead us.*

"I will not say that victory will come easy," Edward continued, "but, God willing, it will come. We are Englishmen, the finest soldiers in all the world. No matter should we face a legion of devils, we would prevail. Nor will Our Blessed Savior or St. George forsake us in our hour of need. Englishmen in London, York, Chester and Canterbury will hold up their heads and walk proud after this day, for the battle of Poitiers will wrap each of us in glory."

Next to Matthew, Lawrence Ravenne muttered, "More likely in a shroud." Throughout the campaign Matthew's brother-in-law had been plagued by boils on his backside and his mood was just as raw. "How can we face sixty, or even thirty thousand French, however many there truly are? 'Tis one thing to be brave, quite another to be foolhardy."

77

Matthew glanced at his father, standing off to one side with other members of the war council. He could not interpret the expression on William's face, but he caught Sir Thomas Rendell's eye, (Throughout the campaign Matthew kept wondering about Lord Rendell's resemblance...to whom? The answer kept eluding him) and when Rendell winked, it reinforced his conviction that his brother-in-law's talk of shrouds was mere doom-saying.

Shouts drifted from the open ground in the valley below. Time was running out.

Edward stood straight and tall. "A thousand years from now, this day will be discussed and harkened back to as England's finest hour. And though our children and great-great-grandchildren will die, our memory will live forever."

Matthew clenched his fist inside his steel gauntlet. *God has granted me this day, this first battle, and should I fight in a thousand such, none will surpass this one.*

As Edward continued speaking, he seemed to grow, to assume proportions larger than life and dimensions beyond humanity. He was not plain Edward of Woodstock, but a symbol of royalty, of England itself. Matthew was pleased with that image, for it was something Harry would enjoy.

"Remember that I will never disappoint you," Prince Edward said. "I will never call upon you to do what I will not. My arm will be stronger than the strongest, my danger greater, my bravery the courage of ten thousand lions. You will never see your prince defeated. Nor will you be defeated. We are Englishmen, and that makes all the difference."

"We are madmen," Lawrence Ravenne muttered, "and the French sun has baked our prince's brain."

But not even such blatant cynicism could mar Matthew's excitement. *This is what life is all about,* he thought, following his prince to the small hill from which they would view the battle. *This is why God created us. For this very moment.*

For Poitiers.

. . . .

A CAVALRY of three hundred French knights raced up the narrow road toward the saw-tooth formation of English archers. The cavalry was to act as a single spearhead which would crash through the hedges. After scattering the yeomen, the remainder of the French, positioned below and on foot in three separate battalions, would attack at predetermined intervals.

Trumpets blared; drums beat in time. "Montjois St. Denis!" the French cried, galloping forward, three abreast. Their destriers strained across the open field, across rows of bleached corn stalks and harvested wheat. Behind the hedges, English yeomen fitted arrows into bowstrings and drew back their bows.

The morning sky darkened as a cloud of arrows arched overhead, guided by keen eyes and silent prayers to St. Sebastian, the martyr of arrows. The French continued straight toward the numerous gaps in the English line, but horses began shying away from the rain of death. Some crashed into the vineyards. Others bucked free of their riders, putting the fallen knights in even greater danger.

Matthew watched the French charge crumple into chaos. Blood gushed from countless wounds—animal blood, human blood, blood as red as the leaves of the turning vineyard, as red as the wine made from the clumps of grapes that still clung to its vines. Unsheathing their long knives, English foot soldiers crept from behind the hedges and pinioned the helpless Frenchmen, slitting their throats.

Situated more than a mile away, unable to see the devastation of his cavalry, Jean ordered forward his first battalion of foot soldiers, under the command of his eldest son, the Dauphin Charles. The battalion, which also contained three of France's four royal princes, began marching toward the English line. More trumpets; more drums mixed with screams and shouts and the thunder of war.

Along with his father, four hundred reserves, and Prince Edward, Matthew surveyed the French soldiers. Having reached its zenith, the sun caught the armor from six thousand men-at-arms. Below, the English archers had re-formed behind the hedges and were now waiting for the enemy to approach.

"They are on foot!" Lawrence Ravenne shaded his eyes against the sun's glare. "The pomp of France, indeed! They look more like peasants than knights."

"But they are much better armed," countered William Hart.

Matthew's gaze never left the oncoming army—row upon endless row, rippling like wild barley grass in the wake of a running horse. Scouts said King Jean held two more battalions in reserve, the last larger than Edward's entire army. Matthew's mouth felt dry.

Soon, he thought. A measure of fear tempered his excitement.

"St. George!" The English yeomen yelled, loosening their arrows.

Marching up the path, the French narrowed their ranks to four abreast. Arrows struck harmlessly against their armor. Toward ragged gaps in the hedges they marched, dodging rider-less horses, stepping across the wounded or dying, meeting foot soldiers in hand-to-hand combat. French knights stabbed with their shortened lances or hacked with battle axes and swords, forcing the English back toward their own archers.

The sun edged westward. Mortally wounded soldiers sprawled on top of bodies already beginning to stiffen. The hillside was slick with blood. Matthew heard the ring of steel upon steel. The cries and screams, chroniclers later wrote, sounded all the way to Nouaille Abbey and the dense darkness of the Bois de St. Pierre.

Led by an inexperienced Dauphin, the French eventually began to give ground, but the retreat was measured in inches.

A sudden shout of triumph exploded from English throats as the Dauphin's standard was seized. Whereupon, the French quickly shepherded Charles and his brothers from the field.

The English needed time to rest and regroup. Bow quivers were nearly empty while jagged gaps in the hedges showed like the yawning jaws of a canine. However, under the command of Philippe d'Orleans, brother of the king, France's second battalion was already moving forward. If this attack proved as devastating as the first, Prince Edward would have to commit his pitifully small reserves. Who would then face King Jean's battalion?

Matthew told himself, *We cannot lose*, but he had no idea how they could win.

On horseback, the Duc d'Orleans and his men came into view. A hush fell across the English line. From the battlefield, the wounded and dying screamed for help and water or the ministrations of a priest.

Matthew watched the French near the point where they would dismount. Upon meeting the blood-soaked, limping, cursing, weeping remnants of their foot soldiers, the Duc's battalion seemed to hesitate *en masse,* then, as if of one mind, retreated in the direction of Chauvigny and the departed dauphin.

"God's nails!" Prince Edward cried. "What are they doing?"

"'Twould appear they are leaving the battlefield," William Hart said. "But I canna believe six thousand men would ride away without striking a blow."

"The Duc is a friend of England this day," Matthew said.

"'Tis a miracle," said the prince. "God is surely on our side."

Many knights crossed themselves and muttered heartfelt thanks to their creator.

Not quite believing their good fortune, the English kept a wary eye on the retreating horses. Why had the Duc decided to flee? Had he been ordered to withdraw? Or was he reluctant to fight on foot in the manner more suited to a common soldier than a knight?

During the lull, archers retrieved arrows from the bodies of the fallen, fetched drinking water, straightened battered weapons, and tried for a measure of rest. Accompanied by Matthew and members of his bodyguard, Prince Edward rode down the hill. Moving among his troops, he tried to instill strength and purpose into his exhausted men.

From a ridge to the north, King Jean marched forward with his final battalion. Overhead flew the Oriflamme—the fork-tongued scarlet banner of the kings of France.

Jean breasted the rise, leading his battalion of ten thousand men. Matthew could actually *feel* the waves of terror that overcame the English, and the strength momentarily drained from his own limbs.

The enemy's silver body writhed toward them, the Oriflamme flicking overhead. Hours of daylight remained. Darkness would not cover the English, nor allow them any rest. Those nearest the shelter of Nouaille Wood began to desert.

"We are undone!" Lawrence Ravenne cried, giving voice to the fear of hundreds. "'Tis hopeless!"

Prince Edward, who had returned to the war council, turned on Ravenne with an expression that would cause the bravest warrior to shrink from his wrath. "You lie, miserable coward! How can you think that I, alive, might be conquered? While I have a breath in my body, 'tis blasphemy to say we are beaten."

Matthew could not blame Ravenne for expressing what so many were thinking. But when Matthew's gaze swung from his father's face to the faces of his father, Thomas Rendell, John Chandos, and the others on the war council, and to that of his prince, he saw only determination. Inside his armor, Matthew unconsciously squared his shoulders and a wave of confidence, if not joy, swept through him. How could anyone doubt men so supremely self-assured? Wasn't the prince the favored son of a golden father? Wasn't England herself a blessed nation?

The French neared.

Edward walked among his troops, cajoling, inspiring, cursing them back to order. "They cannot overcome us! Their numbers mean only that our glory will be greater. Are you Englishmen or French? Only the French run from the field. See how they fear us? 'Tis not I, but the Duc d'Orleans who slinks to the walls of Poitiers. You will not desert. If you dare try, I will slay you before you reach the woods."

Wave after endless wave of French crested the hill. Matthew felt the panic of his fellow soldiers as surely as he heard the cries of the dying, but no one dared run. With a raging Edward behind them and Jean le Bon before them, they were trapped.

Exhibiting a ferocity born of desperation, the English met the French.

Archers shot the last of their arrows.

Holding their shields over their heads, King Jean and his men marched on.

Once their quivers were emptied, some of the archers again tried to break and flee. But Edward stood behind them, flourishing his sword, berating, threatening, *beating* them back into order.

"Fight! They cannot win if we fight. Fight! Fight!" The prince's cries smashed against the English like a gauntleted fist.

The yeomen tore extra arrows from nearby bodies. When the men-at-arms' lances broke, they fought with splintered stubs. Knights who had broken their own weapons took spears and swords from the bodies of the dead.

Returning to the top of the hill, where the war council and reserves waited, Edward said, "Our men will break, I feel it. We must rally them before they all panic."

"What would you do, Your grace?" William Hart asked.

"Attack. Jean will not expect an offensive maneuver, and cavalry still have an advantage over foot, no matter how badly we're outnumbered."

Edward instructed sixty men and one hundred archers to ride north-west, down a hidden track, through a hollow which came out behind the French. "Attack from behind. When you engage them, we shall attack from the front."

William turned to his son. "It would appear you are finally going into battle, lad. I have no doubt you will acquit yourself well enough this day to win your spurs."

Matthew managed a grin. "I might even win me a French king."

Swinging into his saddle, Prince Edward laughed. "Enjoy this moment. War is like a woman. The first is ever the most memorable." Edward then addressed his standard-bearer.

"Bear my banner straight toward Jean le Bon." Louder. "Advance, men, in the name of God and St. George!"

Trumpets sounded. Thrown back by the stone walls of Poitiers, wrote chroniclers, the ear-shattering blasts seemed to make the hills call out to the valleys and thunder crash in the clouds.

Edward's four hundred hit the French at a run. Matthew glimpsed the prince, surrounded by Frenchmen, his sword a silver blur. As one of several squires, Matthew's job was to protect Edward. In the beginning he was able to keep up, but the prince fought so fiercely, no man could match him. His padded jupon contained more arrows than spines on a hedgehog, but Edward attacked with indefatigable fury, mowing down anybody in his way, warding off blows as if he had a dozen eyes and a thousand arms.

Gripping his broadsword with both hands, Matthew stood in his stirrups and swung at the endless knights whose uplifted faces were hidden inside their bascinets. Deprived of their horses, the Frenchmen fell under Matthew's sword and mace as easily as ripened wheat before a peasant's scythe.

The battle passed its seventh hour; the sun edged toward its resting place. Matthew's heart roared in his ears, his breathing seared his lungs, and his sword arm swung with a will of its own. His father, wielding a mace with manic accuracy, fought near the prince. To Matthew's left rode Thomas Rendell, brandishing a war hammer, and Lawrence Ravenne, who abruptly crumpled from his saddle. Matthew did not try to reach his brother-in-law. His duty must be to Edward, no other man.

Slowly, inexorably, Prince Edward pushed toward the Oriflamme.

The French fought as desperately as the English, but their phalanx began to buckle under the onslaught of Edward's attack and the flank assault. Men grappled in hand-to-hand combat. Scarce able to lift their weapons, enemies staggered against each other. With their arrow supplies long since exhausted, the English archers emerged from behind hedges bearing swords, axes, looted household knives, and hammers. When those weapons were unavailable, they grabbed stones or attacked with their fists.

One by one, France's banners fell. Finally, the Oriflamme itself wavered and plunged to the ground. Knowing their cause was lost, one body of eight hundred French lancers galloped off the field without striking a blow.

Scarlet tinged the clouds as the sun hovered above the western horizon. Matthew's destrier, Roland, slipped and stumbled on a field of dismembered arms and legs, a field as slick as a frozen river with blood. The euphoria of battle had long ago given way to weariness, and Matthew found himself looking without emotion upon decapitated bodies—helms trailing the sinew that had once joined head to neck. He looked upon wounds laid bare to the bone, and brains spilling from smashed skulls. One French marshal, butted in the mouth, vomited forth his teeth; others trod upon their own entrails.

The noise of the battle diminished. The groans and cries of the dying reached such a cacophony Matthew began to feel unnerved. He saw Edward retreat from the field, and gratefully followed.

Jean le Bon and a small contingent remained, while the rest fled back toward their horses or Poitiers. English knights, led by William Hart, bore down upon the French king, whose black armor and white surcoat marked by fleur-de-lis made him easily recognizable. Surrounded by his wedge of bodyguards, Jean fought valiantly, seemingly oblivious to the fact that the battle was lost.

"Surrender yourself!" William commanded, pointing his sword at the king's throat.

Jean's helm, once topped by a dazzling crest of plumes, was dented in a dozen places, and he bled from several head wounds. Removing his right gauntlet, he handed it to William.

The Battle of Poitiers was over.

A hush descended. Only the shouts of Englishmen pursuing the retreating French could be heard. The sun set over the jumble of bodies, glinted off armor, edged across faces frozen in death, and crept toward the hill where Matthew and Prince Edward and members of his bodyguard had gathered.

Thomas Rendell planted Edward's banner beside a bush so that returning soldiers would have a rallying point.

William Hart handed Prince Edward Jean's gauntlet "Victory belongs to you, sire."

Edward's favored commander, John Chandos, put his arm around the prince who bowed his head, silently giving thanks to God. Though Edward's face was streaked with grime, Matthew thought his prince had never looked so...princely. Matthew bowed his head, too, but he couldn't pray, not yet. Exultation swept over him, replacing weariness. They had done the unbelievable, the impossible. Eight thousand Englishmen had triumphed over thirty thousand Frenchmen. No wonder God loved them!

A final burst of sunset bathed the battlefield, its rays shining brighter than the blood from countless wounds. Radiant streamers reflected the gaping throats that grinned up at the sky. Injured knights crawled toward the woods. Englishmen captured nobles for ransom, or raced toward the richly accoutered French tents for plunder.

Edward raised his head. His gaze touched upon his troops, then settled on Matthew. "You fought well, lad, as boldly as any knight."

Surprised by Edward's attention, Matthew could only murmur, "Thank you, sire."

Removing his sword, Edward motioned to Matthew and several other squires. "Come forward and kneel. This day you have truly earned your spurs."

Matthew tried to stifle the grin that spread across his face. His dream of being knighted on the battlefield was about to be realized. Wait until he told Harry.

Harry! God's teeth! Harry would weep and chastise him for breaking his word.

You ask too much, Harry. After you understand, you will not begrudge me this honor.

"Come, Matthew," Edward said. "You shall be first."

Edward stretched forth his sword with William Hart behind him. Even through the smears of dirt on his face, even in the fading light, William's eyes shown with pride–and love.

Matthew's heart twisted. Almost imperceptibly, he shook his head. "I cannot, sire. I swore to wait for my brother."

Always impressed by vows and other such chivalric gestures, Edward nodded, said, "So be it," and moved to the next. Matthew stood stiff and straight as the other squires knelt to accept their knight-hood. Shutting out the words of the oath, shutting out the disbelief on his father's face, he closed his eyes rather than watch Prince Edward touch each shoulder with his sword.

Aye, Harry, you asked almost more than I can bear.

Matt had kept his word, as a knight must. So why did he feel such bleakness? Even though he'd proven himself to be a man this day, Matthew found himself very close to crying.

CHAPTER 10

Ravennesfield, 1357

lf leaned his weight against Margery as they left their cottage for the Crown and Sceptre. Villagers had been welcoming home yeomen from Poitiers, and Alf had participated in the celebration by drinking even more than usual.

Margery had heard soldiers regale admiring crowds with tales of the battle, over and over and over again. Their parrot-like voices especially lauded the Black Prince, whose exploits had achieved legendary status. Earlier this afternoon, Robert Wytbread's son, Robert the Younger, had returned to a hero's welcome with a sack of booty slung across his shoulder and a proud grin creasing his plain face.

More than a week had passed since Prince Edward had docked at Sandwich. Now he and his knights were making a triumphant procession toward London. At every village and alehouse the prince had been met by cheering multitudes, anxious to welcome England's champion and glimpse his royal prisoner, Jean le Bon, who was being ransomed for four million ecus.

Even Ravennesfield, so isolated from most events, was eager for every scrap of information. Not for the first time, Margery felt estranged from her fellow villagers with their talk of glory and victory and courageous deeds. To her, death was death, and the rest was just words, hollow as a reed. She imagined the corpses of all the young men, strewn upon the French plains like discarded sacks of grain. Men who had given their lives for the honor of a class that despised them. Sweet Jesu! How could people be so stupid?

Alf stumbled, then clutched at her. Struggling to conceal her impatience, Margery waited for him to regain his balance. She hated Alf's smell, his incoherent mutterings, the pressure of his body against her shoulder, the manner in which he jolted her so that her teeth clicked together. She hated the feel of his rough woolen mantle against her cheek, rubbing her skin raw.

For some reason, the returning yeomen had put Alf in an even fouler mood than usual. "Donna walk so fast," he grumbled. "Wot's yer hurry?" He stumbled and pitched forward. Fearing he might drag her along, Margery did not attempt to catch him.

"Jesu," he muttered, fumbling for her outstretched hand. "The world 'tis spinning."

Margery bit back a caustic reply. Once they reached the inn, she would ask Kate the Alewife to let him sleep on the floor until morning.

Alf's arm closed over her shoulder and he pulled himself up. As they turned on High Street, Margery released a heavy sigh. *If only I could leave Ravennesfield.*

Increasingly, while working the fields, she would gaze at the horizon, as if there she could view England's great cities. She imagined working for a brewer, a baker, or a book binder, though she knew that was an absurd, hopeless dream. Should she step one foot off Lord Ravenne's property, she would be a fugitive bondwoman, subject to fines, imprisonment, even death.

A shame that Lawrence Ravenne hadn't died in France, but perhaps 'twas true what Thurold had once said. Perhaps it was impossible to kill something worthless.

Still, when Margery saw the pilgrims on the road heading toward Ely Cathedral, she longed to join them. Life was moving away from this decaying village and she wanted to move away with it.

Suddenly, she glimpsed a shape in the doorway opposite them. At first she thought it might be a cat or rat scavenging amidst the refuse, but it was far too large. Margery halted, bringing Alf to a swaying stop. Heart thumping wildly against her bodice, she peered into the shadows. Only last month, Walt the Miller had been discovered near here with his throat slashed. The murderer had not been found. In truth, he had not been sought. Violence was too commonplace nowadays.

"Is someone there?" she asked, her free hand resting on the dagger she carried at her waist.

A huge figure stepped from the shadows. "Let me take him from you," the man said. Margery noticed a second smaller man behind him. "He is a heavy burden for such a slight maid."

The shorter man stepped closer. She noted he was dressed in a yeoman's uniform and his face, while young, looked unusually hard.

"Hey, old man, do ye not remember your own son? And ye, Stick-Legs, not an embrace for a returning hero?"

"Thurold?" His voice was not Thurold's, nor did he look as she remembered. And yet his cocksure air..."You are dead," she whispered. "Lawrence Ravenne killed you."

Thurold laughed before wrapping her in his strong, wiry arms. "'Twould take more than that bumbling ass to fool me. I freed meself 'ere the even was out and hid in the fens."

"Then why did you not come back for me?" she wanted to ask, though that was just one of a jumble of questions befuddling her brain. She stared at him. Thurold, alive and walking beside her!

Thurold slipped an arm around her waist and guided her forward to follow the stranger and Alf, who had settled trustingly against his massive chest.

"John Ball," said Thurold, with a nod toward the man. "John be a hedge priest—a priest without a parish. We been travelling together."

John Ball turned around at mention of his name and gave Margery a courteous nod. Ball was perhaps thirty years old, with brown eyes set beneath thick black brows, and a beard that was already turning gray. *A striking man*, she mused, and not only because of his bulk. As he guided Alf, he whistled a melodic tune she did not recognize.

Upon entering the Crown and Sceptre, John Ball settled Alf beside Margery at a table and joined the crowd gathered round Robert the Younger, who was regaling his rapt audience with yet another version of the Battle of Poitiers.

After Kate the Alewife poured him an ale, Thurold gave Margery a shortened version of the past eight years and his absence. "I did na want to leave you but I had no choice. I made me way to London where I found employment with a goldsmith who didna ask an over-abundance of questions. When I lived there for a year and a day I was a free man. But I did na dare return to Ravennesfield, not with Ravenne about and crimes, real or imagined, upon me head. Then the French campaigns came along, and King Edward promised pardons to all who took part. So I hied me to France."

Thurold poured himself a second measure of ale. "I met the hedge priest upon my return."

In the flames from the hearth fire Margery studied her stepbrother. Now she could believe Thurold truly sat before her. The small bright eyes, jutting jaw, the quick decisive movements, the self-sufficient air were all as she remembered.

"My heart is full." Tentatively, Margery reached out to touch his arm, as if to verify he was actual flesh and blood. Thurold captured her hand, squeezed it and they both laughed, as if sharing some private merriment.

Alf Watson beckoned to Kate the Alewife, who was opening the spigot on a cask of ale. John Ball hovered nearby, a commanding, though quiet presence, seemingly content merely to observe. Margery's gaze kept drifting to the hedge priest, trying to gauge more about him, as if his face and form might reveal important secrets.

Brom the Reeve approached their table. After giving Thurold a drunken hug, he said, "We been speakin' about Prince Edward. God be praised for our good prince's victory. Peyters be the grandest hour in England's history, as well ye know, Thurold, for you was there."

"Peyters don't compare t' Crecy," Alf interrupted. "For one thing, our King Edward did not take part and—" He interrupted himself to bellow, "Kate, where's me drink? Me gullet's dry as a dust storm."

After downing his ale, Alf wiped his mouth with the back of his hand, rose from the bench, and lurched back into the crowd.

"I see the old man has na lost his good nature," Thurold remarked.

At that moment, John Ball came over. "Might I sit?"

The priest smiled down at Margery. His tonsured head nearly brushed the low ceiling. Thinking how kind he looked, she nodded. Thurold moved over and Margery knew without being told that John Ball was a man who commanded her stepbrother's respect, even reverence.

"Thurold says you are a hedge priest, Father."

John Ball laughed. "I would not quite agree, for I consider all of England to be my parish."

Thurold nodded solemnly, as if John Ball had just uttered a profundity.

Nodding toward the others, Margery asked, "Are you not interested in listening about the battle?"

"These past weeks Thurold and I have heard little else. I might turn the question around. Are *you* not interested?"

"I do not believe our lords fight to protect us, but for their own honor and glory. I think our lords are cruel and make their own laws and throw the rest of us a bone, or in the case of Poitiers, a piece of silver plate, while *they* bring home wagon-loads of booty. Why should I want to cheer such inequity?"

John Ball's dark eyebrows shot up. He studied her for a long moment before smiling. "Well spoken! I should not be surprised that you would sound so like your brother. He says near the same thing."

Margery glanced at Thurold, whose face bore an enigmatic smile.

John Ball continued, "Methinks you have a fine mind along with a pleasing countenance."

She eyed him sharply, for many priests did not take celibacy seriously though she saw nothing untoward in his expression. "'Tis true I think a lot. But my thoughts remind me of molting chickens. Hundreds of feathers floating around without purpose, falling useless to the ground."

Thurold snorted and John Ball laughed. "It seems a shame such a quick wit is wasted in this decaying village. You'd do better in a place like London, where Thurold and I be bound. In fact, that is why he asked to detour here."

Margery crumpled a piece of goose pie crust between her fingers. "I have thought about leaving, but I am not free. My mother was a bondwoman so I am tied to the land."

Thurold's mouth tightened. "You *are* free, Stick-Legs. And nowadays people leave the land, no matter what their station."

"Times are changing," John Ball agreed. "We can never go back to the way we were before the Death, but what sort of world is being created I canna say. Common folk oft bargain with their masters for more wages since there are so few to work the land. When lords gainsay them, they flee to distant villages, where their services are welcomed with no questions asked."

Thurold turned to the hedge priest and Margery, his eyes shining. "Listen to John Ball, Stick-Legs. More and more our fine lords leave off cultivating their fields and lease them to yeomen farmers, which 'tis a good thing for it brings the yeomen more coin. But the landless, they be worse off than ever. And many of our so-fine lords yet exact dues such as the merchet, which must be paid when a lad and lass would be wed, or the heriot, which enables our betters, upon the death of one of their tenants, to seize their grievin' family's best beast, no matter how poor the survivors might be."

"I do not understand such talk. All I know is that Ravennesfield is dying."

Voices from the group of men and Alf were louder, as if an argument was in the making.

"Unfortunately," John Ball said, "our lords have been passing laws to keep us in our place. For example, Parliament passed the Statute of Labourers, wherein His Grace decreed that labourers should not receive one shilling more than they have ever had. When the peasants try to obey, they're driven to destitution, for prices have risen even if wages have not. Since the statute's passage, some have escaped punishment by hiding in forests and becoming outlaws. I talk to them. Good, hardworking men, driven to crime by the policies of those who are indifferent to and contemptuous of their needs."

Margery had never heard anyone speak so boldly against King Edward, for in most people's eyes he was second only to the legendary Arthur. She glanced at Thurold. Where had he found such a man? "What do you plan to do to better the situation?" Her question encompassed them both.

"For the present, I tell Englishmen that these laws be unjust, and that we deserve better. The time will come when we will demand equality."

"When Adam delved and Eve span, who was then the gentleman?" quoted Thurold, after gesturing to Kate the Alewife for a refill.

Margery had heard that ditty before for it was as ancient as the stones. "I fear you are both whistling in the wind," she said softly. "The lords will always be on top and we shall always be on the bottom."

John Ball fixed his eyes on her, and in their depths shown a light unlike anything she had ever seen before. Margery shivered, as if she had been touched by an invisible hand. The room seemed to fade and she was no longer aware of the low-hanging smoke, the loud voices of Robert and his friends, or the musicians in the corner, scratching their fiddles. Looking into John's eyes, she knew that she was in the presence of an extraordinary being. In him she sensed a bottomless sorrow, an anguish for the pain and injustices which had been heaped on the backs of the common man since time immemorial.

"I hear much talk when I walk around England," John said, leaning forward until his face was only inches away. "I recently heard about a French Franciscan who possesses the gift of prophecy. He has been preaching among the common people, foretelling of a time when they will take up arms against the powerful and rob them of their rule."

Margery found it difficult to breathe. She wanted to tell John that he was a dangerous man—and a saint. But saints did not preach sedition, and men who spoke like John Ball and Thurold were inevitably hanged for treason.

"For as long as I can remember I have heard that the meek must someday inherit the earth," she said. "But the meek do not inhabit castles or possess land, and I cannot believe prophecies to the contrary. Naught is ever going to change, and you will only waste your life if you believe otherwise."

John drew his eyes away from Margery's, breaking the spell. He studied his half empty bowl as if viewing the future in its depths. "This French Franciscan predicted floods, tempests and plagues. After those signs come to pass, common people will rise up, massacre all the greedy churchmen, and take their property."

"You speak as if this will happen in our lifetime," she said with a shaky laugh.

"Perhaps, Margery Watson, perhaps."

John smiled at her. Thurold muttered something about "a thousand years of peace."

Margery shuddered. Such talk was dangerous. Perhaps it was not such a good idea for her stepbrother to have returned.

Thurold leaned in close to her and whispered, "You be different, Stick-Legs. I see the 'ard times etched in your manner. Ye know I did come back to get ye from your hiding place the next even. Ravennes-field was crawling with Ravenne's henchmen, or I would've found a way to stay near."

Margery's eyes filled with tears. Aye, times had been hard but at least he was here, if only for a night. Once again she reached out to squeeze his arm.

Around them, the crowd had grown noisier. Margery recognized Alf's voice above the din; Thurold half turned to study his father and the rest. Suddenly, there was a lull in the fiddle playing. Clearly, Margery heard her stepfather say, "Poitiers could ne'er be fine as Crecy."

Most villagers glowered at him, though some nodded in agreement. "The forest was thick and dark," said Alf, "like lookin' down a well. And up on a ridge, there was a windmill. I remember its blades turnin' slow, and the air layin' thick in me lungs. His Grace rode a white destrier and carried a rod in his hand, and he looked just like a king should."

Margery watched, astonished. Never had she heard Alf, drunk or sober, string so many words together.

"'Twas rainin'," he continued. "The French and Genoese archers marched to the fore to cover the comin' of their knights. When they neared us, the clouds of a sudden parted and the sun came out. Our king said 'twas an omen, a blessin' from God, and 'twas that. The sun shone behind our backs, in the faces of the enemy, blindin' 'em."

"And the English archers won," said Robert the Younger, "just like Peyters."

The others shifted their focus back to Robert, eager to hear about newer battles, more recent glories, but Alf wasn't ready to relinquish their attention.

"When the Genoese stopped to wind up their crossbows, we used our longbows. Again and again. Was as if a snowstorm had taken the place of the rain, for our arrows were feathered with white. And they went through the enemy breastplates easy as a mouse through a 'ole. The soldiers screamed, turned, and ran back to their knights."

John Ball shook his head. "And we all know what happened next," he said, his voice low.

Margery didn't know.

"Their own knights cut 'em down!" said Thurold loudly. "Hacked 'em to pieces for fleeing. We know the story, old man."

Ah, so this is a part of Crecy the legend makers leave out, Margery thought, sickened. Chivalry was a concept that bound together all knights, enemy as well as friend, therefore such barbaric behavior, such lack of chivalry, must be considered a reflection on all knights.

The crowd had grown visibly exasperated with Alf. Some tried to talk above him, but he raised his voice to match.

"Then the French knights came forth, steppin' over the bodies of their own dead archers."

Sensing disaster, Margery rose from the table and headed toward her stepfather. Thurold followed. "Time to take him home and let him sleep it off. He has a way of getting into fights."

"'Twas us yeomen wot carried the day, downin' France's knights!" Alf shouted. "The finest in all of Christendom, they bragged, and we slaughtered 'em easy as a pig sticker butcherin' swine." He made a sweeping motion with his wooden tankard. "The clouds closed again. 'Twas night, but no stars could shine through. We stole forth real quiet, with our knives, and slit their throats…" He paused, shaking from head to foot. "We be the men o' mettle, we common folk. And 'ow was we rewarded? By the Death!" His voice cracked and he began to weep. "Everyone gone."

The crowd tried to edge Alf out of the circle. Robert the Younger put his arm around Alf's shoulders, but Alf pushed him away.

Thurold stretched out his arm. "Come on, old man."

Alf spun around and smashed his tankard against Robert the Younger's jaw. Robert fell. Someone swung at Alf's belly. Alf gave a loud *oof* and dropped to his knees. Other punches were delivered, and a brawl ensued. Thurold was pushed back, away from Alf. Finally, John Ball muscled his way into the fray, tossing combatants left and right in his effort to reach him.

A knife flashed. The crowd staggered back. Alf raised his hands to his throat and uttered a gurgle, then drenched with blood, fell forward, onto the rushes.

"No," Margery moaned. "Oh, no."

John Ball and Thurold both reached Alf's side before Margery. They turned the stricken man over, revealing a gash that ran from ear to ear. Margery's stomach churned. Alf's eyes were beginning to glaze over. She knew she must do something, but she didn't know what. In truth, what could be done? Alf was already near death.

Thurold cushioned Alf's head with one hand while John Ball knelt beside him and began administering last rites. Alf struggled to breathe. His eyes drooped, then jerked open. His hands moved up, as if to claw at his throat, then settled against his chest. By the time John Ball finished anointing him, Alf Watson was gone.

CHAPTER 11

The Road to London

John Ball, Thurold and Margery left Ravennesfield before dawn. For the first several hours, Margery had imagined Lawrence Ravenne's retainers racing after her but the miles lengthened and there was no pursuit. John and Thurold were right—desertion was too commonplace.

John and Thurold settled into an easy rhythm, but when Margery could not keep up they matched their pace to hers. Blisters had long ago formed on the back of her feet, and her toes had forced their way through the worn leather of her shoe tops, but while she was exhausted, she did not complain.

John had said the journey would take at least four days. During their travels, they had passed through mile upon mile of grassland, spreading in monotonous sameness and broken only by an occasional hirsel of sheep and the piping of their shepherd.

John Ball said, "Let me tell you about sheep." Just as he'd told her about swallows and foxes and the mating habits of peacocks. John seemed to know something about every subject under the sun.

"Aye, priest," said Thurold, indulgently. "Tell us about them."

"Sheep are the most obedient of animals. They are devoted to each other, which is why they prefer to remain close together. In Arabia, flocks grow fat upon music rather than fodder, and during the mating season the color of their wool changes with the character of the river from which they drink."

Margery eyed the placidly grazing sheep. "Arabia must breed very different animals from ours."

John nodded. "Sheep are said to know that the north and south winds promote fertility. They know that the north wind produces males and the south wind females."

"I wonder if 'tis the same for people," she said, provoking John's laughter.

They walked and walked. Horizon led to horizon. John's conversation was so interesting and her stepbrother's so comforting, Margery found she could forget about fears and worries and what might be awaiting them in that impossibly mysterious place called London.

Near sundown they met a husband and wife, Bernard and Gunnora, also bound for London. Thurold snared a pair of rabbits and roasted them over an open spit. Bernard and Gunnora settled next to him. Margery sat a short distance away, rubbing her aching feet and studying the couple. Bernard was cut from the same cloth as every male in Ravennesfield—dirtier, perhaps, and a bit young to have lost so many teeth. Gunnora was with child, but her arms and legs were little bigger than stalks of wheat. Her eyes, locked to their impending meal, spoke mutely of her hunger.

"Let me tell you about the hare," John Ball said, smiling at Gunnora. "It is deeply devoted to its offspring. In some parts of the world, the male hare even gives birth, enduring the pain."

Gunnora touched her own swollen stomach and Bernard placed his hand on her knee. His proprietary air annoyed Margery, though she could not imagine why.

Thurold slowly turned the spit. An occasional drop of juice sizzled into the flames, and the aroma of roasting meat made Margery's mouth water.

"A hare is very different from a rabbit, which is far more lustful,"

John continued. "When a rabbit spots a female, it goes mad with desire."

Bernard poked Gunnora in the ribs. *Half-wit,* Margery thought sourly. But his wife smiled in response and rested her head against his shoulder. For some accursed reason, Margery found herself remembering Matthew Hart, which caused her to minutely inspect her dilapidated boots.

I pray they will last the journey.

'Twas that easy to get rid of unwanted musings about someone she hoped had been counted among the English dead. Well, Margery didn't really hope for Matthew Hart's demise; she just hoped she would never meet up with his like again.

After their meal, Margery crumpled up her cloak, rested her weary head, and half-listened to John Ball's rumbling voice as he repeated Thurold's familiar recitations of their lords' wrongs—or more likely Thurold had simply been echoing the hedge priest's jeremiads. Like an Old Testament prophet who beseeched God to smite his enemies.

On the third afternoon they reached the shire of Essex. Dense woods, unlike any Margery had ever seen, blanketed much of the area. The woods had long been designated royal forests, said John Ball, wherein the king hunted at will. They passed enclosed fields, bound by white hawthorn, and Margery gazed upon large herds of grazing cattle with gleaming summer coats.

Their small group was joined by several pilgrims bound for Canterbury.

(Canterbury, home to Thomas Rendell. *I hope YOU also died in France.*)

Bernard, a convert to John and Thurold's way of thinking, urged the priest to repeat his conversation of the previous night. Ever obliging, John Ball spoke this time about the plight of women. Margery noticed that when the priest spoke, Thurold generally stayed silent, save for occasionally nodding in agreement. No one, not even Thurold, could speak with John Ball's eloquence.

"Whatever they save by spinning they spend on rent or on milk and oatmeal to fill the bellies of their hungry children, while they themselves oft starve. Wretched with the miseries of winter, they get up to rock the cradle during cold, sleepless nights. Then they rise before dawn to card and comb their wool, to wash and scrub and mend, to wind yarn and peel rushes for their rushlights."

I would have been one of those women, thought Margery. *I was one of those women, only I did it for Alf.*

She would be forever grateful to John and Thurold for convincing her to leave Ravennesfield. Perhaps God had a hand in her fate as well, turning the tragedy of her stepfather's death, if tragedy it could be called, into a new beginning.

Most of the pilgrims were unimpressed with John Ball's eloquence. "The world will always be a vale of tears because of original sin," said one, and tried to turn the conversation to the relics awaiting them at Canterbury Cathedral.

But a second pilgrim said, "We are the spawn of a defeated nation—"

The same old arguments, Margery thought, shutting them out.

That evening, the last before they would reach London, they camped in a meadow bright with wildflowers. While the others talked around the fire, Margery drew off by herself and gazed up at the full golden moon. But John Ball's voice came to her, deep as a cavern, soothing as a lullaby. Would his words take hold like a gestating seed, or had he set upon himself a hopeless task?

She sighed and closed her eyes, but the moon was far too bright for sleep. She breathed in the cold fresh air, undercut by a hint of wood smoke, then opened her eyes and watched the play of light upon the meadow. The night seemed both lovely and vaguely menacing, for everyone knew that strange things happened after sunset.

Margery recalled one of Kate the Alewife's customers, who had visited the Crown and Sceptre during the last full moon. The woman had been returning from a nearby village, where her daughter had just given birth.

"Whilst crossing the meadow just beyond Ravennesfield, I see a man astride a shining white horse," the woman had said. "His horse 'twas shod with gold and his harness 'twas hung with bells of the same color, like handfuls of gleamin' nobles. The man, a knight, crosses the field afore me, no more than ten feet away. When he reaches the edge, right near the hedge opening, he reins in his mount, turns and stares at me."

Margery had felt her breath catch in her throat. Had the woman seen a faerie? Alice had taught Margery all about faeries, human in form but superhuman in power. During ancient times, they had mingled with mortal man. But as England became more populated, they'd retreated to their underground kingdoms, or beyond to the sea.

"I have ne'er seen anyone so beautiful." Awe filled the woman's voice. "'Twas as if he had been fashioned from the moon and stars. And the look he gave me, I'll not forget it in this lifetime—full of such sweetness and longing, as if he could show me things beyond my imagining. I was tempted to follow him right that very moment, except I knew I could not."

I would have, Margery had thought, even though to follow a faerie meant certain death. In their world time did not exist, so if mortals should return to the earth, they would find that centuries had passed, and their bodies would instantly crumple into dust. *But I would never return. I would live forever in their kingdom.*

Tonight, as Margery contemplated the woman's tale, she pictured Matthew Hart. Such foolishness. Why was he recently so much in her thoughts? Perhaps it was only with the returning soldiers. In the darkness, Margery shook her head, as if to rid it of her memories. The moon shimmered like a lantern in a fog, and she knew that if she questioned it, it would reveal her future.

What will happen to me in London? Will Thurold stay with me or will he disappear again? Will Lord Ravenne hunt me down? Will I be content? Will I be forced to marry someone...like Bernard? Will I ever meet Matthew Hart again?

She extended her arms. The moon's light rippled like a candle flame over her flesh, and she understood with a blinding certainty that she would indeed see the young lord again. She would see him in the dark, when the world was wrapped in shadows, and he would smile at her and hold out his hand and she would take it and follow him into his enchanted domain, if only for one night. And it would not matter, his past, her past, his blood, her blood.

The knowledge both frightened and excited her. A future with a golden knight—

Nay, that cannot be. I do not want that to be.

Margery stared at the moon until it paled and lost its luster and became merely an ordinary part of the sky.

CHAPTER 12

London

Guards, menacing in their chain mail and long swords, were positioned inside the towers of Aldergate which passed by Smithfield, busy with its weekly horse and cattle market. Passing beneath their watchful eyes, Margery feared that everything about her visage and deportment would identify her as a fugitive bond-woman: her walk, her clothes, her braids, a sudden sneeze.

"There be no need to swivel your head like a goose," Thurold said. "The guards are searching for criminals, lepers—"

"And fugitives!"

"Which you technically are not."

"Walk straight," said John Ball. "As if you belonged."

She tried to obey, but she still felt like a criminal. Nay. She felt like a *leper.* During these past several days her emotions had been peeled, layer by layer. Her skin might still be smooth enough, but that was because her decay did not show on the surface. A leper was someone who was supposed to have been mutilated by a morally harmful influence, and she knew John Ball, even more than Thurold, had altered her concept of the world. Once again, she wondered if he was a saint or a very dangerous man.

Odors assaulted her nose as surely as the city's sounds assaulted her ears. Margery inhaled manure from horses and cows, spoilage from discarded waste, and overriding all else, the stench from the city ditch beyond the walls. She had never imagined that London would be so noisy, so crowded, so smelly, so *intimidating*.

Sensing her anxiety, Thurold wrapped a comforting arm around her shoulders. "Someday ye'll not give a second thought to all this," he said, his words nearly lost amidst the barks of the street vendors and dogs. "I got used to it, though I ne'er liked it. But there is much we might not like but 'ave to suffer."

John Ball nodded. "Soon you will be as familiar with London as I am with Our Lord's gospels."

Never, Margery thought. *I'll never make sense of such a place.* The city was a jumble of lanes and alleys and meandering streets, none of which bore any identifying marks or signs. How could a person tell one from the other?

John answered her unspoken question. "We are in St. Martin's Lane, home to the minor trades—woodworkers, vintners, fishmongers, bell founders and the like. I have friends among the apprentices here, though the masters have no use for me. They do not want to be told they are unjust, which they are."

Three-storied houses were squeezed together without so much as a hand's span between them, but Margery enjoyed their bright look, for all were trimmed in vivid yellows, blues and reds, a pleasing contrast to their dark oak frames and daub walls. Many also displayed garlands of flowers or colorful tapestries. A tribute, Thurold said dryly, to Prince Edward's impending arrival.

"They are cleaning the streets, as well," John Ball added, nodding toward a raker. "I have never seen London so bright and shining."

Doubtfully, Margery eyed the pigs rooting in a nearby dung stall. If London was being cleaned, how filthy was it normally?

Blessed Mother, Prince Edward's return! Would Lawrence Ravenne number among the prince's knights? What would that mean for her? Thurold said not to worry, but…She thought once again of Matthew Hart. Would he also be in London?

While making their way through the human press, Margery considered her situation. Wouldn't all the things she found so intimidating be the very things that would protect her identity? As she, Thurold and John passed the Priory of the Holy Trinity, she saw monks and clerks gathered on the steps. Then the foul smelling Shambles with its long rows of butchers' stalls extending toward the Cheap. So many people, so much activity. Among such chaos, who would notice one insignificant creature?

John and Thurold lingered among the tanners, conversing with a pair who were scraping hair from skins thrown across a beam. Trying to ignore the malodor, Margery concentrated on a third apprentice, who was rubbing something into a hide.

Noticing her interest, the apprentice said, "Cold pigeon dung. It softens the skins. Want t' feel?"

Margery shook her head. Londoners seemed uncommonly bold. She was relieved when John and Thurold bade their friends, "Good day."

St. Paul's Cathedral lay directly ahead, rising above the surrounding buildings like an oak tree among acorns. Some said its needle-thin spire was the highest in all the world.

"I will be preaching at Paul's Cross for the next few days should you need to contact me," John told Margery.

Margery glanced at Thurold. Did they mean to leave her here alone?

Thurold pointed out the goldsmiths' guildhall, located across the street from the College of St. Martin le Grand, and with unicorns carved on its massive front door. "We be now at Goldsmith Row."

"Aye," added John. "'Tis situated from Bread Street to the Cross. If you pay attention you'll not get lost."

Margery noticed that each shop was fronted by a sign bearing the goldsmith's richly gilded and painted coat of arms. Everywhere she looked she saw representations of unicorns, which was their symbol.

"Ye'll be fine, Stick-Legs," said Thurold against her ear. "John Ball and I've business 'ere that does na concern ye but I'll make sure ye be taken care of. The gentleman I've in mind has the most lucrative trade in London."

Margery knew very little about rich merchants. Some people said they were arrogant as lords and putting her with such seemed a contradiction of her companions' preachments. But she trusted that John and Thurold must know what they were doing.

"I remember the crucifixes and chalices and reliquaries at Ely Cathedral," she said, and even to her own ears she sounded wistful. "I wondered then what sort of man could fashion such beauty."

"Simon Crull numbers among the most talented goldsmiths in the kingdom," said Thurold. "I apprenticed under 'im and despite 'is peculiarities I learned a good bit of the trade."

"Though a talent for smithing does not mean that God has gifted a man in more spiritual matters," John said enigmatically.

Awed by the mansions lining Bread Street, Margery pivoted her head, gazing from one side to the other. John finally halted in front of a business called the Shop of the Unicorn. The building was four stories high with an elaborate finial of a unicorn's head perched atop its gabled roof. Eaves and lintels were bright gold, doors and window frames intricately carved oak.

"My new home?" she asked. When Thurold nodded, her pulse quickened, for she could not believe her good fortune.

The shop consisted of an open stall fronting the street. A dazzling array of chalices, jewelry, girdles, gold and silver plate, crystal and gold reliquaries lined the shelves. Two apprentices traced elaborate designs in a waxed table. Near a furnace in the center of the room stood a large-boned matron wearing a yellow head dress that lent a greenish tint to her mottled complexion. Thurold explained to Margery that the woman was mixing small amounts of melted gold with mercury.

John Ball addressed the woman. "Dame Gisla, I have a lass with me who is in need of employ." He rested his hand on Margery's shoulder. "I know your home is of high moral character and would be a fine place for my friend. You will take her in, won't you?"

"John Ball." Gisla's homely face settled into lines of disapproval, and her small eyes narrowed until they were but slits. "The last time I saw you, you were being removed from the steps of St. Paul's." She waggled her forefinger at him. "Shame on you for spouting such nonsense." Then she spotted Thurold and a mixture of emotions flitted across her countenance. "You left us in a fine mess last time, Thurold Watson. If you did not have such a deft touch, I'd run you off this moment." When Thurold didn't respond, she added, "If ye be looking to return, we might have room for you."

Thurold's laugh sounded forced to Margery's ears. "Just care for me kin. If I am in need ye'll see me again. My sister, Margery, would make ye a fine maid. You might even teach her a thing or two about the trade."

Dame Gisla studied her with pursed lips. Some faces were pleasant in their plainness and made one feel comforted. Not so this woman's.

"I'll admit 'tis near impossible to keep good help. I had a girl disappear last Lady Day. My husband, however, is a fastidious man. He dislikes filth in anything—" she paused, sniffing "—most especially people."

"We have been on the road for days," said John Ball, with an edge of irritation. "You would not expect us to be other than are most travelers, would you?"

Rather than respond, Dame Gisla turned and shouted, "Orabel!"

A servant near Margery's own age emerged from a doorway.

"Help the girl bathe," said Dame Gisla. "If she suits my husband, we'll keep her."

"The girl's name is Margery," Thurold said with a scowl. "And I expect ye to remember it!"

Chastised, Gisla muttered, "Aye, Margery."

John wrapped Margery in a crushing embrace, followed by Thurold. Watching them disappear around the corner, she felt such an emptiness. She was starting a new life, many miles from home with no family, no friends, and now both had deserted her.

Blessed Mary, I should never have left Ravennesfield, she thought, choking back tears.

Orabel placed a comforting hand on her arm. "Come with me, Maggie-dear."

Orabel was afflicted with a limp that caused her to hunch forward, and made her appear even shorter than her five feet, though she had lively eyes and a friendly smile. Carefully, she navigated the wooden stairs leading to the Crulls' private quarters.

"I know your brother. A fine craftsman he is when he sets his mind to it. But he has a way of being distracted with…thoughts, which sometimes put him at odds with the master." Orabel smiled. "I think we might bathe you in Master Crull's solar. That way we'll not need to carry the buckets very far."

They entered a dreary hall where a handful of faded linen wall tapestries, a trestle table, and a few benches provided its only furnishings.

"Very different from the fancy outside, is it not?" Orabel raised her eyes heavenward. "Master Crull be the richest goldsmith in London, yet he surrounds himself with meanness. He begrudges parting with so much as a crust of bread for beggars, and he'll not bless orphans with more than a 'bye your leave.' He married Dame Gisla for her position. Her father was a powerful alderman and Mayor of London. Master Crull inherited the business, y'know."

Margery did not know, but Orabel's agreeable chatter provided balm to her shredded nerves.

"On the good side, there is all the food you can eat," Orabel continued, critically eyeing Margery's figure. "'Tis a bit light in seasoning for my taste, but I'm not one for complaining." She nodded toward yet another set of stairs. "We sleep on the third floor. Men to one side, girls t'other. The Crulls dislike any mixing, so they have put up a screen to keep us chaste. Not that I'd bother with any of the help, except mayhap Brian. He is downstairs, at the tracing table."

"I am not much interested in men," Margery managed.

"Of course ye be." Orabel's fine green eyes flashed. "A month in London and you'll have far more suitors than I or any of the others at the Shop."

Margery followed Orabel to the kitchen where they were greeted by a blast of heat from an oval stove built into a side wall. The master cook, recognizable by his high hat, flipped fish. Sausages dangled from overhead rods. Several servants stood in front of a long, narrow counter, chopping vegetables and crumbled bread. The seasonings might be niggardly, but the resultant fragrances made her mouth water.

Orabel retrieved four huge kettles from among the frying pans, saucepans, trivets and tongs hanging on the walls. Filling one with water from a nearby vat, she said, "You'll soon find we spend most of our lives bathing. The Master hates dirt. He's a sour old bastard, but so long as ye keep his clothes and rooms clean, he's not impossible."

Startled by Orabel's outspokenness, Margery noted that the others didn't react. A small knot of fear replaced the hunger in her belly. Who was this man? She pictured him in the manner of Father Egbert, had the priest lived and grown old.

"I can make two trips," she offered, mindful of Orabel's affliction.

"My leg looks worse than it is, Maggie-dear. My husband pushed me down the stairs. I curse his memory every time I take a step."

"I am sorry," Margery said, hefting her two kettles.

"No need. He was killed in the king's campaign. Which frees me to wed another."

The solar was located on the opposite side of the hall. After entering, Orabel lit a fire and set the kettles on hooks above the fireplace. "Most of the help is as sour as the master and mistress, which makes me all the happier ye be here. You and I are going to be good friends, I think."

Retrieving a wooden bathtub from the adjoining garderobe, they filled it with water. "I will find ye a gown that will fit. Yours is ready for the rag pile."

After Orabel had limped out of sight, Margery glanced around the solar, which, like the hall, was spartan to the point of meanness. Furnishings consisted of a worn chest, a narrow cupboard, a laver and a bed with curtains as worn as the muslin sheets peeking above the threadbare counterpane.

Margery retrieved a portion of soap, exquisitely molded in the shape of a rose, from a bowl hanging from a hook above the shining bronze laver. The laver and soaps appeared to be the room's lone extravagances. Sinking into the steaming water, she attacked her flesh until the rose was a mere bud and her skin shone more pink than the soap. Finally, she lathered her matted hair, which Orabel helped rinse.

Throughout Margery's ministrations, her fellow maid slipped in and out, chatting all the while. Elaborating on the peccadillos of the other servants, on Master Crull's aversion to dirt; about the hot and cold water taps that King Edward had installed for his personal bath in Westminster Palace, "So says the master;" the French king's imprisonment at the Savoy, "I'm told 'tis the grandest place in all the world;" and Edward of Woodstock, Prince of Wales, impending welcome. While Margery was too distracted to pay much attention, she was soothed by the friendly patter.

Once done, Orabal limped to the door. "After ye've finished up I'll return to help tidy the room."

Retrieving a linen towel from beside the laver, Margery vigorously dried her body, braided her hair, and donned the worn russet kersey Orabel had provided.

"Who are you and what are you doing in my room?"

Margery spun around. A diminutive man, unlike anyone she had ever seen before, stood in the doorway. She was used to short men, but peasants were stocky, even virile. This man reminded her of the elves known to inhabit forests and streams, for he possessed the mean look elves carried on their faces when they performed mischief.

"I am Margery Watson, sir, the new servant. Your wife sent me here to bathe."

"To my room? I think not."

Simon Crull's deep voice possessed an unpleasant ooze, like sap from a tree. It was certainly at odds with his dainty appearance. She imagined him next to Dame Gisla. Half her height and weight; what a pairing. Walking past Margery, he paused to frown at the towel she had dropped, then nudged it with his toe as if poking a dead animal.

"Humph." Still scowling, he sank down on the edge of his bed. "Fetch me my slippers, Margery Watson."

So Margery did precisely that. And put Crull's slippers on his dainty feet. She noticed that his shoulders were as narrow as a boy's, yet a paunch spilled over his girdle.

When she had completed her task, Crull reached out and caught her by the chin.

"Sir?" Margery forced herself to stare into his face, into close-set, watery eyes. His nose was blunt and pitted; spidery veins spread across his pasty cheeks.

Crull turned Margery's face toward the firelight, whereupon he inspected her profile as dispassionately as he would one of his goblets. "Open your mouth, girl."

"Sir?"

"Are you hard of hearing? Open your mouth!"

"Why?" she asked, thinking she had never encountered such a peculiar creature.

"If you are to be a member of my household, Margery Watson, you must obey me. I do not long put up with willful servants."

Pushing down a surge of anger, she complied.

Crull grunted. "You have all your teeth. Some do not, even at your age." Dropping her chin, he gestured toward the tub. "Dump that filthy water down the privy and take that towel to the washer woman. And remember, I will not tolerate dirt in any form."

So this is London, Margery thought, moving to obey. *Thurold, what have you done to me?*

CHAPTER 13

London

Upon his return to London, Matthew Hart took up residence in the Savoy, Henry of Lancaster's magnificent palace. As he gazed out a waterside window, he watched painted barges and wherries glide along the Thames. London Bridge was festooned with banners, yet another tedious salute to Prince Edward and his royal prisoner, King Jean.

Matthew knew that Henry, Duke of Lancaster, had recently spent the staggering sum of thirty-four thousand pounds to renovate his palace. With its cream-colored stone, extensive gardens and lavish interiors, the Savoy was considered the most beautiful residence in England, a fit place for a prince and a captured king.

And a knight, Matthew thought, rubbing his hand across his newly clipped beard. *Which I will be on the morrow.*

"'Tis time," said Harry.

Matthew swiveled toward his brother. For the ceremony, Harry's hair and beard had also been trimmed, which made him look even younger than his seventeen years. He still possessed a disarming vulnerability, not an appropriate trait for a fighter. Matthew had hoped that the passage of time would have hardened Harry, but other than a growth of four inches and a more pronounced propensity toward gaming, he was the same. He still seemed ill at ease with himself, as if he had borrowed someone else's body and was apologizing for the fact. Perhaps after his first battle, he would acquire an appropriate measure of self-confidence.

Harry, Matthew and the other squires were escorted into an adjoining room where six tubs awaited them. As Matthew disrobed, he thought about the morrow. By this hour, the jousting would have begun and the ceremony would have become but a memory.

From the moment of his birth, he had been groomed for this occasion, and yet he felt nothing. His true knighthood, acknowledged or not, had been at Poitiers. God's teeth, how he wished he had never made his vow to Harry. But a vow could not be undone, not from one lord to another, and certainly not between brothers.

Matthew stepped into the steaming water for his ceremonial bath. Leaning his head back against the slanted boards, weary to the bone, he shut his eyes. Last night the squires had pleasured themselves until dawn. The strollers in the stews at Southwark had been hearty Flemish girls, one of whom had even loosened Harry up a bit.

It had taken Prince Edward three weeks to reach London, his booty-laden carts stretching for miles behind. In every town they had been met by cheering subjects, streamers and wreaths, and more free drink and maids than any man had proper use for. That had also been the pattern when they'd wintered in Bordeaux. While the prince negotiated a truce with the French, Matt and his friends had enjoyed themselves to the point of boredom. Now he could think of nothing he'd rather do than crawl into bed—*alone*—and sleep for a fortnight.

Harry stirred in the adjoining tub. "I have prayed for this moment, brother," he whispered.

"Aye," Matt agreed, forcing a smile. "You and me."

"I will be forever grateful that you waited. Today Father has two sons of whom he can be proud."

Overcome, Harry's voice broke and his eyes misted. He tried to compose himself, even though strong emotion was an acceptable trait in a knight. He'd seen knights weep at a sentimental song. He had also seen them slash the throat of a stag without so much as a grimace.

And I am soon going to be one. Might as well say, "I am going to be the tiles on the floor" or "I am going to be a drake and fly through the air in a fiery streak."

He wanted to reach out and clasp his brother's hand, but Matt's eyes were shut and he seemed uncommonly quiet. Had last night's dalliances tired him? Perhaps it was merely the solemnity of the occasion.

Shifting his bent knees until the water lapped over them, Harry washed off a sprinkling of bath herbs. *When Father sees us together, he will note I am taller than Matt. I'll wager my sword swing is longer, too.*

But Harry knew it took more than long arms to make a good knight, and uncertainty bedeviled him. Surely, something would happen during the ceremony to disqualify him. On the morrow, before hundreds of spectators, after his golden spurs had been strapped to his boots, when Henry of Lancaster moved forward to say "Be thou a knight," the duke would lose his voice. He would open his mouth but no words would emerge, and everyone would know that God had rendered Lancaster mute rather than let him knight Harry. Or when the duke tried to bestow his customary sword blow, the sword would refuse to touch Harry's shoulder. Or one of the religious statues would fall from its niche. Or God would strike Harry dead.

Aye, he could think of a dozen signs from heaven, each more dreadful than the last. *I should have been a monk, a holy man, only I am not holy. I should have been anything except what is expected of me, for that is the one thing in this world for which I am totally unsuited.*

With a sigh, Harry submerged himself up to his chin.

. . .

AFTER THE BATH, the squires rested on white-sheeted beds. Matthew was glad that this was a time of quiet contemplation so he wouldn't have to face his brother's earnest cheerfulness.

Just as Matthew was nodding off and Harry had worked himself into a nervous fit over his pending fate, servants entered to dress them. With each piece of clothing, they were supposed to contemplate its meaning. The black hose was a reminder that all men came from earth and to earth they must someday return. The scarlet robe signified humility and the blood a knight was sworn to shed for the faith of Our Lord and the Holy Church. The white girdle conveyed chastity and cleanliness.

Harry furtively studied Matt as a servant clasped a white girdle around his hips. Harry appraised the strong profile, the determined jaw, and the way his brother's hair curled around his neck. *You look just like Father.* Even Matt's hands were William's hands. Harry looked down at his own long, slender fingers, more suited for wielding a quill than a sword. *I do not want to be a knight. I do not belong here.*

"Matt," he said. "Matt, I—"

Friends and relatives entered bearing gifts, so Harry's bid for reassurance remained unspoken. A beaming Sosanna Hart hugged both her sons before handing Harry a small box, wrapped in velvet, tied with fine-spun gold thread.

"Your father will be along presently," she said to Matthew. "Open it," she urged Harry.

Inside the box was a ring, set with a sapphire surrounded by diamonds. Harry grinned his pleasure. "I have never seen such workmanship, Mother."

"It is from the shop of Simon Crull, London's finest goldsmith. I spent most of an afternoon trying to decide what would please you."

"Did Father help select it?"

Sosanna's smile remained bright. "Of course. He is the one who suggested Master Crull. Your father said the ring must be set with diamonds, since a diamond will overcome any enemy."

Matthew untied the ribbon around the cloth of one of the gifts he had received, though he could not recall who precisely had handed it to him. Nestled in the cloth was a dagger, obviously of great age. Its blade had copper strips inlaid with a scroll pattern, and the handle was set with rubies and amethysts, a stone which brought success in the hunt.

After gauging the weight and feel of the dagger, Matthew opened the accompanying note, written in a bold, flourishing script. "Following the glorious battle of Poitiers," it read, "twas my great pleasure to admire you from afar during your stay in Bordeaux. Though circumstances presently prevent me from revealing my identity, I pray that someday you will be able to thank me for my gift in a very personal manner."

The missive was signed with an intertwining D and C. "Do I know anyone with these initials?" Matthew asked Harry, handing him the parchment.

Harry reluctantly turned his attention from his ring to the letter. "David Carrick? Daniel Clairborne?"

"I trust 'tis from a *lady,* brother." Matthew tried to think back to Bordeaux's court women, but there had been so many. There had been one with unusually fine breasts and a jealous husband. Her name was peculiar, Desire something. However, Matthew had never said more than good morrow to her.

Before he could further puzzle the matter, his father arrived. Even nearing middle age, William Hart exuded an animal energy that drew everyone's attention. Striding into the room, his gaze swept the area until he found Matthew. Making his way through the crowd, it was obvious that, at least for the moment, only he and Matthew existed, that the others were mere shadows.

"I have something to show you." William's brusque authority was tempered by excitement as he drew Matthew over to a window, which he swung open, and gestured toward the courtyard below. "Your gift."

A groom held the reins of the finest destrier Matthew had ever seen. The stallion was white and at this distance, he could see that its lines were flawless. "Magnificent," Matthew breathed, scarce believing his good fortune. All knights dreamed of the perfect warhorse to go with the perfect sword and the perfect armor. Father had given him an animal even King Edward would envy.

"His name is Michel, after the warrior saint, and I cannot tell you what a time I had trying to find such as he. He cost a princely sum, but I would gladly pay double." William cleared his throat. "No father could be more proud than I. To ride by your side during the French campaigns. To witness your bravery at Poitiers."

Placing his arm around Matthew, William lowered his voice. "Even that damned foolishness concerning Harry showed that your word is your bond. I thank Our Blessed Savior and all the saints for giving me such a son. You are a true knight. No man could ask for more."

Moved as much by William's approval as his gift, Matthew embraced him. "'Tis all I've ever wanted to be."

"Look at the two of you," Sosanna said, coming up behind them. "Cut from the same cloth, are they not, Harry?"

What cloth am I cut from?

Harry suddenly felt huge and awkward. His ring felt heavy on his middle finger, as if it would fall off. Or worse, as if it misliked its new owner. Perhaps the diamonds couldn't tell one enemy from the other. Perhaps they considered *him* an enemy.

"And you like your ring, Harry?" William asked, his manner challenging.

"Aye, Father, 'tis fine."

"Your mother chose it. While a piece of jewelry can never compare with a warhorse, I told her 'twould suit you better."

Harry heard Matthew's sharp intake of breath, and felt the color drain from his own face. For one fleeting moment, he wished the ring's diamonds would strike William dead.

"Husband!" Sosanna's voice was reproachful. "What your father is trying to say is that you have always appreciated beautiful things, Harry."

"What I am saying, wife, is that Harry has always been more interested in useless ornaments than in fighting, or bravery, or any of life's important matters."

"Perhaps I have a different definition of what might be important,

117

Father." *Throwback, changeling,* his mind screamed. *Where did you come from? Certainly not from William Hart's loins.*

With his gaze locked on the black and white floor tiles, Harry struggled to defend himself. "'Tis not fair to compare me with Matt, Father. When the time comes, I shall acquit myself well in battle. I just happen to believe that life holds something beyond war."

William's lip curled disdainfully. "Which is why you will never be anything but a mediocrity."

Harry flushed and walked away, followed by Sosanna, who glared at her husband in passing.

William turned back to the window as if nothing had happened, but Matthew's pleasure in Michel had been shattered by the exchange. "You should not have spoken so harshly, Father. Harry cannot help it if he has been afflicted with a sensitive nature."

"Knights should not be sensitive. A son who is more concerned with clothes and jewelry than with the sword must always remain a trial. I have tried my best to toughen him, and it is to my everlasting sorrow that I have failed. 'Tis God's mercy that you be first-born. I do not know what I would do if Harry stood to inherit Cumbria."

"But he *will* inherit. I told you years ago that I would never marry. 'Twas not some childish vow."

William's eyes narrowed. "Time has a way of countermanding foolhardy schemes, Matthew, and I would sooner leave my entire legacy to the Church than trust it to your brother."

THE HIGH ALTAR of the Savoy's chapel was shadow-ridden, partially hiding its extravagant display of reliquaries, wall murals and Old Testament tapestries. Armor and weapons rested on the side altar dedicated to St. George, where Matthew and his companions were keeping their ten-hour vigil. Double rows of candelabrum burned, their light catching the jewels imbedded in the pommels of six swords. A faint acrid smoke, incense from an earlier celebration, hugged the air.

Trying unsuccessfully to concentrate on solemn matters, Matthew darted a quick glance toward the lifelike statue of St. George, who seemed to be observing the six squires who knelt or stood before him.

Harry, who had prostrated himself with his arms outstretched in the shape of a cross, inhaled dramatically. The paving stones smelled faintly of dust and felt rough against his cheeks and palms. During this time, squires were supposed to meditate on their obligations to those they would soon be sworn to protect, but Harry found his mind drifting. He could not help but ponder the notion that this entire business of knighthood was passing strange. Surely it was odd to mix killing with God.

We act as if war is God's main passion, and 'tis such an odd passion for God to have.

A pebble dug into Harry's cheek. He shifted his position, which caused the pebble to lodge near his jaw. The saints would never notice such a slight discomfort, so he vowed he wouldn't either. However, his mind refused to stay on religious matters.

I am a warrior who hates war. Why can I not be like everyone else? Did a faerie switch me in my cradle? Is that why I feel so out of place in this world, as if those around me are speaking a language I canna understand?

With another loud sigh, he turned his head so that his other cheek rested against the pebble. It was going to be a very long night.

Situated next to Harry, Matthew stifled a groan. Long ago the feeling in his knees had progressed from agony to numbness. It seemed as if he'd been in this chapel forever, even though the length of the candles and the light filtering through the stained glass windows told him otherwise. He tried to focus his attention on the High Altar, with its enormous gold and jeweled cross. Instead, he thought about Poitiers. He remembered the sun setting across the battlefield and William's proud expression when Prince Edward said, "Come forward, Matt. You will be first."

Matthew flexed his hands, which ached from the cold. Sharp pains shot up his thighs. He had always believed that contemplation should be left to priests, just as fighting should be left to warriors.

During his twenty years, Matthew had seldom felt God's nearness, even though he accepted His love. God had blessed Matthew Hart with little death and much pleasure, and that was that. A hundred hours in the Savoy's chapel would not make God reveal Himself any more completely than He had in any other holy place, so the entire exercise seemed pointless.

Timothy Knolles, who knelt on Matthew's right, had passed the time by squirming, stifling yawns and re-counting all the paving stones within his vision. Tim was nephew to Robert Knolles, one of England's most skilled and respected men-at-arms. After last year's service with the Duke of Lancaster, Robert had chosen to remain in Normandy, much to his own gain and the terror of the French. But Tim had not inherited his uncle's martial prowess. He preferred to spend his time gambling, drinking and whoring. Now, he cleared his throat and still on his knees, edged toward Matthew. Extending his fist, he opened it, exposing three ivory cubes. Then he jerked his head toward the choir loft at the back of the chapel.

"A game of dice, Hart?"

Matthew shook his head.

"I cannot tolerate a whole night of this," Tim whispered. "I've had enough solemnity to last through Lammastide."

Matthew fastened his gaze upon the rood. "Keep your mind on God, Knolles, and stop hounding me."

"Quit sounding like a priest. It ill becomes you. I'll wager my saddle, the one Uncle Robert sent me from France. 'Twould look fine atop your new destrier. Just think what a handsome figure you will cut on the morrow, riding through London."

"Your saddle?" Matthew reconsidered. "Well now, what say we retire to the choir loft?"

THE ROLL of the dice was not favoring Matt. So far he had lost his new sword and, piece by piece, his armor. Soon he would have nothing left to wager.

Undoubtedly, Tim's dice were weighted, but Matthew could not prove it.

120

If I do not discover the trickery soon, he thought, watching Tim whoop over three sixes, *I shall emerge from Lancaster's chapel on the morrow with only my braies to cover me.*

"The Lord is definitely smiling on me," said Tim, "but I feel a spell of piety coming over me. God seems to be telling me that I've enjoyed enough dicing for one night."

At that moment, after Matthew had impetuously wagered Michel, Harry and the other squires emerged from the stairway. Harry handed his brother a trio of dice. "We've been watching. I trust these three will throw more truly."

When Matthew hesitated, Harry said, "Be quick. You've made so much noise we'll not only have the priests on us, but the duke himself."

All the squires squatted round the dice, save Timothy, who rose, shaking his head. "I do not like this whole business. If you canna trust my dice, I am insulted enough to leave right now."

"Nay, Tim. I'll be insulting you with my fist if you leave." Matthew grabbed his wrist. "A wager is a wager, and I'll expect you to honor it."

Matthew shook Harry's dice, then flung them across the floor.

"God's blood! What is happening here?"

Heart plummeting, Matthew rose and faced John of Gaunt, Earl of Richmond and King Edward's third son.

The dice sprawled accusingly; three sixes. Matthew's gaze darted from the dice to John of Gaunt, and back again. Sweat break out on his palms—nay, his whole body. *Father will never forgive me.*

Though three years younger than Matthew, John of Gaunt possessed an innate authority that made him an intimidating figure. And like all Plantagenets, he was known for his volatile temper.

"Someone had best have an explanation for this blasphemous behavior."

"'Tis not what you think, sire," Tim said, sidestepping as if he might shield the dice with his body. "Matt was just...we were tired and...oh, please do not tell my father, for it was truly not my fault and he will banish me to Wales or Ireland as surely as I'm standing here."

John of Gaunt's blue eyes flicked coldly from face to face.

"I will go on a pilgrimage," Tim squeaked, his hands open, imploring. "To Jerusalem even, if only you'll not tell."

Ignoring Tim, John addressed Harry. "I am surprised at *you*. I would not think a member of my household would treat such a sacred time so poorly."

Harry stared down at his feet. Two scarlet spots stained his cheeks. He blinked repeatedly, trying to keep his tears at bay.

Noting his brother's distress, Matthew spoke up. "My lord, 'tis not Harry's fault, nor anyone's save mine. Do not punish others for what was a misjudgment on my part."

John studied Matthew for a long moment before turning to the others. "Go, all of you! Save for you, Sir Hart."

While the squires scurried past with bent heads and stricken expressions, Matthew waited. Unable to meet the earl's steady gaze, he looked over at the railing. Shadows swooped down from the ceiling, toward the altar. His father's words silently mocked him. Would William be proud of him now?

John walked to the railing and clasped the banister between his hands. Unlike Edward and Lionel, his older, more flamboyant brothers, the earl was not one for easy banter but often lapsed into moody silences. He was also famously devout.

He'll consider a harmless prank sacrilege, Matthew thought, shifting uneasily from foot to foot. *I am going to be banished. I shall be a squire forever. I have disgraced the Hart name.* He had never cried in his adult life, but at this very moment he was alarmingly close.

"'Twas a gallant thing you did at Poitiers, refusing knighthood," John finally said. "A true gesture of love for your brother."

"My lord?"

John smiled. "Remember, I have brothers too. Edward and I do talk, especially about that day. I prize loyalty above all else, and your chivalry pleased me."

Matthew nodded warily, confused. He watched the earl's gaze sweep the darkness below. "I have dreamed of being knighted on the battlefield." John's fingers lightly caressed the polished oak railing.

"After Poitiers, this ceremony must seem hollow to you. Is that not so?"

A rush of emotion overcame Matthew. He found it difficult to speak. John understood. "'Tis so, my lord," he managed.

"I believe you and I are a bit alike. I am glad my brother has you in his household." John waved his arm, gesturing toward the darkness below. "Return to your vigil. This matter will go no further."

CHAPTER 14

London

The moon, so full and round it seemed to devour the sky, shone upon the horse and rider. As the knight, whose armor mirrored the moon, guided his mount across a shadowed field, it tossed its head, causing the golden bells upon its harness to whisper like faraway music. She watched the knight, close enough to see the moon's light shining upon his head and the curve of a leg in his stirrup, but far enough away that he could not, in the blink of an eye, be standing before her. Yet here he was, gazing down upon her. Had she ever seen such an expression in the face of a mortal man? Or had the faerie knight returned to her? Whoever he might be, his look was full of longing and such desire, as if he would whisper to her in the manner of the golden bells, and lay before her, as a magician might his secrets, all manner of sweet, wonderful, forbidden things—

Margery's eyes fluttered open. Around her she heard the soft snoring, occasional groan or sigh from the other female servants. Trying to get comfortable on her mercilessly thin pallet, she turned on her side. For eight nights now, she had dreamed the same dream, awakening long before London's bells rang prime.

Yawning, she sat up and rested her chin on her bent knees. Everything was so new and strange and she wondered whether she would ever feel at home in this correct household with its correct master and correct servants and everyone save Orabel seemingly as cold as the ashes from last week's fire.

But I did not feel at home in Ravennesfield, either, she reminded herself. *And I have much to be thankful for.*

Though bland in seasoning, as Orabel had warned, and monotonous in variety, the food at the Crull household was plentiful, and her chores were simple and easy enough, particularly when compared to the hardships of Ravennesfield. After Dame Gisla left at sunrise to shop the Ward of the Cheap, Margery made beds, shook out covers and cushions, and emptied chamber pots. She helped fill the water vat and the big iron kettles. Then she tossed crushed daisy, lavender, rose and other petals onto the floor rushes. Rushes were customarily changed four times a year, but Master Crull had already ordered one change since her arrival. "Rushes stink and carry all manner of filth I'll not tolerate," he had said.

Orabel stirred restlessly, and Margery knew why. Last night her friend had disappeared with Brian Goldman, one of the apprentices to whom she'd taken a fancy. Or Margery wasn't sure how much Orabel actually fancied him but rather what he represented. "Once he finishes his apprenticeship he can go into business on his own. And he's temperate in his habits," she said as if trying to convince herself of his suitability. To Margery, Brian Goldman seemed a bit puffed up with his own importance, but she was more concerned about Orabel's fate should she be caught in a dalliance. While Goldman would be slyly nudged and congratulated, Orabel would be dismissed in disgrace.

The Jesus bells of St. Paul's boomed, followed by a hundred other bells. Margery fancied the sound possessed more dissonance than usual; a harsher quality, a challenge. Or was it just that the bells echoed her dread? Today London would officially welcome Edward the Black Prince from his triumphant Poitiers campaign. Today Lawrence Ravenne would be in London, alongside his prince, of that she was certain. The thought of Ravenne unnerved her, though reason told her otherwise. In such a vast city, they would never meet. And if, by chance they did, Ravenne could not really designate ownership by having her branded, or even hanged. Thurold and John Ball had assured her she had naught to fear, that England's laws, while sometimes nuanced, would actually protect her. And they would know, wouldn't they?

Rising, Margery crossed to a basin of cold water, washed and then dressed in her new gown, an ill-fitting cast-off. She hated the dress, as she did the attire of all Simon Crull's servants. Londoners preferred vivid colors, but the master required that his household wear drab shadings, predominately black, just as he required them to bathe thrice a week.

Black is for mourning curtains, Margery thought, slipping on her sleeveless surcote. *And night. And death. Not people. But I WILL thank the saints for my good fortune.*

Still, what a peculiar place was the Crull household. And how well its peculiarity matched its master.

FIRST CAME the members of London's guilds, all dressed in scarlet, followed by France's king and his captor. When Jean le Bon emerged through Ludgate, he sat astride a high-stepping white stallion and was clothed in the full panoply of state. By contrast Prince Edward, wearing simple soldier's garb and with his head bare, had chosen a plain black hobby.

Huzzahs, trumpet blasts, the booming of church bells seemed to cause London's very buildings to tremble. In Cheapside, beautiful girls, suspended from cages, tossed gold and silver leaves. At St. Paul's Cathedral, the Bishop of London and his clergy greeted the royal personages. Later the procession would wend its way to Westminster where King Edward and a night of feasting awaited.

Following Orabel past Ludgate to Fleet Street, Margery tried to recall every landmark and twisting lane. Should they become separated her friend had said they would meet at the Church of All Hallow's Barking. Margery had never seen so many people and she was so new to the city she could easily lose her way. John Ball and Thurold had already drifted off somewhere, not bothering to inform her. Her step-brother, at least, was in a merry mood, asserting that he and his fellow yeomen had been more responsible than the knights for Poitiers' outcome. As was attested by the stacks of bows, arrows, arms and armor in front of many doors—a silent but powerful reminder that, in the midst of a celebration that was supposed to be one of prayer and thanksgiving—England's citizens were really celebrating their victory.

Since Margery and Orabel had been among the last to arrive, they were shoved near the back. Margery couldn't see much, but she didn't mind. While she couldn't see, neither could she be seen. More than once she wondered if Matthew Hart would number among the knights, but she pushed that thought aside. And with so many warriors, she wouldn't be able to distinguish one from the other. Which should also be the case with Lawrence Ravenne, so, rather than fret she would enjoy the festivities.

As Prince Edward neared, Margery stood on tiptoe to better view him. Among lord and commoner, Edward of Woodstock was univer-sally loved. Even Thurold praised his fighting acumen and his concern, at least on campaign, for *all* those under his command.

Ah, there he is!

Odd that Edward's lack of ostentation only added to his majesty. How graciously, even humbly, he accepted the endless accolades, the women offering kisses and the children running forth to thrust bouquets of lilies and roses in his hands.

Our prince. Margery felt an uncharacteristic swelling of pride. The crowd strained forward, carrying her with it. Edward was nearly abreast. She saw sunlight caress his golden hair, saw one ungauntleted hand raised in greeting. Then Jean le Bon's stallion, nervously side-stepping and tossing its head, hid the prince from view.

It was then Margery realized that she was far too close to the front. Turning and twisting, she sought Orabel, who had been swallowed in the press. Elbows jammed into her; those around her continued pushing forward. Where was Thurold? Why had he and John Ball abandoned her?

Now came the parade of knights, riding three abreast. Arrayed before Margery, high above on their prancing destriers, their brilliant banners snapping in the breeze.

She panicked. *Killers!* It seemed she inhaled them with her burgeoning terror—their size, the cruel set of their mouths, the hard planes of their faces. Everything about their physical appearance attested to the brutality of their profession.

No wonder the French could not defeat you. A hell filled with demons would not prevail.

And, surely, somewhere among them, rode her former lord.

Margery tried unsuccessfully to retreat into the wall of flesh, but there were only a handful of bodies between her and the riders. To the accompaniment of thunderous cheers, Prince Edward's war council approached.

Was Lawrence Ravenne a member of the council? She couldn't remember what Thurold had said. Her head was swimming, blurring her thoughts. She just knew that she must flee.

Closer.

What if Lawrence Ravenne somehow recognized her and had her arrested on the spot?

The crowd scattered and broke, leaving Margery momentarily exposed. Edward's knights rode directly toward her. The crests positioned above their helms made them appear ten feet tall. A cacophony of colors blared from their jupons and shields—mythical griffins, dragons and unicorns, crouching wolves, snarling lions, a hissing eagle. Their crests bobbed up and down. The late afternoon shadows jumped at Margery…*shadows like a smoking torchlight, leaping upon cottage walls.*

She spun away, trying to melt into the crowd. Someone shoved her off balance and she fell. When she rose she saw it—the spread wings of a raven bearing down on her. Margery's gaze jerked from the emblazoned jupon to the raised visor of the helm. Lawrence Ravenne! Aye, her lord. Realities, past and present collided. Soon he would slice her with his sword. Soon his stallion's hooves would crush her to death.

She opened her mouth. Did she scream? She remained rooted to the spot as if, like Lot's wife, she'd been turned into a pillar of salt.

Suddenly, strong arms scooped her off the ground and out of danger. She found herself pressed against an armored leg and the high pommel of a saddle, bouncing helplessly in an unyielding embrace.

Finally, her rescuer reined in near Ludgate, away from the crowd. He then loosened his grip, allowing her to slide to the ground.

"Are you all right, sweetheart?"

Immobilized as she was, it took Margery long moments before she recognized her savior. Nay, it could not be! She stared into the deeply bronzed face, into blue—or was it green—eyes that no longer possessed even the remnants of childhood's innocence.

"My lord Hart!" she gasped.

Matthew removed his helm. "Do I know you?"

Margery tried to respond but the words slipped away without taking form. If Matthew Hart should remember her, he would connect her with Ravennesfield. Then he would tell his brother-in-law—

"By Saint Sebastian, 'tis Margery Watson! But what are you doing in London? Why are you not in Ravennesfield?"

Her thoughts frantically circled. A part of her registered the changes in him—a warrior a parlous man rather than a youth—and while she hated even the look of armor and helms and weapons, not so with Matthew. Not at all. Powerful. Magnificent. Impressions so at odds with the incessant lecturings of her rational mind. So at odds with the danger she now faced and upon which she must concentrate.

"Well?" Matthew prompted her, leaning forward in anticipation of her response.

"I...my lord...I..."

How could this be happening? If Matthew's and her horoscopes were cast, would there be something within the lines and circles and symbols to which an astrologer could point and say, "See here, this is where your destinies are intertwined"?

"I thank you for saving me," she managed, sidestepping his question. Her voice was rushed, breathless and she hoped he'd mistake it for the after-effects of the rescue. "'Twas foolish of me to be so careless." She attempted a smile, though the corners of her mouth felt frozen.

"I am just pleased that you were not hurt. And that fortune has brought us together again."

So his thoughts ran parallel to her own. Exciting. Frightening.

"Please do not feel you must stay, sire. I would not keep you from your fête."

Matthew shrugged. "The speeches and gifts are not for me. I shall miss very little." His gaze, so disturbingly direct, swept her length before resting intently on her face. Now he remembered. As he'd sometimes remembered on campaign. Fleetingly, but more than most others. "You have grown well in two years, Sweet Meg. Even dressed in that dreadful mourning, you are prettier than I remember."

Margery's pulse quickened, and this time not from fear or because of his nearness but from annoyance at his boldness. At the nickname tripping so easily off his tongue, the presumption that he might speak to her so, as if they were resuming a conversation that had been finished days, rather than years, ago. A conversation that had meant nothing to either of them, even though she could recall nearly every word. His manner so familiar, as if he had that right…which he did, of course.

Her cheeks felt hot and she ducked her head so that he would not observe. "Thank you, my lord." She dipped in the slightest of curtsies. "And now…might I bid you good day?"

She turned to leave without his permission but Matthew called, "Wait!" He heard a fading round of cheers, a reminder that the celebration would probably be approaching Westminster and the waiting king. But his head still ached from last night's merrymaking and there would be plenty of time to re-join the revels.

"What you are doing in London, Meg?" he prompted anew. "I'll wager 'tis an interesting tale."

"Please do not tell Lord Ravenne," she blurted.

He frowned. "Tell him what?"

How could she possibly respond in a way that would keep her safe? Acting on instinct, Margery bolted away in the opposite direction.

Matthew called her name, which only hastened her flight. She darted in and out of the narrow lanes tangling like an enormous snake through the city. Racing down yet another alley, she encountered a stone wall and spun around to Matthew, eyes now cold with anger, blocking her escape.

Margery faced him, despair in her heart. *Now I have no hope at all. He will turn me over to Ravenne. I will be branded ere the week's out.*

His destrier's hooves made a muffled thunk among the refuse. She looked behind him, but the space was too narrow to provide an exit. Some creature--a cat or rat--dashed past her feet and disappeared into a heap of rotting refuse. Or was that the Thames she smelled, like offal and over-ripe sewage? Hadn't Orabel said that since the pestilence the king had decreed garbage could no longer be dumped in its already polluted waters?

How can I be so close to the Thames? Where am I? What a fine joke. Thinking to lose him, I myself am hopelessly lost...

"Why do you run from me? Why are you so agitated? When last we met I thought we parted on good terms." Matthew had reined in his horse and was studying her, anger replaced by bemusement.

"We did, but..." Her voice trailed off. She could fashion no plausible story unless she told the truth. Which she could never do.

"Why do you look at me as if I would run you through? I relish fear on the faces of the French, but not on those I'm sworn to protect. Especially you."

How to explain the unexplainable, particularly to someone who by executing his duty would bring about her destruction? God had led her from Ravennesfield, given her a new life only to take it away because of her sinful daydreams and night dreams about a man as forbidden, as imaginary as the faerie knight himself. Was this God's way of mocking her whispered longings to see Matthew Hart again?

"Please do not question me. If you think to protect me, let me go."

"Nay, Meg. You cannot flee from me so you best confess. What are you doing here?"

She released her breath on a long sigh. "Aye, well then." Could she pretty up the truth or turn him aside with a plausible lie? But her wits weren't quick enough to spin out an elaborate falsehood which he would unravel with a few well-placed questions. So be it. If fate had reached out to claim her, she would meet it as bravely as she could. Squaring her shoulders, she returned his gaze. Calmly, she hoped. Should he sense her vulnerability, he would be on her like a hound a hare.

"I am a fugitive bondwoman. I ran away from Ravennesfield after my stepfather died." She paused. "If you tell Lord Ravenne, I am as good as dead." She hated the pleading tone that had crept into her voice. Pleading to someone who would grant her no mercy.

Matthew's eyes narrowed. He would not wish to see her flawless forehead branded, yet she had committed a serious offense. "You cannot take off as you please without regard to your obligations. If every villein had your disregard for the law, our entire society would collapse."

What about your disregard for the law? You do as you please because power gives you that right.

Tears welled inside, but she swallowed down the lump in her throat. She would not give him the satisfaction of seeing her cry. Nor would she beg him to show mercy when he knew not its meaning. She had been a fool to believe otherwise. She lifted her chin and faced him, forcing herself to stand tall, fists balled in the folds of her gown.

Whate'er you think to do to me, do it, but do not think I'll further beg your favor.

As Matthew studied Margery, he considered several options. He hated dilemmas which were not black and white, which could not be handled cleanly with the sword. Laws were for Black Robes, clerks and priests.

"I'll not tell my brother-in-law," he finally said. "Life has changed so much since the Death, who can say what is proper? London is filled with runaways. One more will make no difference."

Margery tried to decipher his expression. She dared not hope Lord Hart would truly keep her secret, or ally himself against one of his own.

"Do not look so mistrustful, Meg. Why do you not believe me?"

Not awaiting an answer she would not be able to give, he said, "Perhaps 'twas propitious we met today."

"What do you mean?" she asked warily.

Leaning over in his saddle, Matt stretched out his hand. "Come along, Meg. I have something to show you."

MARGERY HAD HEARD mention of the Savoy Palace because Jean le Bon was being housed somewhere in this sprawling mass of buildings. Before today, however, "Savoy" had simply been a word. Yet, suddenly her world had veered off course to intersect with epic battles in strange-sounding places. with kings and princes and ransoms and affairs of state that had naught to do with people like her.

"'Tis a city all in its own, isn't it?" Matthew said. They were standing in a deserted courtyard of the Savoy.

Margery nodded. All of Ravennesfield could fit in this area, let alone the rest of the estate. Looking up at the crenellated towers and stained glass, she felt very small. Here it was easy to understand the nobility's arrogance, the origins of plots and intrigues that would ever be implemented to the detriment of those born to serve them. Surrounded by such luxury, why would lords and ladies even notice the beggars congregated at London's gates? Strolling in the Savoy's magnificent gardens, why should they give a thought to those packed in tenements along the Thames? Such privilege might be as God intended, but His reasoning was a mystery.

Intending to guide her from the stable area to the palace, Matthew removed one of his gauntlets and took her arm. The gesture was casual–that of someone who felt he had a right to it. Which he did.

"What are you going to do with me? Where are you taking me?"

"To my room."

Margery's eyes widened. She halted on the green and faced him. Did he mean to hurt her, to force her—because this would certainly not be a seduction when she wanted no part of him? When she'd rather face the plague—well mayhap not that—than feel his lips upon hers, or his arms around her, or the heat of his body molded against her? And why was she being distracted from her indignation by the pressure of his fingers, as if it was more pleasurable than repellant?

"Do not look so stricken. I would have you wait outside, but I do not trust you to be here when I return."

They entered a postern and ascended a narrow flight of stone stairs. Matthew guided her along spacious hallways, past opulently-appointed rooms until she was hopelessly confused. Did Jean le Bon have an entire wing to himself? No wonder he was in no hurry to have his ransom paid. Calling Savoy Palace a "prison" simply meant that the nobility played with the meaning of words however it pleased them.

Following Matthew through this dazzling maze, she found her steps dragging. "I do not belong here, my lord. I do not like this place." She remembered something about its owner, the great Henry, Duke of Lancaster, who boasted that he was particularly partial to seducing peasant girls. Did Matthew think to mimic his overlord?

"Jesu, Meg, you are as flighty as a hare." He pulled at her arm to hurry her along. But the Savoy struck her as sinister somehow, as if even now she could hear an echo of its future—and theirs—in the swish of their footfalls, the rhythmic clank of Matthew's armor, in their voices, which sounded so strange and lost in its vastness.

"Ah, now we're here." Matthew opened the door to the small room he shared with Harry and a half dozen others. "I've not had time yet to have my things removed to our townhouse."

When Margery hesitated in the doorway, he gestured for her to enter. Gingerly, she complied. So, now here it was. Would he ravish her and would it be so brutal that she would cry the way her mother had cried following her encounters with Lawrence Ravenne?

Or would it be like in her imaginings, when he held out his hand to her...

She studied him from lowered lashes, trying to gauge what would happen next. Despite her aversion to him, she had to admit that, had Matthew Hart been of her station, she would have found him compelling.

Irresistible, even, as he was when he came to her in dreams.

And if today he had an immoral purpose in bringing her here, why waste time on this elaborate charade? Any hedge or doorway would have served as well.

Tossing his helm and gauntlets onto a pallet, Matthew bent over his trunk and began rummaging through its contents. Finally, he withdrew a small box.

"I had meant to detour to Ravennesfield before visiting my sister at Bury St. Edmunds. I should be thankful you saved me the journey."

He handed her the wooden box which was delicately carved with a design of intertwining vines. "I've had this since Bordeaux, early on in the campaign. I promised I would bring you back something from France. Remember?"

Matthew had seen the piece in a shop packed to the brim with oddities, and had immediately remembered a promise to which he'd given little thought since uttering. And the part about detouring to Ravennesfield, well, he'd not really *meant* to do so. The possibility *had* crossed his mind, and he wasn't really lying for he would have gotten round to it. Otherwise why would he have brought the trinket in the first place?

"Open it," he urged.

She turned over the container. Was this some sort of trickery, improvised on the spot to soften her defenses so he might more easily seduce her?

She lifted the lid. Nestled inside was a wooden robin, so tiny it fit into the palm of her hand. Its eyes were made of jet, and it possessed the brightest scarlet breast she had ever seen.

"You said you preferred robins once," he said softly. Watching her, Matthew wondered once again whether larger forces were at work for why would he step into that very shop and why would he remember a casual conversation and why had he carried the bauble with him only to meet her here in London, of all places?

Margery traced a finger across the bird's breast. "'Tis truly wondrous." He'd remembered a conversation that she'd run round in her mind far too often. What to make of this? He could not pack around gifts to proffer to every maid he thought to seduce. Or he could, but not one so tailored to her. Margery felt something shift inside her. Matthew Hart looked so sincere...but he was standing far too close.

She could feel him, feel that pull, as if she were caught in a dream in which she had no power over her actions.

"Few take promises seriously, my lord. I canna believe you did."

"As a knight, I consider all my vows important," he said, a trifle pompously. "Our family motto is *'Tout est perdu fors l'honneur,'* after all. If I should lose everything save my honor, I would yet possess all I need. It would be dishonorable to deliberately break a promise, which I would not do."

Matthew's use of French and his mention of the word honor, a term his kind frequently abused, helped Margery return to her senses. Still...

Sometimes I am so confused. She did not realize she'd spoken aloud until Matthew repeated, "Confused?"

Margery shook her head. She would not even attempt to explain something that she herself did not understand.

"What do you want from me? Why did you really bring me here?"

He gestured toward the robin. "For this very purpose." Not quite true. Now he was thinking of bedsport. At seventeen years, or thereabout, Margery Watson should no longer be a novice to love, especially with that face and figure. And, despite the debaucheries of the last several days, he suddenly wanted to twist up her gleaming mass of hair and kiss the nape of her neck. He was certain she would smell fresh, that her skin would feel soft as rose petals.

"'Twould be simpler if you had not done this." Margery's voice was so hushed she might have been speaking to herself. "If you were heartless like all the others—"

"What others?" Margery's words jolted Matthew from his amorous mood. Did she have other lovers? "What do you mean by heartless?"

Margery felt the change in atmosphere and told herself she was relieved. The other was too dangerous. She had found herself weakening, allowing those impure thoughts to once more intrude, and sensed her safety lay in goading him. Replacing the robin in the box, she closed it and folded her fingers over it.

"I have known the cruelty of your kind, sire," she said, her manner challenging. "Your natural calling oft runs more to ruining lives than protecting them."

Matthew's eyebrows shot up. "Why would you even think such a thing? You need only look to our prince, who is unfailingly generous to those in need. Or our king and every lord whose retainers guard his lands. If we were not here, who would defend you from England's enemies? Who would give alms to the poor? Who would provide the beneficences to build churches? Who would goldsmiths fashion their pieces for, or cordwainers their shoes, or weavers their cloth? We are well aware that with privilege comes obligation. That you think otherwise surprises me. Is it because of my brother-in-law?"

Margery gasped and took a step backward. "How did you know?"

"I said I would not tell Lord Ravenne you had run away. Why will you not trust me?"

Margery assumed he'd been referring to her mother's murder. She waited until her heart ceased its frantic pounding, until she'd regained a measure of self-control. Matthew's words were truthful. Just because she had experienced a different reality did not mean that he was trying to trick her. She opened her palm and studied the box before raising her eyes to his.

"I want to trust you," she finally said.

The room was hot and stuffy. Sunlight filtered through a narrow window, catching dust motes dancing in the air. It was so quiet she fancied she heard his breathing; certainly her own. She had a sudden image of him embracing her, sweeping her into his arms and carrying her to his pallet where he would lay atop of her. Well, he would have to remove his armor so she need not worry about that but if circumstances were different, would she struggle or would she welcome him? She had seldom had such thoughts, only fleeting wonderings with the boys and men she'd known, but this was very different. And something she had played over in her mind more times than she cared to count…

Reaching out, Matthew caressed her cheek with a touch that seemed to burn her skin. If he kissed her, if he slipped his arms around her, if he drew her to him. Such a shame that he was safely encased in iron…

His eyes darkened and his gaze lingered on her lips. She felt that

137

pull to him, as inexorable as the tides. *And if I succumb, I will surely drown.*

"'Tis so close in here. Please, might we go now? You will miss all the festivities, and I have a friend awaiting me."

Matthew stepped back without protest. She assured herself that she was relieved, though relief felt more like disappointment. Why didn't he press the matter or order her so that she would have no choice but to obey? Then she would not be responsible, then she could pretend that she had been forced to do something that she confessed in her heart she desired.

Matthew took her arm and so politely guided her from his quarters, back down the hallways and out of the Savoy.

After depositing Margery near All Hallows Barking, where she requested, Matthew said, "I will be in London for a time. Where might I find you?"

Margery reminded herself she must not disregard her past merely because Lord Hart had given her a trinket. To pursue anything with this man would lead only to tragedy. As it had with Alice Watson and Thomas Rendell.

"I live on Candlewick Street. I am servant to a draper..." She searched her memory for the name of one of Orabel's suitors, the one who had lived on Candlewick. "Nathan Dwyer, my lord."

Matthew leaned over in his saddle. Margery found herself taking his large calloused hand in her own and gazing up at him, as she'd done in dreams. How handsome he was, how masculine, as if he might indeed protect her from anything. Which he could not. And would not.

"Thank you, my lord, for my robin."

"Soon, Sweet Meg."

She watched him until he disappeared before heading through the emptying streets to the Shop of the Unicorn.

I did the proper thing by lying.

Even so, Margery touched the box tucked safely away in her sleeve and imagined the wooden robin inside, the wooden robin with its bright eyes and its scarlet breast.

And wished...oh, how she wished...

CHAPTER 15

London, 1359

In 1358, King Edward's mother, Isabella, once called the she-wolf of France, died peacefully at Hertford Castle. She had requested burial in her wedding dress beside her husband, Edward II, whom she and her lover were said to have murdered some thirty years past. His Grace ordered London's streets cleaned for Isabella's funeral. As her procession crept through the city, bells tolled and people prayed for a woman they could scarce remember. Isabella was a remnant from a bad time long ago, when England had been in chaos—a time that, like the Death, was best forgotten.

Edward III's perennially popular reign—the chronicler Froissart would later write about the king that 'His like had not been seen since the days of King Arthur'—enjoyed several quiet, peaceful and prosperous seasons. Unlike his father, Edward II, who would have preferred being a gentleman farmer to a warrior king, his son was both a brilliant tactician and knight nonpareil. By mid-century, thanks to Edward and his able councilors, England was in command of both sea and land. Recently, the ever troublesome Scots had accepted a ten year truce and France's dauphin had his hands full battling foreign marauders and his own rebellious *paysans,* leaving Edward III free to attend to domestic matters. He expanded Windsor Castle, home of his Order of the Garter, and built or renovated holdings throughout the kingdom. Domestic and foreign trade flourished, leading to over-flowing money chests and an increase in the number of wealthy merchants, particularly those engaged in the wool trade. Parliament remained in an uncommonly mellow mood; England's civil servants performed their services so efficiently that even the most critical found little to complain about.

If a certain amount of unrest existed among the lower classes or those permanently displaced following the 1349 pestilence, few heard and even fewer took note. Only men like John Ball decried such injus-tices as Parliament's Statute of Laborers which decreed that a man was bound to his employer in the same manner as before the Death, and at the same wage. Some subjects who declined to be thus indentured formed criminal bands to rob their betters traveling the king's high-ways and byways. Others pointed to the closing of so many churches, which had subsequently fallen into disrepair, for what they lamented was an alarming increase in immorality.

"Things were better in the old days," they said, "In the days before the Death."

But with up to half of England's men, women, and children moldering in plague pits, who could actually even remember those "old days?"

For the royal family, the months passed in a pleasant haze of pageantry and tournaments. On May 19, 1359, eighteen-year-old John of Gaunt married Blanche of Lancaster, Henry, duke of Lancaster's thirteen-year-old daughter. King Edward and Queen Philippa were ecstatic with the match, not only because their son was clearly smitten with the pious and beautiful Blanche, but because she was heir to a fortune that would someday make John the richest man in England. Furthermore, though the king and queen had been blessed with an abundance of offspring—twelve with eight living—so far only one had married, and the couple had one legitimate grandchild. By John's age, Queen Philippa had already cradled their firstborn son and England's heir, Edward of Woodstock. (And, while the king and queen whole-heartedly celebrated John's wedding, they *did* fret about Prince Edward, who at twenty-nine remained a bachelor. Had he followed in His Grace the King's wake, the prince would already be father to nine. As his parents oft reminded him.)

Following their wedding at Reading Abbey, John of Gaunt and his young bride were showered with presents befitting their wealth and status, including an enormous eagle-shaped brooch bearing a huge diamond in its breast and surrounded by rubies, pearls and other jewels crafted from the Shop of the Unicorn. Then the royal entourage was off to London, where a lavish celebration, including a three-day tourna-ment, was to be held in their honor.

At the Shop of the Unicorn, which had enjoyed such profitable business these past months, Master Crull had given the help an extra day of leisure. Now that the year and a day was well past and Margery no longer had to worry about her bondwoman status, she found life in the Crull household pleasant enough.

Well, not exactly pleasant. Rather, when she contemplated her circumstances, she defined them more by the "nots": she was not hungry or overworked; she was not beaten by either her master or mistress and fellow servants were not unkind. She did not mind the times she shopped for Dame Crull at Cheapside or watered and weeded her mistress's plants in the back-side. In fact she felt real pleasure tending the various flowers. She would pluck petals of lilacs, lavender, and peonies to decorate stews; violets, onions and lettuce to create salads and flavor broths; and roses and primroses for dessert. As she'd once done in Ravennesfield. The flowers were a link to memories that, with each passing month, became more smudged around the edges.

On free days, Margery and Orabel might watch the great proces-sions of the various guilds or mystery or morality plays in season. They might go caroling in churchyards, singing and dancing away the after-noon. They might watch archers practice on the green, bending their bows back so far and with such keen eyes they could split sticks from a hundred yards or more. Twice she'd attended St. Bartholomew's Fair, where she'd enjoyed acrobats, jugglers and fire-eaters and mingled with the nobility to cheer on the bull and bear baiting. On Shrove Tuesday there was cock fighting and football, a rough and tumble game that King Edward had banned, citing frequent injuries and less frequent deaths.

While Margery was prime marriage age, she continued to spurn the tentative advances of apprentices like Nicholas Norlong and Brian Goldman, who had long ago shed himself of Orabel. Orabel was as unlucky in love as Margery told herself she was indifferent. Orabel's latest had been a white tawyer—leather dresser—who had given her both a ring and a promise of marriage. After she'd lain with him, his words had fallen apart as quickly as her ring, which had been made of wound rushes. More recently, Orabel had cast her eyes upon Thurold, who promised Margery that after the next campaign he would buy them a cottage with a small garden so they could "leave this piss-hole." Since that was Orabel's dream as well she'd spun fancies about they three living in a tidy cottage, in the village of Romford or Maidenhead, mayhap. Anywhere outside of London.

"Thurold will forget as soon as he exits the Shop," Margery warned to dampen her friend's enthusiasm. "He is faithful to his cause— nothing beyond that."

Freedom. Justice. Equality. Those were Thurold's passions. What did Margery feel passionately about? Children? The laughter of toddlers never failed to bring an answering smile to her own lips and she enjoyed watching the Crulls' nieces and nephews, as well as those on the green chasing butterflies with nets or soap bubbles from a pipe or playing hoodman's blind. Oh, but the pinch-faced urchins who begged for food, that was heartbreaking. And she'd witnessed a seven-year-old hanged for stealing a merchant's purse. And so many died so young…

A love of God? Sometimes when John Ball spoke of their creator, she could float to heaven upon the power of his words. She was stirred by the majesty of St. Paul's Cathedral when sunlight would pierce its stained glass to create glorious patterns upon its paving stones, and its monks would chant their hours with voices that echoed forlornly off its high ceilings and sifted down from all the dark places. Those times God seemed both impossibly remote and so close she could feel Him at her elbow. Still, Margery knew she was no holy woman, particularly when Father Crispin gently chided her on her sins during confession.

What was left, marriage and a husband? No, she didn't yearn for that; she found the very idea distasteful. Sometimes she wondered whether something might be wrong with her. God had given women a physical need to desire regular sex so that their seed wouldn't coagulate and suffocate their wombs, which was one of the reasons many wed so early. So, why didn't she feel such a need? When marriage was impossible, women were supposed to travel, exercise and ingest various medicines to counter their base desires. But unless one called a stroll to Milk Street travel, household duties exercise, and an occasional potion for monthly cramping "medicine," Margery should be fainting from the effects of lust.

Which she most definitely wasn't.

And yet...

She hadn't forgotten *him*, not at all.

Since the Shop of the Unicorn catered to the most exalted clientele, she'd spotted several patrons wearing the hart badge, the Lancaster rose and the Prince of Wales' ostrich plumes, but Matthew Hart never numbered among them. His brother was a frequent visitor—though Harry would not have seen her for she spent most of her time in the private quarters. And even if he had, he'd surely never recognize her from their long ago meeting in Ravennesfield. After Harry's departure, she would casually question Nicholas Norlong, who could recall a customer's previous purchases down to a farthing, and was eager to impress her. Judging from Harry's selections of bracelets, arm-rings, neck chains and hair pins, Harry Hart either had many lady friends or hoped to have many lady friends. A pity Master Crull wasn't in the weapons business for then Matthew would most likely attend the Shop as regularly as most attended mass. Margery sometimes imagined a chance meeting during a Sunday stroll or a visit to one of London's many public gardens, but that never happened. And, should they meet, she would have to explain her lie.

If Lord Hart remembered her at all.

Margery had devised a clever tuck in each of her three gowns so that she might safely carry her robin with her throughout the day. As if it were a talisman, though she refrained from sleeping with it. That would have been too foolish.

As I am more than foolish. I am a fool.

Here in London she was hourly reminded that Matthew Hart was so far above her station that, had it not been for their Ravennesfield connection, he'd never have given her a glance. When she recalled Alice's talk of noble blood, Margery dismissed her mother's assertions about her being "special" as the fevered ruminations of a woman who had been hidden away in a tiny hut in a no-consequence village, and whose idea of a great city was Cambridge. Had Alice ever set foot in London—even after such losses that ten thousand plague victims had been buried in West Smithfield just beyond city walls—she would have been undone by its sheer size. And immediately shed of her grandiose notions. Here Alice would have been exposed to lovely women with painted faces and dazzling clothes, with sophisticated airs and education. Had she merely stood in front of the Shop, she would have counted an array of nationalities, miens, dress and languages (though English was now nearly universally spoken), and overheard conversations where curious names like Antipodes, Byzantium, Constantinople and Danzig were tossed about as casually as she and Joan Tomsdoughter had once chatted about the weather.

Surely, then Alice Watson would have realized her naiveté. Believing that a moderately pretty face could secure favor! That teaching a daughter to enunciate and speak properly would outweigh the fact that she could neither read nor write! And most ludicrous of all, that being the bastard child of a lord would be enough to secure her fortune!

And yet…

At night, when she tossed on her pallet, Margery still conjured *him*. And after she slipped into sleep, Matthew Hart still came to her. Upon awakening she would remember flashes, impossible to disentangle one from the other—the moon huge and round as a gold plate, dazzling armor, high-stepping stallion with its silky curtain of a mane and tail shining as if from an inner radiance. Moonlight resting upon her lover's head like an anointing. Leaning forward, beckoning to her. Her faerie knight...*him.*

She carried those flashes around as surreptitiously, and as faithfully, as she did her robin, and reminded herself that the moon had surely promised her *something*, when she, Thurold and John Ball had been London bound. But so many months had passed and she worried that she might have misread its message.

Not because she was desperate, she assured herself, but because she was curious, Margery had become adept at casting and interpreting horoscopes, even without the knowledge of letters, and hers foretold a period of monumental change. A woman healer in Southwark, who was supplementing Margery's knowledge of the medicinal and magical properties of plants, had also taught her the ancient art of scrying. The process was simple enough. Margery would gaze into a shallow bowl of water and allow her mind to drift on a cloud of vapor. Images were supposed to form in the liquid. Once interpreted, the images would provide a glimpse into the future.

Margery would patiently study the smooth surface until a simulacrum appeared. Sometimes she fancied she saw the face of the man in the moon and sometimes...others. What could the faces mean? Was the man in the moon a reminder of her vision? Or was it an affirmation that the vision had simply been a dream concocted from the cloth of her desire?

Surely, all the signs pointed to that unnamed *something,* did they not?

ON THE THIRD day of the tournament held in honor of John of Gaunt and his bride's nuptials, Margery and Orabel attended. Located beyond London's walls, the lists consisted of an enormous field of hard-packed earth surrounded by stakes. The knights' silk and velvet pavilions, with their brilliant colors and banners, were located west of the wooden galleries. Save for squires and yeomen, who were relegated to the lower tiers, the cushioned or carpeted stands were reserved for the most exalted—which included Jean le Bon. While remaining officially imprisoned, the French king, now ensconced at Windsor Castle, continued to live as he pleased.

Margery wedged herself between Orabel and a friendly candle-maker. The pair flirted while Margery kept her eyes upon the field, lightheaded with anticipation. Not because today, she knew, Matthew Hart would number among the participants, but because of the sun, which was unusually warm for this early in summer. So she told herself. And knew, once again, she lied.

Trumpets announced the beginning of the joust. The crowd murmured, then stilled in anticipation. Margery shaded her eyes and waited impatiently. After all this time she would at least glimpse him. She was hungry, starving for some contact with him, even so far away, even when she was but one among hundreds.

Row upon row of knights circled the lists to the accompaniment of enthusiastic applause. Ribbons, sleeves, stockings, scarves and other favors streamed atop their lances and helms while from the stands, ladies tossed yet more gloves, girdles, and flowers.

Orabel turned. "Do ye see him yet?" While Margery kept her own counsel, Orabel knew enough of her friend's heart to understand that today's lone attraction would be a glimpse of her knight.

Margery nodded and pointed, drinking in the sight of Matthew Hart. Circling the field with the rest of the challengers. Helm off, a breeze ruffling his hair, a multitude of favors upon his lance—surely more than most anyone—which returned her to reality. She need not gaze down at her drab gown to be reminded that, compared to the court ladies, she looked like what she was—a peasant from the countryside.

She touched her ever-present robin, hidden in a pouch that looked to be part of her embroidered sleeve. *Then why hasn't he married?* She knew he hadn't, he was of an age, and he was first-born. Love and attraction weren't generally involved in marriage, but could his continued bachelorhood mean something?

That he is pining for you? Margery Watson from Ravennesfield? Dim wit!

In the light of day, in light of her lie to him, in light of the social chasm separating them, she knew there would be no rendezvous beneath the moon. Or anywhere else.

It does not matter. I will enjoy this day and the sight of him and then I will return my robin to its box and, as Father Crispin says, put away childish things.

Challengers and defenders, who had not removed their helms, lined up on opposite sides of the lists. Matthew, now recognizable by the identifying banderol on his lance, numbered among the twenty-four challengers. A second blast of trumpets signaled the start. The screaming crowd, the thunder of racing destriers, and the knights' battle cries were deafening. When the two sides met, the very ground seemed to shake with their impact, reverberating through Margery's body.

The field soon became a chaos of armor, men and horses, all tangled together. Orabel jumped up and down, clapping excitedly, but Margery had to refrain from squeezing her eyes shut to black out the violence. Instead, she clasped her hands tightly together and searched among the flashing swords until she spotted Matthew battling John Lovekin, London's mayor.

"There is your knight!" cried Orabel, waving as if he might see her. "Why is he having such trouble besting the mayor? Lovekin's but a fishmonger."

Margery winced, unable to look away. She could almost feel the blows thwacking Matthew. Back and forth across the lists, he and the mayor advanced and retreated, slashed and parried. "This is madness," she breathed. Sweet Jesu! Such brutal games these lords enjoyed—nay, all men enjoyed for those of her class were as rough in their own fashion.

Given their ranks, the defenders were fighting far more skillfully than one would expect. In fact, they seemed more like berserkers than ordinary guildsmen, and had little trouble overwhelming their challengers. Soon riderless horses circled a field littered with crumpled bodies and shattered lances, until only a handful of challengers remained mounted, including Matthew.

Margery watched as he went knee to knee against the mayor. Lovekin repeatedly slammed his sword against Matt's helm, and finally sent him toppling to the ground. Her breath caught as Matt's squire and body servant raced onto the field, grabbed their lord's arms and legs, and carried him to safety.

"I pray he is unharmed," Margery said to Orabel, but her voice was drowned out by the jubilant roar of the crowd, signaling the defeat of the last challenger. The victorious defenders removed their helms, which caused the crowd to cheer all the louder. London's mayor turned out to be, not lowly John Lovekin, but King Edward himself. Edward's sons were all there too, disguised as sheriffs.

"No wonder your knight could not best him." Orabel squealed with laughter. "What a fine jest."

"A fine jest, indeed. What if Lord Hart is hurt?"

"Go find out."

"Nay, I could not." Women did not invade a male bastion.

Orabel turned to face her friend. "Think ye I donna know why you sigh so and canna sleep? Why you turn aside any man who dares approach?" She pulled Margery toward the back of the crowd. "What harm is there in offering your services? Are you not skilled with herbs? Come along, Maggie-dear. 'Tis time to give fortune a bit of guidance."

The more Margery considered the idea, the less transparent it seemed. And it had been so very long since she'd seen him. And he had such a way of stirring her emotions...

They searched among the pavilions for Lord Hart's identifying shield. Tethered hunting dogs bayed at their passing while squires called out lewd comments. Margery dodged riderless destriers, dizzy, battered knights being led to surgeons for a restorative bloodletting and servants scurrying hither and yon.

Finally, she spied Matthew's shield with its hart rampant. There were no barber surgeons or priests hovering about the tent, which meant he could not be too badly hurt. "This is a poor idea," she said to

Orabel, hanging back. Had a woman ever been so bold about her intentions?

"We've come too far to stop now." Orabel smiled at Matthew's groom, who was currying his master's warhorse. "My," she breathed. "What capable hands he has!"

While her friend struck up a conversation, Margery approached the open tent flap. Inside, she saw Matt's squire, his barber, his brother, and Matthew himself, his back to her. His torso was bare, his legs clad in the braies and chausses that served as undergarments beneath his armor. His broad shoulders fairly rippled with muscles, then angled to a narrow waist and lean hips. He looked very much alive—and very well.

Margery felt light-headed. How brazen she was, how inappropriate, but how often the last long months had she wished she'd told him truly, "I live here," imagined him coming to the Shop, imagined days and nights that need not have been so barren and empty…

Matthew drank from a wooden goblet, then spat out a mixture of wine and blood. "Who would have thought I'd cross swords with His Grace?" he lamented, limping toward a wooden stool. "No wonder I could not best him." He tossed a discarded sponge into a nearby bucket of herbal water and with a muted groan, eased onto the stool, facing Margery.

Slip away, she thought. *This is a mistake. Do not let him see you.*

At that very moment, Matthew *did* see her. "Margery Watson!" He bolted to his feet, one arm across his bruised ribs. "What are you doing here?"

She reddened under his hostile scrutiny. The others turned and stared. She dipped in a curtsy.

"I am sorry for my boldness, my lord, but I watched you fall and was concerned." Of course, Lord Hart saw through an explanation that was flimsy as gossamer. "I know a bit about medicinal herbs."

She tried to focus on his face, but he was so clearly displeased by her presence that her gaze fastened to the damp hair shading his chest, hair that she might accidentally brush while treating him. Or she might gently probe the bruise that was beginning to disfigure his upper stomach—his hard, flat stomach.

"You have an interesting way of appearing and disappearing, Margery Watson." His legs were spread in a truculent stance, his voice challenging. "Have you become confused? Lost your way?"

"I see my fears were unfounded." All amorous thought had been shattered by his coldness. "I am relieved your injuries were not grievous."

She turned to leave, but ignoring his injuries Matthew moved more quickly, closing the distance in a few strides. Catching her waist, he spun her around. She fell against his chest and jerked back as if scalded.

"Why did you lie to me, Margery Watson?" he asked, ignoring his brother and the rest, who were openly gawping at the exchange. "I inquired at every chandler, weaver and draper's residence on Candlewick, trying to find you. I am not over quick. It took me some time to figure you had deliberately deceived me."

"I was afraid you would tell...that you would reveal my where-abouts," she replied breathlessly. "I could not risk it."

"Meaning you do not trust me." He released her and stepped back, as if too disgusted to be in her presence.

Striving for a measure of calm, Margery inhaled deeply, only to capture his scent–a combination of leather and lavender, chamomile and bresewort from the herbal water. His skin gleamed softly from a mixture of perspiration and the sponging his barber had administered.

"I hope you will forgive me."

Matthew studied her, as if her expression, some nuance or gesture would provide a more satisfactory answer than her words. To what question, Margery could not say, but she was unnerved by the intensity in his eyes.

Harry approached. Following a nod to her—*Might he remember?* —he said, "Well, brother, we will be going now. Let us know when you are finished with...well..." After a final, unreadable glance at Margery, he and the others left.

In the charged silence that followed, she said, "My treatment of you has weighed heavily on my conscience. I am sorry for that."

Did she detect a softening of Matthew's mouth, of the hard expression in his eyes? He moved, as if he might touch her, but then grimaced and cradled his ribs. Turning his back to her, he limped back to his stool.

"God's nails," he swore softly. He took deep breaths, as if to manage the pain. She tried not to focus on the swell of his bare chest. Rise and fall. Inhale, exhale. Father Crispin would have her saying *Pater Nosters* until the feast of Mary Magdalene.

"My lord, I am skilled with poultices and potions. Might I not help?"

A long pause. Finally, he opened his eyes, gazing at her as if he'd forgotten her. "Nay, 'twill pass."

She stood awkwardly before him until the silence became unbearable. "I will fetch your barber then."

He nodded.

She hurried toward the exit. Such humiliation. Why had she listened to Orabel? Why had she listened to her heart? Her foolish, treacherous heart?

"Meg!" He beckoned her back. She hesitated. Was he seeking to detain her in order to further embarrass her? Slowly, she complied, stiffening her shoulders and striving for an outward dignity at odds with her inner abasement.

Matthew seemed caught in some internal dialogue for he did not speak for a good while. "I have been known to accept apologies from beautiful women," he said finally. Something in the pitch of his voice caused her limbs to turn liquid.

She managed a nod. "I am grateful, my lord."

"And I know you reside at the Shop of the Unicorn."

Margery's eyes widened. "How—"

"Harry. He saw when I rode away with you at the Poitiers celebration. And he recognized you later, at the Shop."

She tried to keep her face expressionless. Why pretend anger over a lie when he'd known—how long had he known?—her true where-abouts. Yet he'd made no effort to renew their acquaintance. Yet he said he'd searched for her. Matthew Hart was a puzzle...

"If you do not vanish again, mayhap I will pay the Shop a visit."

"I would like that, my lord," she whispered.

Matthew closed his eyes, as if against more pain. "And now, would you fetch me my barber?"

152

CHAPTER 16

London

In the summer of 1359, talk of war with France resumed largely because Jean le Bon's ransom remained unpaid. Though the southern provinces of Languedoc had responded, no money came from a north ravaged by the Jacquerie, an uprising in which peasants revolted against their lords, as well as the incessant raids of various Free Companies. An impatient King Edward pressed Jean to a second treaty with terms so outrageous that Jean's sons and the French Estates General adamantly refused ratification.

"We have dallied long enough," His Grace declared. "We have no choice but to declare a "just war" against their perfidious rejection."

It was at this time that Edward III also began entertaining ambitions of being crowned King of France. Through his recently deceased mother, Queen Isabella, who had been sister to the French king, Philip the Fair, His Grace could support his blood claim.

And so he did.

With August's arrival, Edward, along with thousands of other knights and yeomen, again fastened greedy eyes upon France.

. . .

WHEN LEARNED men expounded on the human constitution, they explained that each person's body is composed of four contraries—hot, cold, moist, and dry. While males are generally of the sanguine type, women, because their nature is melancholic, are primarily influenced by cold and dry humors, which push them more readily toward death, the coldest and driest state of all.

Margery often pondered the word "melancholic," for that was exactly how she had been feeling. Throughout the day, as she went about her chores or snuck away to check the turf seat built into the side wall of the Crull back-side for a message from Matthew, that word kept rolling around in her mind. *Melancholic*.

But why wouldn't she feel thus with war once again at her door readying to take away her stepbrother, but most especially, Lord Hart?

Since the tourney, she and Matthew had met a handful of times. He had devised a secret system, paying one of the urchins clustered on church steps or at the side doors of mansions, to sneak into the back-side and deposit an appropriate number of stones in the turf seat. Two small flat stones and Margery and Matthew would meet that day at the Tower Garden at terce, three at sext and four at nones or thereabouts, depending on how quickly she could slip away.

During their assignations—well, Margery could scarce call them assignations for that intimated they were lovers—Matthew was always attentive, but he never transgressed boundaries. The space between them fairly crackled with sexual tension—at least *she* felt it—but he never tried to seduce her. Why? Did he have another? Was he secretly affianced? Did he find her dull, homely? But no lord would seek out a plain woman of her station for conversation, for anything save a sexual dalliance, so why wasn't Matthew Hart dallying?

Oft times she suspected Matthew was so enamored with the talk of war that he had no room in his heart for another mistress. Then why did he dispatch the beggars with their stones? At her most frustrated Margery considered concocting a love potion, as she occasionally did for Orabel. She need but search the back-side for yarrow, passion flower, motherwort, and all the other necessary ingredients, mix them together and chant her wish. But such activities smacked of black magic, and, even in this enlightened England, 'twould be dangerous to be labelled a witch. While gardeners were encouraged to crumble consecrated hosts over their gardens to kill caterpillars and priests used holy water to drive off grasshoppers or exorcise ghosts, certain boundaries could not be transgressed. So long as the rituals involved religious symbols, it was deemed acceptable. But for a woman, and for love potions?

Still, Margery felt so restless, so discontented, so…so…melancholic between the times Matthew summoned her.

As he did today.

Four stones tucked in the corner of the turf seat.

Margery raced through the noon meal and her chores before seeking out Dame Crull for permission for her and Orabel to leave. Gisla was in the back of the shop, before the furnace. Master Crull stood nearby, explaining some gilding technique to Nicholas Norlong. Margery spoke quietly so as not to be overheard. Her master could be querulous for the most insignificant reasons.

Gisla assented with an indifferent shrug, but Simon Crull called, "Where are you bound?" He approached her, waving his dainty hands as if shooing away an unpleasant odor. "Who are you seeing? Someone among that hedge priest's band of mercenaries, cutthroats and pickpockets?"

Dame Gisla ceased working her bellows to glare at Margery. "Husband—"

"You think I do not know what you are about? I'll have you followed, and if I find you've been whoring around, I'll have you removed from this house."

"*Husband*, I need you to tend the furnace." Gisla jabbed a bellows in Simon's side. "Off with you, girl, before I change me mind."

TOWER HILL, where the Tower of London was located, possessed an abundance of private gardens, as well as a royal garden which specialized in exotic pear trees. Its slopes were terraced with vines and orchards. Margery considered this part of London one of the most beautiful, for flower and vegetable gardens also stretched all along the city wall and down to the Thames.

Once at their destination, Orabel, who always accompanied her, would discreetly tend to a strip of garden designated for the Crull household while Margery and Matthew met.

During her three years in England's capital, Margery had come to consider London as alive as any human and fancied she could read its many moods. Today the city seemed charged with excitement, like an animal before a storm. No need to be a soothsayer to understand the reason.

"Why does combat so enthrall men?" she asked Orabel, as they turned up Tower Hill. "It unites them as nothing else can."

Her friend shrugged. She enjoyed these outings because of the opportunities they provided for gossip with other households, not to ponder weighty matters. "Men be just big boys and boys are allus looking for a fight."

Margery nodded. From camp cooks to commanders, from the merchants who readied supplies to the boys who bid their fathers farewell–all men seemed to embrace the very concept.

'Twould be fine for all the nobility to go off and die, she told herself. *All save my Lord Hart.* She had ceased questioning Matthew's power over her, for she deemed it elemental and inevitable, a force of nature. Beyond that, Margery was so grateful that he'd rescued her from that netherworld she'd inhabited before the tourney, when she'd been neither alive nor dead and where lassitude had been her dominant emotion.

They entered the grove. After Orabel retreated to the Crull garden, Margery drifted to the enclosed arbor where she generally met Matthew. Her favorite area brimmed with Rosa Gallica—the rose used on John of Gaunt's coat of arms; the rose his retainers wore as an identifying badge.

The king and his sons and my lord Hart off to France as if enjoying some grand game, with the French merely set pieces for them to smash as they please.

To escape the cloying smell of fallen fruit already beginning to rot, she brought a dazzling purple rose to her nose, inhaling its fragrance. She closed her eyes.

War...Melancholia...

"What a fine sight you make, alone in the garden."

Margery turned, startled. "I did not hear you, my lord." She gave him the slightest of smiles, as if no frisson of excitement accompanied her first glimpse of him, as if every part of her had not been immediately shaken to life. "How long have you been there?"

"A while. I enjoyed watching you. Such a refreshing change from court ladies, who keep thinking to marry me." Matthew laughed as if such a possibility was ludicrous, and approached her. He leaned down to kiss her on the forehead. As he might a child.

Margery studied him, not daring to speak until she was sure she could trust her voice. "Someday even you will have to bow to convention and marry."

"Never. I will remain a bachelor like Prince Edward."

Margery released her rose. "At the shop we are always hearing talk of marriage for the prince. 'Tis just a matter of time."

"I am not a prince. I can do as I please," he boasted. "And it pleases me to remain just the way I am." Matthew took both her hands and smiled into his eyes. She felt his excitement, as surely as she had that of the city, and knew he had come to say good-bye.

"In a week's time we'll be bound for Dover, and I would not waste our time speaking of unpleasant things. Come along, Meg, let us walk. I am too restless to stay hidden in a garden."

With Orabel trailing discreetly behind---she'd fallen in with another pair of maidservants headed in the same direction—Matthew and Margery headed toward London's outskirts. Margery tried to concentrate on the river traffic, the various street vendors, the noises and smells and bustle, but she kept thinking, *In a trice you will be gone. I may be seeing you for the last time.* She found it hard to speak, though she assured herself she need not fear for his safety. *You are going off to war, and if there is one thing you excel at, 'tis combat.*

"I know you are pleased to fight, but there is always so much suffering...'tis women and children who are most affected. Before you ride into France, they will be wives and sons and daughters. After your leaving they will be widows and orphans."

"The French refuse to pay their king's ransom. What else can we do? You must never forget that the French are not people so much as they are England's enemies. I know few woman can see the joy in war but only the sorrow, so I canna criticize you for not understanding. Mayhap there are things about women I could never understand." His tone made it clear that what he did not understand he did not care to contemplate.

Matthew's assuredly flawed logic reinforced the gulf between them, which she once again chose to ignore. Rather, Margery would concentrate on the fact that they were first and foremost man and woman, enjoying each other's company. Without past or future, but merely the present. It was a delicate maneuvering act, like a juggler balancing his balls. The slightest mistake might send them all crashing—and reveal the fragility of their relationship. If relationship it could be called. For didn't that imply something between equals, something that would lead somewhere? When this never would. Still, she would smile and revel in the touch of his arm on hers while pretending otherwise.

As they strolled along with Matthew decrying the latest French duplicity, Margery fancied she could read the impending war on the faces of passersby. She tried to imagine which women had said good-bye to their lovers or husbands or brothers, which men were readying to leave and whether, if she looked closely enough, she could read their fate in their eyes. Who would return and who would die in France?

"Almost there," said Matthew, his words breaking through her fog.

"Where is THERE?" She noticed they were in Holborn. And that by the sun's position many hours remained before she must return to the Shop.

"Hart's Place." He said it so casually, as if 'twas their usual destination.

Margery halted. "Why?" There could only be one reason for him to take her to his townhouse. Seduction. Was this the moment she'd been longing for?

"Meg." He uttered only her nickname but his look left her weak with desire. A part of her seemed to detach, to drift overhead and survey them from above, to view her, so soberly attired and looking, what?—frightened, wary, eager—for she felt all those things. And Matthew, brimming with the supreme self-confidence of a man who's won his courtship and is about to claim his prize.

They reached Hart's Place. Beyond noticing that his residence was detached—a further reminder of familial wealth—her concentration had narrowed to the burning of his palm as it slid down her arm to lace her fingers with his own, to the lust in the depths of his eyes when he turned his gaze upon her.

As if in answer to a question he had not asked, Margery nodded.

Matthew drew her to the front door. Once inside, he wrapped his powerful arms around her, pulled her close and kissed her long and slow. She had to stand on tiptoe to fully reach him, for her own arms to slide around his neck.

When he finally released her, Margery remained pressed against him. She closed her eyes, the better to imprint this moment on her memory.

For later, before it would all have ended in sorrow...

"I wanted to be alone with you, where we would not be interrupted." He brushed his lips across the crown of her head. "I would not force or hurry you, but sometimes events have a way of sweeping people along with them."

Might she beg him to stay in England, to pay a scutage rather than fight? But that would be a foolish, womanly thing to do, as well as a waste of precious moments. More than that, she wanted him to lead her —now—to wherever they might have privacy so that he might complete his conquest.

Matthew kissed her again. She drew back, noted the pulse racing in his throat, felt the evidence of his desire and whispered, "Take me, my lord...if you please."

Matthew swept her up as though she were light as a lamb and carried her upstairs to the solar. With one booted foot he kicked closed the door behind them. Margery slipped from his arms and stepped back from him, dimly aware of her surroundings—of the massive canopied bed and the shuttered mullioned windows swathing the room in shadow. They faced each other. How to feel simultaneously breathless and totally still inside? Should she tell him she was a virgin, that she was frightened of what was about to unfold? But the first seemed unimportant and the second would be a lie.

Matthew reached out. Carefully, he loosed the braids coiled on either side of her ears so that her hair fell free down her back. Margery stood as if paralyzed. His actions seemed oddly gentle in so large a man. He ran his fingers through a tangle of hair, brushing her breast in passing. "Monks say the sight of a woman's unbound hair will drive any man to lust." His hands settled upon her hips. "They must have been speaking of you."

Matthew kissed the corners of her mouth. His breath smelled sweet. Though his touch remained light, there was no mistaking the power, even danger, behind it. That threat of danger she ever found intoxicating.

"I have waited so long," she whispered. For it seemed so, at least a lifetime. Her fingers curled in the thick hair at the nape of his neck. Bringing his head down, she kissed him. Boldly, inappropriately. And she did not care. She pressed against him, delighting in his hardness. She might decry a warrior's occupation, but the result of that training was the man who stood before her, a man with a body nonpareil. She remembered the sight of him, half naked after the tourney, and felt such an unfeminine eagerness to have all of him revealed, to make love to him in the magnificent flesh, as she'd made love to him countless times in her imaginings.

Matthew whispered against her ear, "I knew we'd be a fine fit." His lips trailed down Margery's neck, to the cleft above her breasts. His manner became more demanding, as did hers. Slowly, insistently, he worked her toward the bed, both removing their clothing in the process. His hands and tongue seemed to be everywhere, caressing, probing, raising her emotions to an unbearable intensity. In turn, Margery hungrily explored every inch of him. She tasted the salt on his neck and in the hollow above his collarbone. Her lips travelled downward, along the muscular chest to his flat stomach, down to where the golden hair tapered into a vee.

More, she silently demanded, *more*. He might think he would take her upon the canopied bed, but she would be the one doing the taking.

Matthew pressed her back until she sank into the brocade coverlet. Then he straightened, to better view her. His gaze swept the curves of her body, in a look as exciting as his touch. "You are fine, indeed, Meg. Even finer than my imaginings."

"As are you, my lord."

She held out her arms to him and pulled him on top of her. *So this is what the priests mean when they say we are insatiable.* It was as if she were inhabited by a wanton, a harlot, anything but a blushing virgin. For that she was not.

As his movements became more urgent, Margery dug her fingers into his back, not minding the pain, wanting only for him to go deeper and deeper until he could never extricate himself, so that she would devour him. He might think to claim her, but he was wrong, she told herself, as he released his seed. Matthew Hart would be the one forever branded by her desire.

WHILE MATTHEW DOZED, Margery tried to sort out these past hours. Who had she been, certainly not the Margery Watson who spurned the very touch of a man. Nor had she behaved like an innocent, though her body was already feeling the after effects. She would be sore, but that would be a reminder that today had not been a dream. She reached out to gently stroke Matthew's arm and he sighed in his sleep, shifting toward her. She had done what she'd said she would not, what she had longed to do and had schemed to do.

This once. Never again would they, should they be together. Hadn't she always vowed she would never end up like her mother and Thomas Rendell?

But we need not repeat others' lives. Please, God, I would rather just live my own. And how, after tasting such sweetness could she ever return to the wasteland that had been her life?

Margery folded down the sheet to expose Matthew's chest. In the light from the shutters playing across his tumbled hair and those perfectly sculpted arms, he was indeed her faerie knight. They need only the rising of the moon to complete the tableau. And he *had* been hers, if only in passing.

Turning aside she stared into the gloom. With the ebbing of passion, with the understanding that from now on everything—and nothing—would be different she felt once more that familiar melancholia. She closed her eyes to stop the pricking of tears.

I chose this man knowing that we had no future, and I did it all the same. Do I think to punish myself? To run headlong toward desolation even as I insist I will not?

A whisper of footsteps beyond the door. Had the Hart servants been listening? Or Matthew's brother? For the first time she was aware of outside traffic, of London going about its business. Judging from the mouth-watering smells wafting into the solar it would soon be dinner time, meaning she must find Orabel and return to the Shop, as Matthew would return to his routine.

Which would be upended by war.

So you sail for France and I will pass the days at the Shop and there will be no further intersection between us. I know it, always knew it, and yet I insisted on having my desire. Why did I choose the waywardness of my heart over the wisdom of my head?

She felt a panicked need to hunt through her discarded clothes for her robin which acted as a talisman whenever she was in need of comfort, or during the times Matthew had seemed lost to her. Retrieve it from the folds of her gown and crush it in her fist.

Matthew stirred and opened his eyes. "Why do you look so sad, Sweet Meg?" He caressed her stomach, the curve of her hip. "I did not hurt you, did I?"

She shook her head and managed a smile.

He leaned on his elbow to face her, his free hand toying with a strand of hair tumbling upon her breasts. "What is it then? The campaign? You know you need not fear for me."

She nodded at his mistaken assumption, pretending that were so.

"Aye, then, we'll not think upon unpleasant matters. When I ponder today, I would rather remember other things."

He brushed his lips against hers and she nestled against him, her head upon his chest.

If I could capture this moment in time…

A part of her was as misguided as Orabel, fancying she could spin yearnings into reality. Next she'd be conjuring a tidy cottage awash in roses and toddlers with Matthew sitting before the fire like some simple yeoman.

As she'd bent over star charts, and stared into bowls of water pretending they might portend the future when they'd simply been… bowls of water.

Slipping away, Margery scooted to the edge of the bed and leaned over to gather her clothes. "I must be off. Master Crull gets angry if I'm gone too long. And Orabel must be bored having waited so long."

I will spend years, into old age, remembering this moment. When I chose something as ephemeral as a wish, as uncapturable as a longing. And I had thought to brand you? When I'll never be able to remove your mark from my soul.

Matthew looped a forearm around the front of her waist and pulled her back against him. "Your master must be a rich man. Does he ever try to buy your favor?"

Margery recoiled in horror. "Why would you even say such a thing?"

He stroked her shoulder and planted a kiss. "An old man. And a beautiful young woman."

"Simon Crull loves naught but his work. And he is so miserly he will not buy enough wood for the hearth fires, let alone frivolities."

"I know his shop has a fine reputation, but there is something repellant about him, like when you come across a dead animal unexpectedly…a dead animal swarming with maggots."

"Jesu!" Of a sudden she felt peculiar, as if by bringing her master into the conversation in such a grisly fashion Matthew had tainted their tryst.

"I do not see him often."

"Have you ever thought of seeking employ elsewhere?" he persisted.

"I have a good friend in Orabel. I would not want to leave her. Besides, life at the Shop is simple enough. Another household might be far worse."

Margery retrieved her chemise and the rest of her clothes, pretending to be distracted by a high neck and long tight sleeves. She brushed against her robin and suppressed the urge to clutch it to her breast. When she reached for her cote, Matthew stayed her hand and forced her to face him.

"If you find that you are with child, Margery, I will care for thee."

Margery felt herself flush. "Why would you say such a thing?" Blessed Virgin, what had she done? Now God would punish her by making her pregnant and Master Crull would banish her from his household and she'd end up begging on the steps of St. Paul's.

"What would you do for me and my babe if it did happen?" she asked sharply. "Bring me a handful of coins when it pleases you?"

Matthew was surprised by her bitter tone. "Of course I would not. I would do whatever you require. I take care of all my offspring."

"Is this another of your bastards?" Beatrice Rendell had asked her husband. *How many bastards did Matthew have? How many other women?*

Margery retrieved her leather slippers from the carpeted floor. "I will not become…in that way." She placed her slippers on her feet and began plaiting her hair. Would Orabel be in the garden or chatting with some of the Hart servants in the kitchen? She would find her and they would scurry back to the Shop like wayward children fearful of being caught. "Do not worry about me. I would not have you distracted during the campaign."

Reluctant to end their lovemaking on a tense note, to ruin memories he would re-imagine during long nights in France, Matthew teased her. "What would you have me bring you this time?"

Margery flinched. Carefully coiling a braid around each ear, she said, "Only yourself."

"'Tis a foregone conclusion. Something else."

She shook her head. "I do not want anything else."

"Look at me, Margery."

Reluctantly, she complied.

"This was not a careless bedding for me. I promise you two things. I will not forsake you and I will come home to you. Do you believe me?"

Margery considered the question. He ran his fingers along the back of her neck, the line of her chin.

"I believe you," she whispered. *Like a work of filigree, repeating a pattern over and over and over...*

"Say it then. Say you believe I will not forsake you."

Margery parroted the words, almost convincing herself in the saying. *If only I could spend a thousand nights with you and make love to you and bury myself in your physical presence and never engage my mind. Tragedy must lie at the end and yet even knowing, I would risk it all.*

"Do not look so solemn, Meg." Matthew embraced her once again. In the honey of his kiss, she momentarily forgot her doubts. He murmured against her ear, "Would you like me to tell you I love you?" And with the uttering he was willing to do so and even to mean it. After his fashion.

Margery shook her head for she knew love had naught to do with any of it. "Just come home to me, my lord. France is no fit place for an Englishman to die."

CHAPTER 17

London

Margery and Matthew were able to meet a handful of times before his leavetaking, and during their final rendezvous she presented him with a necklace made of draconite, removed from a dragon's head. This particular stone had been drawn while the creature was still alive, which meant it would protect him from all poison, and if borne on the left arm, overcome all enemies.

After Matthew set sail, Margery could almost believe she'd made love to a ghost. She found it increasingly impossible to connect Matt with Lord Matthew Hart, as well as the larger events around her. With him—and Thurold—departed, London seemed emptied, as empty as her soul without her beloved.

While Margery largely kept her own counsel, she knew she must beg absolution for her sin. Rather than seek out Father Crispin at St. John Zachary, where the Crull household worshiped, she chose the anonymity of St. Paul's.

There, at the western front of the cathedral, she spotted John Ball, moving among a motley assortment of beggars, tradesmen, laborers and strollers wearing hoods of scarlet rey. Of course John Ball would be about, though knowing that Thurold was absent from his side caused a twinge of sadness.

She heard John address a rough-looking lad. "Avoid luxury, avoid causing people needless pain, don't be fooled by a Papal pardon, and finish your soup." His laughter thundered as he clapped the lad on the shoulder.

Margery also smiled for John's laugh always warmed her.

"Hedge priest," she called and waved, though she did not stop. John so seldom drew crowds it would be selfish to demand his attention. Besides, he was a great one for questioning her about every facet of her life, and so perceptive she sometimes worried he might be able to read her thoughts.

Traitor to your class, she chastised herself in his stead.

Circling to another entrance, Margery paused inside at the *Si quia* door, which was a popular place for posting notices. During other visits, Thurold had read to her some of the bits and pieces of other people's lives.

'Please help me find my coin purse, stolen Tuesday last.'

'Please save my six-year-old son who be coughing blood.'

'Please restore the feeling to me hands for I canna use me chisel.'

If she could read and write, would she have tacked up her own plea? What would she have written?

'Please right the wrongs of this world?'

'Please rid your children of pain and suffering?'

'Please make Matthew Hart desire me evermore?'

She entered the gloomy interior and crossed to the main altar where she lit three candles—one for Lord Hart's well-being, one for Thurold's and one for the souls of her dead relatives. Then she knelt on the paving stones and gazed up at the altar, which still had loaves of bread left over from Lammas Day.

Margery remembered other Lammas Days when her mother had woven yellow flowers through her hair symbolizing the sun at its strongest, drawn a circle and placed fresh-baked bread in its center as an expression of gratitude to the earth for its bounty. Odd that after all these years, she could recollect such ceremonies so vividly when she could recall little else.

She heard John Ball outside and knew by the pitch of his voice that he had launched into a sermon, though she couldn't distinguish individual words. Rather it was like a vibration passing through stone walls and pointed clerestory windows, across the carved cannons' stalls and the jumble of tombs and brasses. It seemed to thrum like ten-thousand insects, carrying with it the knowledge of hope and failure.

And death, of course.

The death of injustice and poverty, for what else did the Lollard priest ever speak of? Unfortunately, Margery knew the ghosts John so skillfully exhumed would be exorcised in the brutal light of reality. While those now enraptured by his message would carry it home and mull it over, they would ultimately discard it like a worn-out piece of clothing.

Raising herself from the stones, Margery sought a priest to hear her confession. She knelt before a middle-aged cleric who looked unusually well fed beneath his robes.

"Father." She made the sign of the cross and bent her head while reciting her mortal sins in order to be spared viewing his expression of displeasure. However, before granting absolution, the priest delivered a spirited lecture.

"You are a wicked woman. All women are wicked and weak and responsible for ALL the world's ills. If Eve had not tempted Adam to eat the forbidden fruit, mankind would still be in Paradise."

To Margery, it seemed as if God Himself were condemning her. She'd never before had to confess such serious transgressions, or at least those involving sexual matters. She felt her face redden with embarrassment and kept her gaze fastened to her clasped hands, though she felt the tiniest flicker of rebellion. Wasn't the purpose of penance to be washed clean of one's sins? And surely this priest had heard worse.

Now her confessor castigated the biblical and secular Jezebels who forever preyed on simple, unsuspecting, blameless men. "Shamelessly leaving their hair and arms and shoulders uncovered and tempting us with the hint of your breasts."

While Margery's head remained meekly bowed, she surreptitiously checked her neckline to ascertain that the priest could not be referring to her. Perhaps he was one of those who kept a leman, for he seemed mightily preoccupied with sins of the flesh.

I should have gone to Father Crispin. He would have granted forgiveness and forgone the lecture.

"Harlots all, leading men astray with your seductive wiles, forcing us to give in to our base desires."

She remembered how she'd felt with Matthew—aye, a harlot; he was right about that.

Margery was glad this part of St. Paul's was nearly empty so that others would not overhear the priest's rant. While she accepted that she was but a simple creature, she could not ignore a major flaw in his reasoning. Since women had fewer rights and lower intelligence than men, how could they be powerful enough to be responsible for all the world's travails? To be able to knead the superior sex as easily as a bowl of dough?

But she kept such thoughts to herself, meekly accepted the priest's penance and absolution once he deigned to grant it and quickly exited the church.

In the bright light of the precinct she paused until her eyes adjusted. The crowd around John Ball had grown and was obviously mesmerized by his jeremiad, which seemed to be dealing with the Jacquerie of 1358. Margery leaned against a wall and closed her eyes, allowing his words to paint a horrific vision, knowing this was her real penance for Matthew Hart. Not *Pater Nosters* or a trip to a nearby shrine but this reminder of the cruelty of the nobility and how she'd betrayed John Ball and Thurold with her fleshly weakness.

She imagined the entire uprising…one hundred thousand peasants, dressed in tatters and driven to desperation by war taxes, picking up their scythes, pitchforks and hatchets and marching upon their tormentors. In her mind's eye, she saw faces like those of the lepers at London's gates, the urchins with their begging bowls. She imagined them swarming like angry locusts across the countryside, putting castles to the torch and causing French clergy to tremble in their monasteries.

Until, as was inevitable, the Jacquerie was defeated.

"Knights chased them through their hamlets, rode them down, and slaughtered them," cried John Ball. "Women and children, old men and suckling infants, even those who had not taken part in the rebellion. Then the lords captured their leader and crowned him 'King of the Jacquerie' with a circlet of hot iron. They beheaded him, hoping they'd behead the cause. But 'tis impossible to destroy an idea. It will continue to grow and spread. Our lords should heed what happened across the sea."

Margery slipped away. She was sorry for those poor French peasants. But she was also glad the uprising had been put down, for that meant one less danger for Lord Hart.

And she felt comforted, knowing that John Ball was wrong, that such a holocaust could never happen here in England.

CHAPTER 18

France, 1359-1360

ccompanied by three of his sons—Edward, Lionel and John—
Edward III left Calais on All Saint's Day, 1359. His destination was Rheims. Since ancient times, all French kings had been anointed in Rheims Cathedral and His Grace planned to be crowned King of France there.

In order to more easily find provisions, England's army was drawn up into three divisions, positioned twenty to thirty leagues apart. Because The Black Prince shared command with John of Gaunt, Matthew and Harry Hart often rode together.

In one respect, this *chevauchee* mirrored the last. Incessant rains crept into the bones like the fog that crept across the bleak horizon. There was never a sign of the sun, simply a gray mass of clouds bleeding to black where the rains descended. Water pummeled Matthew's armor, slapped his helm, ran along his nose guard into his eyes, and soaked his skin.

This is a God forsaken country, he thought, as the supply carts left their trail upon the bleak plains like the tracks of giant snails. *Hostile, wet and ugly.*

They encountered few people and no French armies. After strengthening the towns along the enemy line of march, the Dauphin Charles had ordered his captains to remain behind city walls.

As the days passed and the English penetrated more deeply into the desolate French interior, it seemed to Matthew that he and his fellow soldiers remained the sole inhabitants of an empty world—an earth not only devoid of people but even of animals. He seldom glimpsed a deer or a darting fox or heard the call of a nesting bird. Any land that hadn't previously been destroyed by Robert Knolles' mercenaries and His Grace's marauders had been put to flame by the French themselves. Enormous clouds of smoke mushroomed on the horizon before dissipating in the wind, silent signals that another town or wheat field had been destroyed rather than surrendered. Each cloud meant more nights without shelter. Each cloud meant half-filled bellies. Since the English lived entirely off the land, their horses suffered most of all. When the weakened animals could no longer pull the carts, forever bogged in sucking mud, they were slaughtered for meat.

Hardship piled upon hardship, like a child's building blocks. No one complained about the lack of food, or the rain, or the cowardly French. Discipline remained perfect, and there were no stragglers.

Our time will come, Matthew assured himself, *turning his face away from the relentless rain. Our time will come when we reach Rheims. And none of this will matter, except to the chroniclers.*

By the first of December, Edward's army still remained far from Rheims. The jagged and charred remains of countless towns taunted them in passing, even though many of the skeletons were months rather than weeks old. Matthew sometimes spotted a madman amidst the ruins, or a crippled peasant, ugly reminders of last year's Jacquerie.

Harry sometimes tried to discuss such matters. "'Tis sad, is it not?" They were passing through yet another razed town. A skeleton hung from a gnarled tree limb, its bones clacking in the breeze like a child's wooden-jointed doll. "First the Death, then we came, then their own rebelled."

Matthew gave the skeleton no more than a cursory glance. It was, after all, merely a pile of bones. "If they treated their classes as they should, as we treat ours, the rebellion would ne'er have happened." Swallowing a cough, he turned away, successfully suppressing all save a bark. Matthew's cough had descended with the rains. Once begun, it tore relentlessly at his lungs and chest. Others had been similarly afflicted and some were beginning to die.

"God is dealing harshly with the French," Harry said solemnly.

"God is on our side, brother. Do not forget that."

"Aye, but I hope He never so turns against England. The French are God's children, too. Listen! Can you not hear their cries?"

"'Tis but the wind, Harry." A spasm of coughing wracked Matthew's body. Kicking Michel, he bolted away, seeking privacy until the fit passed.

I'll not spend the greatest moments of my life sick and shivering like an old woman.

And yet, no matter how he willed it, he could not shake his illness.

AFTER CONVERGING into one enormous division, the English finally reached Rheims. They were not greeted with flowers and cheers, nor did the French fling open their gates in welcome. The Archbishop did not proclaim Edward III the Lord's appointed and anoint him with holy oil. Instead, the townspeople brought in supplies and prepared for a siege.

Intent on being voluntarily crowned, King Edward refrained from attacking. Rather he attempted to persuade by negotiation. And a blockade. While his men set up camp in the bogs, located miles beyond the city walls, His Grace and his advisors resided at the abbey of Saint-Basle. From its location, perched high on the edge of the Forest de la Montagne, Edward need but look south to see the towers of Rheims Cathedral. When diplomatic efforts frustrated him, he studied the twin Gothic towers, assuring himself that his goal was indeed within reach.

"I *will* be crowned King of France," he told members of his war council. In his late forties, Edward was yet a comely man, with a humorous curve to his mouth. His light brown hair was beginning to gray, as was his beard, but his carriage was erect, his walk purposeful.

The campaign had been grueling, but Edward firmly believed he would prevail. "Because it is right and proper and God's will. Remember Crecy and Poitiers? Have we ever failed before?"

Christmas approached, sparse and dismal. Only the excellent local wines provided even the pretense of celebration. Daylight was short; rain mixed with sleet as inevitable as rumbling bellies. Morale plummeted with the rain. Matthew began spitting up blood. The first time he noticed he was frightened, but soon he ignored it. He did not tell his father or Harry. As his condition weakened, he isolated himself from them.

I'll not have their worried looks and comments, he thought, seeking a warm, dry place to sleep only to find the smothering embrace of the quagmire. The cough tore at his chest and seemingly into his bones, but he was confident he could overcome it. He was twenty-three. No one died at twenty-three. He forced his mind from other similarly afflicted young men whose lifeless eyes would never again gaze upon the sweet hills, forests and valleys of England.

Sometimes he pictured Margery Watson, and those memories strengthened him, but more often that past seemed unreal. Hard to believe life existed beyond these accursed days which seemed to stretch into the future like an endless string of penances.

With the coming of spring, 1360, Matthew's cough improved but Edward III's dreams of being crowned King of France dissolved like smoke borne upon the wind. He had been thwarted by the weather and illnesses, by the length of the campaign, and by the cowardliness of the French. Not once had the enemy met him in battle, no matter how brazenly Edward provoked them.

To appease his frustration, King Edward ordered his men-at-arms to ravage the surrounding countryside around Paris. Then he retreated toward Chartres. Hunger was omnipresent. The countryside could no longer yield its bounty, for no bounty remained. The entire area had been picked clean, like the bones of a dead animal.

"The besiegers are in worse shape than the besieged," Harry said glumly, after His Grace had ordered a long march toward an area free from devastation. "If I never partake of another campaign, I'll consider myself a lucky man. War always sounds so much finer when related from the lips of minstrels."

Harry had not had a true bath in months, nor a decent meal. When he had not been cold and hungry, he had been bored senseless. What Matt and his father saw in such hardships he could not fathom, though both professed themselves optimistic over the final outcome.

"Just wait," Matthew said cheerfully. "Before 'tis finished, something grand will happen. Somehow His Highness will force the French to battle and all this will be of no consequence."

Harry stifled a snort. Matt had nearly died from a wasting disease and he acted as if the experience had been nothing more than a bothersome crease in a newly-pressed bed sheet. Although Harry admired his brother more than anybody else in the world, not for the first time did he wonder about his mental acuity.

On Monday, April 13, as the English army broke camp, the eastern horizon showed ominous. The month of March had been so temperate. God had given the English that much, which had helped ease the sickness. Men were now dying in handfuls rather than droves. Standing near King Edward, the Black Prince and John of Gaunt, Matthew watched the sky darken.

"I do not like the look of it," said His Grace. "We'll not break camp until it passes."

The blackness crept toward them; a bitter wind sprang up. From the clouds, lightning flicked like serpents' tongues. The tethered destriers neighed and pulled at their ropes. Matthew felt the same restlessness as the animals.

Coming forth from the tent he shared with his sons, William Hart said, "'Twill be a rough one."

Matthew nodded. "I canna remember such darkness of a morning."

"I must go. All the members of the war council have been summoned to His Grace's tent. Look after your brother," William called over his shoulder. "See that he does not blow away or get struck by lightning."

The wind sliced through Matthew's body, buffeted the baggage carts, lashed at the tents, and scattered the flames of the cooking fires into oblivion. Mounted knights tried to soothe their anxious horses. A mist emerged from the approaching darkness, whipped along by the wind, stinging Matthew's face. He drew his cloak around him only to have the wind tear it from his grasp.

Harry emerged from their tent. At the sight of the clouds, impenetrable as a midnight sky, his eyes widened. "What does this remind you of, brother?"

Matthew shrugged, his gaze on the horizon.

"Remember the plague?" Harry's nervous laugh was snatched by the howling wind. "Remember when it was told how a dark cloud would cover the earth? I still have nightmares about those times." When Matthew did not respond, he asked, "Do you truly think this looks like an ordinary storm?"

The wind blew raindrops hard as rocks into their faces. Lightning skittered toward the earth, accompanied by thunder which shook the tents. The rain now showed white and hard, coagulating into hailstones. Grabbing Harry's arm, Matthew shoved him back inside the tent. "We will wait it out here."

Harry crouched down beside his brother on one of the sleeping pallets and began muttering various disjointed prayers.

"France's storms are not like England's," Matthew said, attempting to cheer him. "I saw worse than this during the Poitiers campaign."

A lie, but it seemed to relieve a measure of Harry's anxiety.

The wind rattled and whistled at the sheltering canvas. Matthew rolled over to fasten the tent flap, but the wind jerked it away. Hail attacked the exterior. A hailstone the size of a pigeon's egg tore through the canvas. A flash of ground lightning illuminated the tent, followed by thunder which boomed like the wrathful voice of God. The tent ripped from its pegs and took off in an erratic flight, like a bird struggling against a headwind.

Exposed to the full force of the storm, Matthew and Harry rolled into protective balls. The hail assaulted Matt's exposed back, slamming against his hauberk with the force of a sword. He slapped his bascinet over his head. Even through the pounding hail he felt the hair on the back of his neck stand and knew that lightning breathed upon them.

Ground lightning danced around destriers' hooves and silhouetted horse and rider in sheets of fiery orange. Both began plummeting to the ground as readily as if God's own hand had smote them. The blackness swirled overhead; torrents of rain began to lash the earth.

"'Tis the end of the world!" cried Harry.

Matthew tightened his arm around his brother. He was certain today was not the end of the world, but a storm unlike any he'd ever witnessed.

When it was over, six thousand horses littered the ground, as well as a thousand men—more dead than in all the campaigns combined. As they carried away their lifeless companions, or sought shelter amidst the streams of water and hailstones, the men had already begun to refer to the episode as Black Monday. A bitter cold settled like the breath of a giant over the camp. It was the kind of cold that neither fire nor blankets nor the warmest mantle could lift from the bones.

King Edward, his sons, and his war council walked through the camp, surveying the devastation. Matthew had seen them all unflinchingly face countless hardships, as well as death by the sword. Never once had he seen fear on their faces. Until today. Even his father appeared shaken.

"'Tis an omen," King Edward said, voicing the others' apprehension. "God has sent me a sign."

Earlier, the revered John Chandos and most of the other members of the war council had strongly advised Edward to end the campaign. They'd been in France six months and not been allowed a decisive battle, nor taken a major walled town or capital city. Chandos, especially, was beginning to believe that France could never be conquered by pillage or siege.

"Our position is yet strong." Despite the loss of an eye in an early battle, John Chandos was one of England's most accomplished knights. Many credited him with orchestrating the victories of Crecy and Poitiers. He pressed his advantage. "We will win more by negotiating this time than continuing. We have fought a grand war with much profit to it, but 'tis too expensive for our resources. If we do not stop now, I do not doubt this campaign could continue the rest of our lives."

177

King Edward gazed from Chandos to his sons. Then he walked away, seeking a private moment in which to collect his thoughts. The storm had terrified him. Edward knew himself to be a great warrior, but he was foremost a humble servant of God. In his heart he believed his Savior was displeased with him, and he feared for his soul.

Looking up at the sky, Edward said in a loud voice, "I renounce before God all claim to the crown of France."

Some of the watching lords crossed themselves. Others added private prayers of their own to strengthen their king's vow. Even the Black Prince was uneased, but it was not only the storm that had confused him. War Edward of Woodstock understood, but the subtleties of this campaign and its incessant tilting with ghosts had debilitated and frustrated him.

The prince turned to his younger brother, John of Gaunt. "The French will rue this day, as well as all their cowardice. I swear by all that's holy, Charles will pay full measure—in blood."

John of Gaunt nodded. "There will be other campaigns."

Matthew overheard them, but with a rare flash of insight, thought, *The Dauphin Charles might be a woman and a coward, but his unorthodox tactics have won. His Grace was not crowned king of France. We gained no new territories, nor fought any epic battles. We accomplished naught that we set out to do.*

John Chandos, whom the chronicler Froissart would describe as being "wise and full of devices," assured himself that this was only a temporary setback. War was much longer than life; but his life at least was long enough to understand that they would live to fight another day. Still, as Chandos returned to the remains of his pavilion, his bones ached as much with weariness as the cold.

Perhaps the days of Poitiers and Crecy are forever past. Perhaps they are passing with our youth.

He could not quite believe 'twas so, but, like some others, he was no longer certain.

CHAPTER 19

London, 1361

In February of 1361, Englishmen and women began whispering about strange happenings they'd witnessed in the night skies. Burning lights in the shape of a cross appearing at midnight; two castles, as if painted from moonlight, out of which rode two hosts, one black and one white, to do battle with each other. What could such visions mean? Surely nothing good, particularly when followed by an eclipse of the sun. And in the spring the rains declined to return, causing crops to wither and die in the fields.

In London, gloom had descended—a gloom that metamorphosed to terror. For following the signing of yet another treaty with France, soldiers and lords had begun returning home. Along with the Great Pestilence.

Ah, now the portents could be divined. And all of England trembled at their meaning.

Cemeteries were reopened to accommodate the hundreds, then thousands of victims. Ordinary folk fled London on penitential pilgrimages while noble men and women withdrew to their remotest holdings, praying the plague would not follow.

As if to challenge the Death, King Edward held his Order of the Garter tournament at Windsor exactly as he had during the first plague. But privately His Grace had begun to fear, or at least to allow himself a niggling doubt, that God might be withdrawing His favor. In addition to Black Monday and the frustration of the last campaign, all around him long-time advisors and friends were dying. The most prominent was Henry, Duke of Lancaster, which made King Edward's third son, John of Gaunt, the richest man in England. But riches could not replace friendships and King Edward was losing so many who'd been his youthful companions, then his wise and trusted advisors, men he'd counted upon to accompany him into old age. Now they were being taken from him.

Finally, unwilling to risk more casualties, His Grace suspended the actions of all the law courts and the Exchequer, and retreated to what he hoped would be the safety of the countryside.

MARGERY WATSON LEANED against a small table scattered with medicines and gazed absently out the narrow window overlooking the street. The window was set in diamond panes which distorted the view. Not that there appeared to be anything to see. London's streets were deserted. Gloom had settled over the city as decisively as the fog descending upon the upper stories of the apartments extending into Bread Street. Sighing, Margery shifted her position to ease an ache in her left calf. While the weather had turned cold, the solar itself was oppressively hot. The windows had been ordered closed to keep out unhealthy airs that carried the plague. However, it was not only the return of the Death and the stirring of painful memories that accounted for Margery's melancholy. Twenty months had passed, and she'd not heard from either Thurold or Matthew Hart. Both could be long dead, and she would not know. Margery touched her hidden robin for comfort. She had told her heart so many times that of course Lord Hart would not contact her, that his sweet words had been cheaply given, and she castigated herself for continuing to hope, for not being able to forget...

Below on the street, a figure approached the shop. The man appeared tall to Margery, and wore the dress of the nobility, though in the wavy glass she could not tell much more. Something was wrong with his gait, which was as slow and hesitant as an old man's.

Mayhap he has the plague, Margery thought, with a sudden shiver.

Hearing a stirring from the master's bed, she shut her eyes. She sometimes wondered whether the Death could be any worse than her present position.

"I am thirsty," came a whining voice. "Get me something to drink."

Margery forced down a surge of annoyance, forced herself to feel nothing at all. She noted that the figure had paused directly below, in front of the closed shop. She wished she could stand forever, gazing down at a stranger, idly speculating on identities and activities that did not touch her. Even more fervently, Margery wished she'd never again have to breathe the air in this stuffy room or respond to Dame Gisla's querulous demands.

Reluctantly, Margery faced her mistress. "Would you like some brandy water?"

Gisla's face was of a color with the iron grey hair framing it. Her mouth worked, then the corners drooped downward, indicating her disapproval. "I hate water. Mix it with wine. And be quick about it."

From the medicine table, Margery poured a small amount of brandy into a goblet, then filled it half way with wine. Doctors said Gisla suffered from vermin in the womb. Brandy was said to have curative powers, but since Gisla had fallen sick near Candlemas in early February, nothing had helped. Not the barber with his bleeding, nor the doctors nor Margery's knowledge of herbs. She had been cooped up with her mistress the entire time, and the only change she'd witnessed was a deterioration in Gisla's temper.

"You are worthless, Margery Watson," Gisla said, as she approached the bed. "Lazy and insolent."

Margery shut her ears to Dame Gisla's criticism. When she'd been healthy, Gisla had been a woman of few words. Would to God she'd soon regain her health.

Bending over, Margery encircled the back of Gisla's head and helped her drink, holding her breath so she would not inhale her mistress's odor. Though Master Crull insisted the room be daily cleaned, it still reeked of his wife's sickness.

A trickle of liquid slid down Dame Gisla's chin. Coughing, she pushed Margery's hand away so forcefully the brandy wine spilled on Margery's gown.

Trying to remain calm, Margery bit the inside of her lip. She'd rather help her mistress with this task than some of the more intimate ones, such as applying poultices to Gisla's womb in order to draw out any offending vermin.

After Dame Gisla slumped back against the pillows, Margery returned to the window. Below, the stranger had just stepped from the interior of the shop. He could not be a customer, for the shop had been closed for days. She watched his retreat, the labored walk. Though Margery did not have much faith in signs, she crossed herself.

"Where are you from, Margery Watson?"

Margery eyed her mistress warily. She knew Gisla was not interested in a pleasant chat. Somewhere, the conversation would take an ugly twist.

"Cambridge." Thurold had once told her half a truth was better than a lie, and less easily uncovered. When Margery had obtained her position, Dame Gisla had entered her basic information into the household book. Surely, Gisla knew so was this some sort of trick question?

"They must breed useless help in Cambridge." When Margery did not answer, Gisla continued, "Are your parents as worthless as you, Margery Watson?"

Margery clenched her fists, trying to curb the flash of anger. "My mother is dead." Dame Gisla should know that as well. "She died during the first plague."

Shifting position on the pillows, the old woman scrunched her eyes and mouth, as if tasting something sour. The Death was a subject that greatly vexed her. She began mumbling to herself and did not cease until Simon suddenly popped into the doorway.

Charging that the place was filthy, Simon seldom entered the solar. Nor was he solicitous of Gisla's health. Now, he fixed his gaze, not on his wife, but Margery. "You are a busy woman for being so quiet, Margery Watson."

Simon's conversations were so filled with similar enigmatic phrasings that Margery had long ago ceased trying to decipher them. "Dame Gisla is a bit better today, master. Her appetite seems to have improved."

"How old are you, Margery Watson?" Simon crossed to the table and, as was his habit, poured himself a bowl of hippocras.

"Twenty-one or thereabouts." Birth dates were a chancy matter at best.

"It seems strange you have not married Brian or Nicholas or one of the other apprentices." Simon eyed her over the rim of the drinking bowl. "Perhaps you reach much higher than a tradesman. Will you sleep your way to position, Margery Watson?"

As always, Margery ignored his jibes.

"I think I will do a bit of checking on you."

"Come here, husband," Gisla interrupted.

Simon reluctantly approached his wife. The skin on her face sagged like that of a hound; her fingers, picking at the faded coverlet, were gnarled and bony as a skeleton's.

"Any more word on the Pestilence?" Gisla's voice wavered.

"The cases remain sporadic."

"God will smite us all for being wicked, wicked." Gisla rocked her head from side to side and began to cry. "Nothing is as it should be." She launched into a familiar lament. "Englishmen have given themselves over to lawlessness, gluttony, and lechery. I've seen ordinary women with bodices so low and breasts laced so high a stroller would blush with shame. God indeed be punishing us for our sinfulness."

Simon studied his wife with the same ill-concealed distaste he showed the beggar children who congregated at the front door. "Do not trouble yourself with this sinful world. We are good people. We have naught to fear." He raised his eyes to Margery. "Though others in this room should have a care."

. . .

TWO DAYS LATER, Margery visited her herb patch to replenish the yarrow used in Gisla's poultices. London smelled of brimstone, uncollected garbage and excrement. The sun baked the earth or slunk away in the wake of angry rains. Margery was surprised and heartened that through it all the back-side had prospered. The vibrancy of her flowers belied the possibility of death lurking just beyond the garden while their perfume obliterated any encroaching scents of decay.

After picking several pink and white clusters of yarrow, Margery headed back to the shop. As she passed the turf seat, she glanced down by force of habit.

"Mother Mary!" she breathed. Two pairs of smooth stones lay upon the seat's hard packed earth.

"He's back." Margery tried to estimate how long the stones might have been there. Today, perhaps, a fortnight, even a month? She hadn't been in the garden for nearly a week, and then she hadn't checked the seat. Or had she? She couldn't remember.

"My lord Hart is in London," she whispered, savoring the news. "He is well and wishes to see me." The wonder of it all immediately erased months of misery.

Margery did not know how, but this afternoon she would await Matthew in the Tower garden. And if the stones had been put there days past she would continue on to Hart's Place, where he would surely be ensconced.

As nones neared, Margery left the shop saying that she needed more special herbs. While walking along largely empty streets and passing occasional doors marred by red crosses, she found herself trembling.

But this time the Death prefers children. And I am no longer a child.

Upon reaching Tower Hill, Margery waited in the orchard. Everything appeared mournful and neglected. The trees were grey and shabby; the plants drooped toward the ground, as if trying to hide their faces.

Margery waited and waited. With each inhalation of breath, she worried she might be inhaling pestilential vapors. Without the protective shelter of four walls, the comforting presence of other humans, she felt vulnerable.

Finally, she decided Matthew was not going to arrive, which meant the stones had been placed in the turf seat days past.

Mayhap he has already left London. She began walking northeast, toward the opposite end of the city and Hart's Place. *Mayhap he will think I do not even want to see him.* Margery prayed that Matthew would still be at his residence. She prayed that he would be well.

"Lord Hart canna see you." Margery recognized Francus, one of Matthew's squires, peering from behind a narrow opening in the door. From the fear on his face, Margery might have already broken out in plague boils.

"He left a message that I was to meet him."

"That is impossible. Lord Hart has not been from his bed in days."

Francus slammed the door.

Margery stared numbly at the wooden surface, trying to assimilate the squire's words. If Matthew was bedridden, that meant he had the plague. She closed her eyes and slumped against the wall. A wave of sickness welled upward from her soul. Her past was repeating itself, over and over like the refrain from a funeral dirge. *Dirige Domine, Deus meus…*Dying, dying, dead.

Margery whirled around and began hammering on the door. "Let me in! I must see him!"

The door opened, more widely this time. Margery recognized Matthew's brother. Francus stood behind Harry, glaring at her.

"I am Margery Watson, my lord. I insist on seeing your brother."

"I know who you are," Harry said. "You are the reason we are stuck in this accursed place. Even the servants had enough sense to flee." Harry's eyes were bloodshot from drinking and lack of sleep. "I told Matt we should go to Cumbria with Father, anywhere away from people, but he would not listen. He said…" Harry stumbled to a halt. He shook his head, as if to clear it, then motioned her inside.

Harry's words were so confusing, Margery wondered whether he might also have contracted plague. Silently, she followed him and Francus up the wooden staircase. After pushing open the door to the solar, Harry stepped aside. Margery peered in. The room was large and shadowed, though a huge bay window took up part of the far wall, and a fire burned in the massive fireplace. A large candle flickered beside the canopied bed, which dominated the solar, as she remembered. She could see very little of the figure propped against the pillows.

Slowly, Margery approached the bed. Though a part of her feared contamination, a greater part was reluctant to witness the extent of Matthew's decay—the swelling, the black spots, the desecration of that magnificent face and form.

She swallowed down tears. *I never thought you would die. Of all men, you were the most alive...*

"My lord," she said, "can you hear me? 'Tis Margery, Margery Watson. Do you remember me?"

"Of course I remember you, Meg. Why would I not?" Matthew sat up. She saw at once that he was not suffering from plague. In fact, though his face looked gaunt, he looked exactly as he should.

Margery's legs buckled, causing her to nearly collapse upon the bed. It had all been cruel mummery. Matthew was fine.

"I stopped by the Shop," he said. "Your master said you were gone. He said—"

A spasm of coughing wracked Matthew's body, and tore at his lungs and chest, causing him to bend forward. Francus hovered over him, holding a cloth to his mouth. When Francus removed it, Margery saw that it was bright with blood.

What did this mean? Matthew did not have the plague, but he was spitting up blood. She studied him more carefully. He was not thin; he was emaciated. In the orange firelight, his eyes appeared bright with fever. Save for two scarlet spots on his cheeks, his face was the color of wax.

"Do not look at me like that." Though a pain stabbed his side, making each breath a torment, Matthew managed a smile. He had lived with the pain so long, he had conditioned himself to ignore it. "'Tis just a slight cough I picked up during the Rheims campaign. It came back a few weeks ago, during the crossing from France. I've had a bit of trouble shaking it."

"In case you need reminding, that slight cough killed hundreds," said Harry. "It very nearly killed you."

"No one dies at twenty-four."

Harry poured himself some wine from an available pitcher. "'Tis a pity someone forgot to tell all those twenty-four-year-olds who will remain forever behind in France."

The corners of Matt's mouth lifted. "At least I know I will not die puking and sweating from some bothersome wasting sickness. 'Twould be no fit end for a knight."

"Not even you, brother, can choose the way to die."

"I can choose the way I'll NOT die."

Harry shook his head at Margery. "What little common sense he possessed seems also to have been left in France. Otherwise, we would be hundreds of miles away by now."

Margery could scarce believe that Matthew would return to London because of her. But he had said she was no casual affair, and now his actions seemed to prove it.

After draining his goblet, Harry poured himself more wine. "I'll grant she is comely," he said to Matthew, "but not enough to risk all our lives."

Another spell of coughing choked off Matthew's reply. Francus held out a clean cloth, Harry retreated to the bay window at the opposite side of the room, and Margery watched helplessly.

When the coughing finally subsided, Matthew acted as if nothing had happened. *But ignoring it will not make it disappear. You look much worse than Dame Gisla.* That the wasting sickness could so ravage that powerful body was proof of its strength. Reaching out, Margery took Matthew's hand in hers. It was hot. And as bony as her mistresses'.

She raised her eyes to Francus. "Where is his physician? How is he being treated?"

"Brother Timm left two days ago and has not returned. He either ran away or the pestilence took him."

"I can speak for myself," Matt said. He gestured toward a chest covered with vials, mortars, small sacks of herbs, all manner of paraphernalia. "Brother Timm stuffed me with potions which were as useless as they were foul. Death would be preferable to some of his remedies."

"Do not joke about such a thing," Margery said sharply. Fear made her disregard her station and address Matthew as an equal. Again turning to Francus, she said, "I know a bit about herbs, but not enough to feel competent in treating him. We must find someone with more knowledge."

"Who? The best physicians fled London with their patrons long ago. As for the rest..." Francus shrugged. "I would not know where to find them, and I would risk the plague myself in the hunt."

"Perhaps Brother Timm will return," Margery said. "If he does not—"

"Then you will nurse me," Matthew said, squeezing her hand. "Will you not, Sweet Meg?"

"I cannot. I would be missed at the Shop. Master Crull would—"

"Master Crull can go to the devil," Matthew interrupted. "I went to his shop and he told me you no longer worked for him."

"So you were the man I saw."

"I have a score to settle with that bloody bastard, and I canna believe that you would rather do his bidding than mine."

Despite the seriousness of the circumstances, Margery found herself smiling. "I would much rather do your bidding, my lord."

FOR THE NEXT WEEK MARGERY, with Francus's help, ministered to Matthew. When Harry wasn't drinking, he prepared marginally edible meals and paced the solar, paternoster beads in hand, sending endless prayers heavenward imploring God and the saints to cure his brother.

Ever mindful of the plague, Margery concocted drinks containing Angelica Archengelica, which she had found in the Hart garden. Because rue was supposed to expel pestilential miasmas, she strewed it throughout the room. When Matt was feverish, she sponged his wasted body with tepid water containing pennyroyal, spearmint and black mustard. She spoon-fed him salty gruels, which he frequently vomited. When she was too exhausted to continue, Francus or Harry replaced her.

In the beginning Matthew had tried to wave away their help, but his condition deteriorated so rapidly he could not even stand without risking dizziness. Soon he could not stand at all.

After a particularly bad night, when Matt's skin and even his fingernails had turned blue, Francus drew Margery away from the bed, to the bay window, and went to get Harry.

Margery gazed idly outside. She could not remember when she had last noticed the weather. Not that it appeared to have changed. In the distance, she saw a portion of city wall, London's ragged skyline.

What is happening in the city? she wondered. *Does the plague still rage, or has it peaked? Is anyone left alive, or have they all perished?*

"Mayhap I should search out a priest," Francus said, when Harry reached them. "I do na think my lord can last the night."

"My brother cannot die," Harry cried. "What will I do without him?"

Margery was too exhausted to feel much of anything. 'Twould be the way of life, to have Matthew return to her only to die. Still, sending for a priest seemed too blatant an admission of defeat. "Sometimes there is a crisis. Sometimes they improve after. Mayhap he will get better now."

"He is going to die," Francus said flatly.

Harry began to weep.

"Stop this," Margery said. "Your tears will only upset him. Besides, my lord said he has no intention of dying, and we all know how strong-willed he is. If 'tis humanly possible to survive, he will."

Harry poured himself a cup of wine, drowning his sobs as he gulped it down, then reached for his paternoster beads and renewed his pacing and praying.

Margery returned to the bench beside Matthew's bed. Bone weary, she dozed, leaning her head and a shoulder against the mattresses for support. She settled into such a deep sleep she was not even aware when Matthew awakened in the predawn, his body wracked with such violent chills that the coverlet trembled and his teeth chattered. Hugging his arms about his body and drawing up his knees, he tried unsuccessfully to control the shaking, the merciless pounding in his head. How long did the torment last? Until the nearby candle guttered? Or had it already been close to its core? The onslaught of a fever was beginning to disorient him.

Francus slept on a pallet near the door and Harry near the fire. To keep himself from crying out and awakening them or Margery, Matthew clenched his teeth until his jaw hurt. This was certainly not the first time he'd experienced these symptoms, but their intensity uneased him.

I will overcome this. He hugged himself until his body felt bruised. *As I did in Paris. As I always have.*

Margery stirred, then bolted upright. In the light from the bed candle, she saw Matthew hunched against the pillows.

Immediately she was at the medicine chest, searching for betony, hyssop and the other herbs used to ease violent blood and chills. After mixing the potion, which smelled strongly of oranges, she thrust it beneath Matt's nose. His mouth was partially open; his breath came in painful shallow gasps. She thought she glimpsed a fuzz on his tongue. What horrors were corrupting his insides?

"Drink this. It will soothe you."

Matthew managed only a few swallows before the goblet slipped from his fingers onto the bed. Margery looked from the dark stain spreading upon the sheets to him, taking note of his glassy eyes. He seemed unaware that he'd dropped the cup.

I must do something. But she had no idea what. Medicines were always haphazard, as was the entire practice of doctoring, and so far her potions had done him no good at all. She placed her hand upon Matt's forehead, which was clammy with sweat, and he trembled, as animals did during a thunderstorm.

I cannot just stand here and watch him die. But what can I do?

Matthew collapsed against the pillows. "Cold," he muttered. Drawing his body in a ball, he pulled up the covers. Slipping into bed beside him, Margery pressed her back against his shaking body, forcing him to mold against her, forcing her warmth into him.

His shivering gradually lessened. Margery remained pressed against him, even though her body slickened with his sweat, and his skin was hot to the touch.

"I came back for you, Meg," Matt murmured, nuzzling against the back of her neck. "I could not break my promise..." His hand curved around her breast, and he slept.

"IS MY BROTHER TRULY BETTER?"

"He has not vomited since last even, and his fever seems to have broken."

The voices wafted to Matthew from a distance, as if he were struggling awake from a deep sleep. Sounds and events were beginning to register, though he could not yet summon enough energy to properly think on them. For the first time in days, however, his head did not hurt.

A cool hand cupped his forehead. Matthew opened his eyes. "What have you been doing, Meg? You look awful."

"So do you, my lord," Margery replied. She cradled a bowl of gruel in her hands.

"'Tis a pity you have lost your most interesting shade of blue," Harry said, attempting levity. "I have always wanted a blue brother." Measuring a spoonful of gruel, Margery motioned for Matthew to open his mouth.

"I thank you, but I can feed myself." Matt struggled to a sitting position. Now that his mind had cleared and the fever passed, he had no intention of being treated like an invalid. With shaking fingers he reached for the bowl, brought it to his lips, and managed by sheer force of will to drink more than he spilled on himself.

Afterward, Matthew fell back upon the pillows. His entire body felt bruised and battered, as if he'd been in combat, but he knew the worst of his sickness was behind him. He groped for Margery's hand, and held it in his own.

"Will you lay with me, Meg?" he murmured. As he began drifting back into a fatigued sleep, he felt the pressure of her head against his chest. "I have to tell you..." But Matthew didn't know whether he spoke the words or thought them. He had something very important to say to Margery, but he was asleep before he could remember what it might be.

CHAPTER 20

London

"'Tis time for me to go," Margery said. Each day of Matthew's recovery reminded her of her absence from the Crull household. "'Twill be difficult enough now to explain a fortnight's disappearance."

"Not if I am with you," Matthew said. "That weasel goldsmith would not dare object to you saving my life. You might be a member of his household, but he does not own you. And I will never forgive him for lying to me. Now that I am hale, perhaps 'tis time to confront your master."

"I do not want anyone at the Shop to know anything about my private life." Master Crull or his wife would just find some way to use that knowledge against her. "I will think up some appropriate lie."

Matthew grinned. "I cannot imagine you lying. 'Twould be an interesting performance."

"With some people it does not really seem like a lie."

The pair were seated opposite each other in the "She and I" seat cut into the bay window. Afternoon sunlight illuminated Matt's face. The planes had softened, the hollows had begun to fill out. Each day he grew stronger and less inclined to remain cooped up indoors without physical activity. As the threat of plague receded, some servants had also returned, including the cook. A good thing since Matthew's appetite was voracious and Harry's culinary efforts had been uniformly dismal.

Matt leaned forward and rested his hands atop Margery's, which were folded in her lap. As he struggled to formulate his question, he absently stroked her fingers. For days he'd been trying to decide how best to broach the subject preoccupying him. "I asked you once before about leaving the goldsmith's household. From what you've said, both he and his mistress are unpleasant."

"Where would I go? They are better than most. I have been cold and hungry before. I would gladly put up with a little inconvenience rather than risk being a beggar."

"You would have no trouble finding someone else to take you in."

Margery shook her head. "At least I know what to expect with the Crulls."

Matt cleared his throat. "What would you think of mayhap...have you ever thought of becoming part of *my* household?"

Margery's eyes widened. "Why would I wish to do that?"

"So that we could be together."

"Nay." Margery left the window seat and retreated to the canopied bed, so that Matthew's proximity would not distract her. She looked about the room as if seeing it for the first time. Since the servants had administered a thorough cleaning, it had lost the look of a sick room and now looked what it was. The solar of a great lord.

Following her, Matt placed his hands upon her shoulders. "Why could you not, Meg? 'Twould mean much to have you always near me."

Margery closed her eyes. She would be a servant of the most menial kind—a chambermaid, perhaps. She would have the privilege of making Matthew's bed, of cleaning up the after-effects of a night of lovemaking between him and one of his court ladies. Perhaps she would even be called upon to bring them their sop in wine afterward.

Now I do not know what you do so it does not matter. Then I could never forget. "I would not like that, my lord. I would most likely see less of you than I do now."

"I think not." Matthew twisted her shoulders, forcing her to turn and face him. He groped for a tactful way to impart what was in his heart without frightening or angering her, though he'd never been proficient at word games. "Did you know that even King Edward has had dalliances?"

Margery was taken aback by the implications behind his words. "But his queen is so kind!"

"She is also in poor health and His Grace is a lusty man." Though King Edward, who genuinely loved his wife, had strayed even when Queen Philippa had been young and vigorous. It was just the way with men.

Matthew asked, "Does that seem wrong to you?"

"Aye. After all their children, and all their years together—"

"Even Prince Edward has illegitimate children, though he remains a bachelor." Mathew's voice dipped. "As do I."

Margery stiffened. So such things went. They sired their children, then abandoned them. "What has this to do with me?"

"I am just trying to say 'tis a common practice for a man to have a mistress."

"I do not care how common it is," Margery said sharply. "'Tis the mother and child who suffer the consequences."

"Not if they have a considerate lord." Matthew thrust his fingers through his hair in a gesture of exasperation. Margery was either totally ignorant of his meaning, or refusing his offer. "Damme, Meg, but you are difficult to reason with. 'Tis glad I am that you are not nobly born. I believe I would have to ask you to wed."

Margery gasped. "I do not understand. What are you saying?"

"I have been trying to say that I want you to come live with me, to be my leman. I will care for you and hold you dear. Jesu I am not good at this. I have not asked before."

To have the question asked so boldly did not seem proper, but then the entire business was improper.

"I could not."

"I do not feel about you the way I do other women." Reaching out, Matt cupped the side of her cheek. "I am grateful to you, of course, for caring for me. But it goes deeper. I will confess something. I tire easily of women. After I've bedded them, they lose their attraction. 'Twas not that way with you. During the Rheims Campaign I thought about you...often. Instead of being sated, sometimes 'twas like a hunger to be with you again. I knew then 'twas different between us."

He tilted her chin, so that she looked into his eyes. His lips turned up in a half smile. In an echo of their first encounter, he asked, "Would you like me to tell you I love you?"

Margery shook her head. "Words are not necessary." *Had Thomas Rendell ever professed love to Alice? 'Tis impossible. Noble and commoner cannot mix. But I am neither, and both. How do I fit into this world? What rules apply specifically to me?*

"If love is what minstrels sing about and poets compose boring verses for, then 'tis so," Matthew said, "I do not love you. But if 'tis something I've not felt before, then I do. Is that enough?"

"'Tis more complicated than that."

"You care for me, do you not?"

Margery nodded, but she found it difficult to describe her feelings. Once such things were uttered, she would be even more vulnerable.

If I do not speak, I can still deny my emotions. If I do not admit to love, 'twill not be so much a betrayal of my past.

"We both know how short life can be, and how precious," she said carefully. "And I do care for you, more than I can say."

"Then why do you hesitate?"

Margery balled her fists. "'You know so little about me, and there is much in my past that makes trusting someone like you difficult. I do not want to be suspicious, but I find myself expecting treachery instead of love."

"We generally find what we are looking for. If you seek treachery you will find it." Matt kissed her lightly on the lips and drew her into his embrace. "But if you would look for lasting affection, you need only come to me."

Margery rested her head against his chest. She would like to believe that, to spend her days and nights with him and cease worrying about the future or dredging up the past. "Before I give you an answer, I must tell you something."

And so she confessed the truth of her parentage and about the way her father had sent her off with a handful of coins. But if she'd expected shock or outrage, she received neither.

"There is no shame in being illegitimate, Meg, especially with a father like Thomas Rendell, for his family is an exalted one. And I am sorry for your last experience with him but the plague times were difficult for everyone. He would not have meant to hurt you."

"My experience of treachery goes far beyond my father." She had also meant to tell Matt about Lawrence Ravenne, but he had such a way of championing his own, and she did not want to hear him rationalize murder. "I want to trust you, but if I did consent to be your leman and you discarded me...who would I turn to? No respectable household would employ me. And London's mayor has banned begging within the city limits. Where would I go? How would I survive?"

Matthew took her in his arms. "You are the daughter of a powerful lord, Margery. You seem to be uncomfortable with that fact, but 'tis truth. You could find service in any household. But I promise you, there is no need. I will care for you." He kissed the crown of her head. "I am sorry for your past, but believe in me. My word is everything to me, and I vow I will not weary of you or cast you aside."

"Love is not the same thing as a battle oath. One cannot dictate to the heart."

"My word is my bond, on or off the field. And I have seen enough of battle to know that men recover from wounds which are gently cared for. Since your heart has been wounded, I promise I will be extra gentle with it."

Margery was touched by Matthew's clumsy attempt at gallantry. She could spend the rest of her life testing his loyalty and trying to protect herself. Or by a conscious act of will, choose to trust him. Slipping her arms around his neck, she whispered, "I will be your leman."

With the declaration came a certain peace. Or so she told herself. Or was she simply feeling numb?

As if to seal their agreement, he kissed her. "Now that I am feeling strong enough, I will hie me to Cumbria to see my parents. But I will be back by summer's end. Then I will set you up in a grand house, grander than Hart's Place, and we will spend our days and nights making love. Would that please you? I assure you I can think of no pleasanter way to pass my time."

Margery laughed and nodded. Matthew leaned over to brush her lips, then trailed kisses down her throat. "What say you we enjoy a foretaste of what is to come?" he murmured against her ear.

"You are still a sick man. You must not over-tax yourself."

His lips found the swell of her breasts above her bodice. "I cannot think of anything that would cure me faster."

"Or make me happier," she whispered, following Matthew to his bed.

So, Margery had risen one step above her mother. Was it happiness she felt, drowning herself in the physical presence of the man she loved? Or was she simply engaging in a distraction, allowing herself to be caught up in Matthew's imaginings of a future she knew could never come to pass?

BLACK SERGE DRAPED the front door of the Shop of the Unicorn. Upon entering, Margery noted that all the other doors were similarly draped, and that death garlands of periwinkles decorated the walls.

She reached the dining hall before meeting anyone she could question.

"Who has died?" she asked Orabel, who after the shock of seeing her, imparted the news.

"Dame Gisla two days past. We thought you'd done the same, Maggie-dear." She hugged her friend. "I was so worried. By the saints, where have you been?"

Margery sidestepped the question. "Did our mistress pass of the plague?"

Orabel shook her head. "'Twas the sickness. The master believed you had also died. He will be surprised to see you alive, as we all are."

Margery opened her mouth to explain her disappearance, then pressed her lips together. She would save her excuses for Simon Crull. She feared she was going to need them.

CHAPTER 21

London

Dame Gisla's funeral was a somber affair and sparsely attended because of lingering fear of plague. When her month-mind was celebrated with a second funeral service, relatives and prominent burghers and their wives came out in force, a sign that London was returning to normal. Why was it then that Margery felt so uneasy, an unease that went beyond the death of her mistress? She was certain something sinister, something naught to do with plague or illnesses, tainted the air, though she could not reason what.

I wish my lord had not left, she oft told herself. *I wish we'd already begun our life together.* She counted the days until summer's end and her lover's return. Sixty more days in the Crull household. Matthew had already sent two letters which she'd had read by a copier, one of many in various precincts who performed related services for a pittance. Each letter warmed her heart and reinforced her decision. Soon...

On the feast of Saint Shenute, which fell on the first of July, Simon finished his evening repast and remained at the table sipping a cup of wine, watching Margery, as he so often did, before abruptly rising and retreating to his chamber. As was her custom, she gathered food scraps for the handful of vagrants who dared defy the mayor's ban on begging, until interrupted by Orabel.

"The master would see you," she said, retrieving the basket.

"Why?"

Orabel shrugged. "Who can say? 'Tis best to just nod and obey and go about our business."

An uneasy Margery found her master seated on a bench close to the hearth fire and in the process of removing his street clogs.

She hesitated in the doorway.

"Do not stand there like a dolt," Crull said as he massaged his hosed feet. "Enter. And close the door."

Warily, Margery obeyed. She misliked this, a man of habit summoning her for no apparent reason.

"I've something to show you." Simon stood, crossed to the linen wall tapestry behind his bed and lifted a corner to retrieve a locked wooden casket, banded in iron, from the uncovered niche. After fumbling with the key ring at his waist, he fitted a key into the lock.

As her master bent over the box, the light from the hearth fire played across his scalp, gleaming through sparse strands of hair. Margery noticed that the hands resting upon the lid were as delicate as the filigree he so expertly fashioned. She fervently hoped their meeting would be short.

Crull tapped the chest. "What do you think I have in here?"

"I could not guess, sir."

"'Tis a locked box and 'tis kept in a secret place." He enunciated his words as if were speaking to a half-wit. "What do those two conditions imply?"

Rather than look at him, Margery studied her hands. "That there is something of value in the box."

"Be more specific, Margery Watson. You are capable of deduction, are you not? Tell me what the box might contain."

"Money?" She hoped 'twas a viper that would sink its fangs into his wrinkled flesh.

With a flourish Simon flipped back the lid and held the contents toward the fire's light. "Jewels!" Plunging his hand into the casket, he emerged with a handful of stones. Rubies, sapphires, diamonds, amethysts trickled through his fingers. "Have you ever seen anything so lovely?"

Since Margery handled the various wares in Simon's shop and occasionally performed the most rudimentary work associated with goldsmithing, she was hardly a stranger to gems, though she'd never seen so many in one place.

"Jewels are for the wealthy, sir. For myself, I prefer flowers."

"Nonsense. A flower's beauty is transitory. These last forever." He held out the box. "Touch them. Hold them."

Reluctantly, Margery ran her fingertips over the jewels. Cold to the touch; lifeless, cold and hard. And one was probably worth more than she would earn in a year's time. "What would you have me say, sir?"

"There is a fortune in this casket, and it all belongs to me. Did you know I am one of London's wealthiest merchants?" Extending a sapphire toward the firelight, Simon rushed on. "Did you know you are very like these jewels? The color of your eyes. Your lips like rubies." He held a topaz up to her hair. "The highlights are the very same."

Stunned by Crull's sudden metamorphosis from businessman to suitor, Margery stammered, "I do not understand."

"Like my stones, you are beautiful even in your unpolished state. I've known it for years. I am going to refine you, transform you into a thing of beauty, an adornment for my house." Simon stroked his stones while imparting his vision of the future Margery Watson. "I will give you fashionable clothing and improve your manners. I will build us a fine mansion and with you by my side, I will entertain royalty should I so desire."

Frightened by his babbling, Margery backed away. "If you'll excuse me, sir, I have chores to attend."

Simon grabbed her arm. "I appreciate beauty in all its forms. Dame Gisla was a proper matron and furthered my career. But she is gone and I shall replace her with a woman more suited to this time in my life."

"Pardon me, master, but I have no idea what you are saying."

Simon Crull's lips turned up in a smile that did not expose his teeth, which were discolored and beginning to rot. "Beauty and intelligence seldom go hand in hand. 'Tis God's way of providing a measure of justice in this world."

He loosed his grip on Margery's arm and returned to caressing his jewels. "My father was a leatherworker," he said, his voice low with remembrance. "A lowly enough trade in the best of times. He preferred to spend his life in taverns rather than make a proper living. He was filthy and disgusting, and died as he should—with his head bashed in during some brawl. From an early age, I knew God had created me for greatness, but I also knew naught would be handed to me. I turned to goldsmithing because 'tis the most prestigious and lucrative craft. I married Gisla because her family owned real estate throughout London. Those who possess property possess power as well as wealth. I have accomplished nearly everything I have set out to do, and when I am elected mayor, as I intend to be, everyone from lord to alderman to the miscreants in the stocks will know my name. When I pass Londoners will say, 'There goes Simon Crull. He is an important man. Do not anger him. Cultivate him.' They will envy me not only for my position, my house, my friends—but also for my beautiful wife."

"I do not understand. I have never heard you talk this way, master, and I am confused—"

"I will speak as plainly as possible then. We are going to be wed, you and I."

"What?" Margery gaped at him. "Is this a jest? Have I done something to displease you? Do you think to trap me somehow by this pretense? You and I both know that—"

"You heard me correct, Margery Watson. We are going to become man and wife."

"But I do not intend to marry anyone," she blurted. "Most certainly not you."

Simon smiled complacently. "'Tis not unheard of for an important man to marry beneath him." He ran his fingertips over her hand exactly as he had his jewels. "And you are not really so far below. Your blood is most exalted." He paused. "Or at least a portion of it."

Margery stiffened. How could he know about her heredity?

Upon her service, Dame Gisla had asked the usual questions, "Where are you from?", "What work can you do?", "Name me your relatives." She'd noted each answer in her account book, but with so many dead and so much changing there would have been little chance of checking out Margery's answers, true or false. And in her four years at the Crulls, she'd never discussed her past with anyone save Orabel. Had Thurold said something?

"You look surprised," said Crull. "I assure you I know all about you. 'Twas not so difficult to find out. London is filled with such as you, but a man like myself has connections."

"My past is unimportant," Margery said, with more conviction than she felt.

"You are the bastard daughter of a peasant woman," Simon said. "Your father is the Canterbury knight, Thomas Rendell. Rendell's mother was Maria d'Arderne, the fabled mistress of Edward II's half-brother, Richard of Sussex. The Rendell family is most influential, especially in the south of England. So 'tis not only your physical attributes that intrigue me."

"I have a dowry consisting of exactly sixteen shillings," Margery managed, though she could scarce hear herself above her heart's pounding. "Even if I am who you say, I have no material goods to bring into a partnership. Marriage to me would make you a figure of ridicule. Such matches cause talk even when the bride has something to offer, which I do not."

"You have noble blood, nay, even royal blood, for rumors have long circulated that Thomas Rendell's father was really Edward II's half-brother. If that is so, then Thomas Rendell's grandfather would be Edward I, the same as our own King Edward. When His Grace and I sit together upon Westminster's dais after I am elected mayor, we will have much to discuss."

"None of this can be proved," insisted Margery. "You are constructing genealogies out of air." Fear made her drop her usual respectful pose and speak bluntly. "I am worthless to you, I do not want to marry you or *anyone*, and I will not."

Her mind raced, sketching plans. She would head north for Cumbria. She would leave Crull's employ immediately, slip out the first thing tomorrow, and if she had to attach herself to a band of pilgrims or merchants and walk to Matthew, that she would do...

"'Tis best, master, that we both pretend this conversation never took place." She retreated for the door only to have Crull grab her wrist and spin her around.

"When I said I knew everything about you, I was speaking true. Before coming to London, you were bonded to the Ravenne estates in East Anglia. You ran away." Simon's voice dropped an octave. "You are a criminal, Margery Watson. Who would have thought?"

Margery fought down a wave of panic. Simon was trying to trap her with words, and doing a fair job of it. But he was wrong about her status. "Even if what you say is true—and I am not admitting to it —'twould make no difference. Anyone who lives in London a year and a day is considered free. By law I am a free woman."

Simon laughed. "You know enough of the law to know absolutely nothing. A woman can only be free should she marry a free man."

Margery hesitated. "I do not believe that." She desperately wished Thurold or John Ball were here to reassure her, to confirm whether Simon actually spoke truth. They would know such laws, but Thurold remained in France with English mercenaries and she'd not seen John Ball in months.

"You would question an alderman who deals daily with the law? You insult me, Margery Watson. Did you know I can impose extremely severe penalties for your slanders?"

"I did not mean to anger you," she said, her manner placating. "But I am certain the law will protect me."

From the interior of his robe Simon retrieved a document, removed the seal and unrolled it. "Read this. It will tell you."

Margery stared at the unintelligible lines. "You know I cannot read."

Simon smiled his closed-mouth smile. "Let me read it for you. 'According to the Westminster Decree signed by our most benevolent majesty, King Edward III, any woman who is born a bondwoman must remain so, without exception, unless and until the time she should marry a free man.'"

The words sounded as official as the seal looked. She raised her eyes to Crull, trying to determine the truth by his expression. "'Tis correct, then?" No fleeing London or seeking employ elsewhere or taking charge of her own fate?

Simon nodded, folded the document, which contained detailed instructions from one of his clients requesting a set of golden goblets, and thrust it back inside his robe. "If you do not marry me, I will turn you over to the proper authorities. They will throw you in Ludgate or Newgate, or the Clink mayhap. You would not want to die in prison, would you, Margery Watson?"

She swallowed hard. "Nay, sir."

"Good. 'Tis settled then." Reaching out, he grabbed her hand. "Before God, here in this chamber, I will have you as my wife."

Stunned, Margery shook free from his grasp, but he merely grabbed her other hand and forced her to look into his eyes. "You, Margery Watson, will have me as your husband, will you not?"

Even in her distracted state, she knew that Crull was attempting to intimidate her into consenting to marriage. Such an agreement, whether uttered neath the spreading leaves of an ash, in front of a ruined tower, or in a room like this one, was considered to be as solemn and binding an oath as one uttered in church. Nor did witnesses have to be present. Should she dispute the oath, she would have to take Crull to court to determine its legality, a process that could take months.

"I do not want to commit myself to anything without thinking upon it. Please, do not rush me so."

Simon squeezed her hand. "You will take me for your husband or you will end up in prison. You *will* have me. I do not make idle threats. Either you agree now or pay the consequences."

"I will take this to a hearing," Margery cried. "They will say 'tis entrapment. You canna force me. Any oath given under duress will be ruled invalid. I know that much of the law, at least."

"If the courts so rule, I will inform them of your true status, which would lead immediately to your death. Do not fight me, Margery

Watson. You are no match for me. I have long anticipated this moment, and your reluctance only strengthens my resolve."

Margery tried to decide what to do. It was inconceivable that she might actually become Simon Crull's wife, but Simon was right about one thing. She was no match for him—at least not in an open confrontation. She had spent her life watching those with power trampling on those without. But the powerless, like Thurold and John Ball, kept re-grouping for another skirmish.

I can give lip service to anything in order to stall. Matthew promised he would return by August's end. He'll thwart Simon Crull, regardless of a thousand clandestine oaths or Westminster Decrees.

She nodded. "I do agree."

"Say it. I will have you, Simon Crull, as my husband."

Margery repeated the words.

Simon's expression was smug. "We are bound together now for eternity. Before God, we are man and wife."

The pronouncement of the oath sickened her. *I should not have uttered it under any circumstances. 'Twill prove my undoing.*

"When are you planning on the official church ceremony?" she asked aloud.

"As soon as the banns are posted." Three weeks before a wedding, banns were placed on the church door in order to allow anyone knowing of a prospective spouse's bigamy or consanguinity to raise objections.

Quickly Margery calculated. If Simon meant to be married around Lammas Day, Matthew would still be gone. She tried to keep her voice steady as she asked, "Why so soon, sir?"

"Because it pleases me. As all things will be done at my pleasure. Understand?"

"'Twould be inappropriate so soon after Dame Gisla's death. Think of the scandal. You are running for mayor. Such an act might harm your political ambitions."

"I shall keep our marriage quiet for a time, though I have been assured that my election is a foregone conclusion. Besides, the world has changed since the Death. Proprieties do not matter as they used to. A man like me can make my own rules."

That might be so, Margery thought, after Simon dismissed her. But whatever rules you might think to make, I will think of something. I must.

Never, NEVER would she become Simon Crull's wife.

CHAPTER 22

London

Harry Hart and Lady Desiderata Cecy sat on opposite sides of a table in front of the solar window. Afternoon sunshine pooled upon the wooden Merrills board which sat next to a ewer of wine and two jewel encrusted goblets. While Harry studied the playing board, consisting of three squares within squares, Desire, as she was commonly called, drummed her fingers impatiently on the tabletop. Desire's relentlessly black hair, swept on either side of her ears in a caul of gold, revealed a heart-shaped face with intense brown eyes. Though she was skillful in the use of cosmetics, the sunlight betrayed Desire's pitted complexion. But Harry considered that a minor imperfection when weighed against the lushness of her figure.

"Would you please make your move?" Desire said. "You've been contemplating that board since Christ was a babe."

Harry took a long swallow of wine. "Patience, my sweet. I am almost ready." Desire had an undeniably sharp tongue, but she could drink a tremendous amount without becoming incapacitated, possessed remarkable cleavage, and best of all, was an abominably poor Merrills player. He'd already won a noble.

Desire sighed loudly. "I cannot concentrate." Scooping her goblet from the table, she retreated to the bay window where she could view the Hart garden below with its pebbled path meandering through bright patches of flowers, and beyond, a portion of Holborn, that most magnificent of London's garden suburbs. Church dignitaries, lords, and courtiers all coveted a town house there—as did Desire. But her primary requirement was that any residence she rented be as close as possible to Hart's Place.

Plopping down in one of the window's cushioned "She and I" seats, Desire contemplated her foul luck. She had first seen Matthew Hart near five years past, following the English triumph at Poitiers. Prince Edward and his men were being welcomed back to Bordeaux by thousands of cheering townspeople and Desire had been there to dutifully greet her husband, Guy Cecy. However, after glimpsing the young knight among the celebrants, she had forgotten about Guy, about everything save Matthew Hart. Before her marriage, Desire had enjoyed many affairs, but she'd never experienced such an immediate and overwhelming attraction. Whenever possible she'd put herself in a position where she might watch Matthew from afar. Plagued by a jealous and ever-vigilant husband, she could do no more.

What did she find so intriguing about Hart, what caused her to single him out among all those larger-than-life creatures who so carelessly tottered on that knife's edge between civility and brutality? To a man they fairly swaggered when they walked, seeming to tower above ordinary men like giants among dwarves. Yet even among the others, so deliciously cocksure and with a seemingly insatiable penchant for drinking and whoring following months of campaigning, Matthew commanded her attention.

And left her frustrated by a husband who kept her on a tighter leash than his hounds.

Unused to being observer rather than participant, Desire tried to channel her vexation by spending endless hours stitching a mental tapestry of the object of her obsession—his personality, which she simply *knew* would fit perfectly with her own, his unparalleled prowess at the joust and war and lovemaking and any other activity in which he chose to participate, and finally the incomparable affair she would someday enjoy with a man she had never yet spoken to.

Fortunately, fate, though slow-moving as a crone, finally intervened when Guy Cecy died during the Rheims campaign. Following a conventional, albeit extremely brief mourning period, Desire had sailed for England.

Only to be thwarted again.

For the third time since the game's beginning, she lamented, "Who would have thought your brother would leave London just as I was arriving?"

Harry sighed inwardly. "While Matt is famous for his bad manners, he can hardly be blamed this time since he knew naught about your arrival. 'Tis lucky I was here or your entire journey would have been wasted."

Desire swirled her wine and stared moodily out the window. The trees in the Hart garden were in full spread. From her position she could see a sun dial and a water fountain, its drops spilling like diamonds in the afternoon sun.

"Compared to Bordeaux, London is impossibly provincial. Even the current intrigue involving Lady Joan and Prince Edward cannot hold my interest." Desire had attached herself to Joan of Kent's household because it was in close proximity to the Black Prince, and Matthew was one of Prince Edward's retainers. It seemed simple enough. One would naturally assume that Matthew Hart would be at Kennington along with his lord, but he was off to some wilds no one had ever heard of, while Desire had to content herself with watching Prince Edward and Joan's unfolding love affair.

During the time Harry and Desire had known each other, he had heard identical complaints more times than he cared to count. Long ago he had decided he'd far rather watch Desire than listen to her.

Desire drained her goblet and placed it on the tiled floor. "If it weren't for your brother, I would leave London tomorrow, never to return."

"'Twould be London's loss, I assure you."

Harry rearranged two of Desire's playing pegs so that he could position three of his own in a line and form a mill. He calculated that by evening's end, he might win an entire pound. Desire probably knew he cheated at Merrills, but she was wealthier than he could ever hope to be and would never miss the money. Confident that he would end the day a richer man than he began it, Harry experienced a sudden wave of affection for the lady who would make it possible.

"I mislike seeing you so gloomy. Brooding over Matt will not bring him back one whit sooner, so why not forget him and go to bed with me? Everyone agrees I am by far the handsomer brother."

"You are a child," Desire snapped. "I had enough of children during my first marriage."

Harry was so offended by Desire's bluntness that he moved several of his pegs to a more advantageous position while her back was turned. "I am feeling lucky today. What say we raise our wager?"

Ignoring his question, Desire placed her arms on the window ledge, leaned her chin upon her hands, and contemplated London's skyline. After a time, she said, "I think 'tis true what the gossips say, that Lady Joan really will snare the prince. 'Tis being whispered that Prince Edward's esquire has recently sailed for Avignon to obtain the necessary marriage license. Joan personally told me that she and Prince Edward have already plighted their troth."

"A match will never happen. Besides being his cousin, Joan has been married twice before. The scandal that erupted over her double marriage is still discussed." Harry poured himself more wine. "As you should recall, Joan wed the earl of Salisbury only to have Thomas Holland step forward, charging that they had already exchanged secret vows. While you and Joan might be afflicted with faulty memories, the rest of England remembers that the pope himself upheld Holland's claim and dissolved Joan's second marriage. His Grace would never allow his son to marry someone thus tainted."

"You are so naïve." Desire glimpsed a group of children playing tag in an adjacent garden and swung shut the window to drown out their laughter. "'Tis a condition you share with my late husband, who contemplated life in similar simple terms. Should I so much as look at another man, Guy would threaten me with strangulation or disembowelment, depending on his mood. He never understood that while his threats might have kept me physically faithful and dissuaded all who might wish to woo me in the usual way of the court, he could not control my thoughts. 'Do you desire that comely form?' he would ask." Desire mimicked Guy's voice. "'Nay, husband,' I would respond ever so sweetly. It never occurred to him that I might lie."

"I trust your husband died a happy man."

Harry studied the board, trying to decide whether he could rearrange any more pegs. But all were lined up so that no matter how he moved, 'twould be impossible to lose. Gulping down the rest of his wine, he decided to think of some way besides cheating to re-pay his opponent's sarcasm. *Naïve, indeed!*

Desire turned to face him, her arms crossed in a dismissive manner. "You men might be masters at war, but not so much in love. We just pretend so that we can better lead you where we wish you to go."

"Is that what you believe Joan of Kent is doing with our prince?"

"Ah, Harry Hart, you are not so dull as you appear. I'll wager she has long plotted to snare him, and now that she is between husbands, will succeed."

"A wager, you say!" Harry poured the last of the wine and rang for a replacement. "I'll bet two pounds they never wed. Prince Edward has escaped marriage for thirty-one years. He is a confirmed bachelor."

"He only thinks he is. Being a chivalrous lord, Prince Edward cannot resist a helpless female, and Joan is skilled at playing the vulnerable heiress in need of protection from fortune hunting knights. Edward of Woodstock might not realize he is being manipulated, but everyone else in the kingdom does."

Harry scooted back his stool in order to better view Desire. Dropping his bantering tone, he said, "If you are thinking to emulate Joan of Kent's actions, I warn you, you will end up disappointed. My brother has never been one to listen to minstrels' prattle about love, but he will remain loyal to Margery Watson. I am not saying he won't occasionally tumble a wench when the fancy strikes him, but he'll not give his heart to anyone else. Besides, Matt has long vowed he'll never wed, and once he gives his word, neither heaven's angels nor Satan's minions will dissuade him."

Desire's dark eyes seemed to glow with an inner fire. "And I am neither. I will achieve what heaven and hell cannot."

Harry shook his head. "After all I've told you about my brother and his paramour, I canna believe you would cling to such delusion. Besides, your obsession with him makes no sense. You two have never even spoken."

Desire made a wide arc with her arm, as if to sweep aside a bothersome cobweb. "That matters not. I know what I want, and I want Matthew Hart. The very first moment I saw him, I understood what the troubadours mean when they tell of instant love."

"'Tis not physical love they are referring to," Harry countered, "but spiritual. And 'tis the knight who pursues the lady, not the other way round. Besides, you've left out the most important part of your scenario—"

At that moment a servant entered, carrying more wine. "Pardon, m'lord," he said, placing one ewer on the table and retrieving the other. "A woman has arrived who gave her name as Margery Watson. She says 'tis imperative that you see her."

Harry's eyebrows lifted in surprise. "And speaking of the most important part of your scenario, she appears to be downstairs at this very moment." After instructing the servant to tell Margery he was on his way, he stood and faced Desire. "I admire your persistence, but 'twill come to naught. My brother is truly smitten with his doxy. And I canna blame him. Despite her base origins, she is good-natured, easy to look upon, and most probably saved his life."

While Harry normally never complimented one woman in the presence of another, he deliberately did so to goad Desire. As he headed for the door, he said over his shoulder, "The court is filled with men who would give a decade of their lives to bed you. Why pursue a man who doesn't even know you exist?"

AFTER EXCHANGING THE CUSTOMARY GREETINGS, Margery said to

Harry, "Something terrible has happened." She handed him her letter which had been penned by a copier at Paul's Head Tavern in St. Paul's Churchyard. "You must put this in your brother's hands as soon as possible. If he does not arrive in London by Lammas Day, my life will be ruined."

"What has happened?" Harry turned the letter over. It had been sealed with the imprint of a robin, which might mean something to Matt, but nothing to him. "I will be happy to do as you wish, but Cumbria is a far distance. Might I somehow help you now? Please tell me what your problem is, and I will try to solve it."

Harry always sounded so sincere, but Margery could smell the wine on his breath and was familiar enough with his behavior to realize that he was intoxicated. She also knew that Harry Hart could only be given simple tasks, and not too many of those. Otherwise, he might become overwhelmed and accomplish nothing.

"Thank you, m'lord, but the biggest help you could provide is to send the letter." Carefully choosing her words in order to impart just enough information, she further explained, "'Tis a problem I am having with…Master Crull. I know Lord Hart can help me solve it, but if he does not change his plans, I am doomed. He must return to London immediately."

Though Margery's words made little sense, Harry willingly agreed to help. "I will have the letter sent personally by one of our retainers. I've known Matt to reach Cumbria in seven days by riding night and day. I'll instruct my man to do the same."

Margery calculated. A week for the messenger, a week for Matthew, and the wedding little more than a week after that? That left little room for bad roads and bad weather but what choice had she? "You will not forget, m'lord? 'Twould destroy me if your brother does not receive it."

Harry leaned down to kiss Margery on both cheeks. "I have never properly thanked you for saving my brother's life. 'Twill be my repayment for tending to his health. I will send for a rider posthaste."

Margery's eyes filled. Harry might have faults, but he loved his brother. She was glad she'd thought to enlist his help.

Harry, in turn, was touched by Margery's tears. He had never understood Matt's affinity for lower class women, but she seemed to please him, and had certainly earned at least this in repayment.

"My brother will not forsake you," he said, his voice gentle. "Cumbria might be a great distance but that will mean naught to Matt. He can do things the rest of us would consider impossible."

"Aye," Margery said. "That is why I am here."

"SHE HAS A PRETTY FACE," Desire called down from the landing after Margery's departure, "though not so pretty as mine. And her figure is at best average."

Harry strode to the stairs and gazed up at his grinning companion. "No wonder you are so admired at court. You have a talent for being where you should not. And your assessment of Margery Watson matters not. 'Tis Matt who cares for her, not you."

"I just wanted to view my competition. I did not overhear your discussion."

"You lie as charmingly as you do all things. Your hearing has been sharpened by all those years of intrigue in Bordeaux. You probably heard her conversation more completely than I did."

Desire had certainly heard enough to realize that God had just granted her a boon. She would emulate Joan of Kent's strategy—take full advantage of a situation and exploit it to her own ends.

Harry called one of the servants and instructed him to go to the stables and return with Jerome Graf, who had a way with horses and could coax more miles out of his mount than anyone else. Graf was also one of the few men Harry knew who was tough enough to withstand several days and nights in the saddle. "Tell him I will await him in the solar."

He then ascended the stairs. When he reached Desire, she held out her hand for the letter. "I am curious as to what has distressed the poor servant girl so."

Harry brushed past her into the solar, holding the letter above his head and beyond her reach. "Nay, sweetheart. Not for marriage to the richest lady in the kingdom would I risk Matt's wrath. His leman asked me to deliver this and I mean to do it, exactly as she asked. I'll not have you or anyone else tamper with it."

Crossing to a writing desk he stuck the letter in one of its cubby-holes. "Until Jerome Graf arrives, that is where it stays. Now let us resume our game, and no more wearisome talk."

Desire smiled, displaying small even teeth and a dimple that Harry often maintained was delightful. During her marriage she had learned patience—and when to be silent.

Refilling their goblets, Desire obediently sat down across from him, contemplated the Merrills board, noticed that he had been cheating, increased her bet and lost it all. While Harry separated the pieces for another game, she waited, outwardly quiet and inwardly teeming with possible plans and strategies. First, she must read the letter. She could get Harry so drunk he would pass out and she would have as long as she pleased to study the letter's contents and decide on a course of action. Jerome Graf was a different matter. Once the document left Hart's Place, she wasn't certain how she would be able to retrieve it. Perhaps she could have Graf waylaid somewhere along the route...

The servant Harry had sent to the stables entered the solar. "Sir Graf cannot be found. Some say he is in Gropecunt Lane; others at Boar's Head Tavern."

"Very well," Harry said. "Just leave word that the moment he returns he is to contact me."

Afraid that her expression might betray her delight, Desire ducked her head as if to study the playing board. Fortune was indeed smiling upon her.

Now I will get Harry inebriated as quickly as possible and turn my talents to Margery Watson's letter.

USING HER DAGGER, Desire carefully worked the wax seal from the parchment. She was proficient at removing seals from others' correspondence and replacing them so adroitly no one was ever the wiser.

Given the intrigue inevitable at any court, it was a skill one soon acquired to survive.

From the bed, Harry sputtered and snored. By Vespers, he had finally succumbed to the alcohol.

"Do not fret for me," she'd called as he'd collapsed upon the gold threaded counterpane. "I will have my carriage called round and leave you to your rest."

Which of course she had not done.

Retrieving the oil lamp from the stand beside Harry's bed Desire opened the parchment.

'My Esteemed Lord,' the letter began.

'I fear something terrible has happened. My master thinks to marry me against my will. The ceremony has been set for Lammas Day. He has threatened me and I fear for my safety—and our future. If you care for me as you say you do, my dearest lord, please return to London as soon as possible.'

"God's balls!" whispered Desire. "This is wonderful." What to do? She might pen Matthew a letter, ostensibly from his paramour ending their relationship. Nay, that would not work. He would probably sprout wings and fly down from Cumbria on the next air current. Then the truth would come out. She must think of something else.

Desire stared at the oil lamp's dancing flame. Finally, she opened the lid from the inkhorn and retrieved a quill and clean piece of parchment, which she placed atop the slanted writing desk. After smoothing the parchment with pumice stone, Desire dipped quill into ink and began writing. She would be brief and speak in such simple language that Matt could not misconstrue her meaning amidst a confusing tangle of words.

"Margery" wrote her "lover" that Master Crull was getting married to a...widow...a burgher's daughter...who??...and because of the extra preparations asked Matthew to delay his return until Michaelmas. Margery and Simon Crull would be long wed while Matthew Hart was still dallying in Cumbria.

A knock interrupted Desire. She opened the door to Jerome Graf.

"M'lord Hart sent for me."

"Lord Hart is indisposed at the moment. Return on the morrow at matins."

Afterward, Desire signed Margery's name, folded the letter, slashed it on either side with her knife, and passed a cord through it. Then she softened the wax slightly above the lamp flame and positioned the seal between the two strands of cord in order to connect them. Tossing the original missive in the fire, she placed her copy in the original space.

Now she could leave.

On the return ride to Joan of Kent's residence, Desire contemplated her plan from every angle, ferreting out flaws. The carriage in which she and her servant, Sybil, traveled clattered noisily through rapidly emptying streets.

Though Hart's Place was beyond London's gates and not subject to curfew, few townsfolk ventured out after dark. In the poorer parts of London, taverns frequented by criminals and ne'er-do-wells crammed every lane. Any law-abiding citizen so unfortunate as to be in the area risked being stabbed, smashed with quarter staffs, or robbed and beaten by midnight revelers wearing animal masks.

Mentally weighing and measuring every permutation of her scheme, Desire stared unseeing out the window. In this part of Holborn only an occasional wall torch in the garden of some prosperous vintner or wool merchant cast flickering shadows across the fruit trees, iron gates, and walls. The lone sound inside the cramped space came from her maid's soft snoring.

First, I will visit the Shop of the Unicorn, bribe a member of the household to spy on Lord Hart's simpleton, and make certain she doesn't write any more letters or try to contact him in any other way.

Desire would order any messages Matthew might send Margery to be intercepted and, following the wedding, turn all correspondence over to Master Crull. *'Tis a sure bet he'll never let his bride near her former lover.*

Sybil's head slumped against Desire's shoulder. "How much longer until we're home, m'lady?" she murmured, after Desire pushed her away.

"Quiet. I do not like to be interrupted when I'm thinking."

In ten days or so, Desire would compose a letter from Matthew, assuring his doxy that he was even now bound for London. Desire would pay her spy, whoever he might be, to monitor all of Margery's movements and keep Desire updated.

And in three weeks 'twould all be over.

Up until the moment Margery Watson uttered her marriage vows, she would believe that Matthew Hart meant to rescue her. Anticipating the moment when she would realize his betrayal, Desire smiled. Fool! Who did she think she was, grasping above her station? Aspiring to attach herself to an actual lord?

And Matthew, what would he do when he discovered that his leman was married? *Will he be furious or brought low by love? If that is the case*—and Desire could scarce believe that Matthew Hart would long mourn a commoner—*I will be at his side to comfort him, to remind him of Margery Watson's treachery and show him how sweet life with me can be.*

CHAPTER 23

London

August 1, 1361, neared. Even though Margery and Simon Crull's wedding ceremony would be private out of respect for Dame Gisla's passing, much still remained to be done. As a wedding present Crull had chosen for his intended a magnificent wardrobe of velvets, samites, cloth of gold, and brocaded silks in colors that flattered Margery's complexion, and in styles that best showed her figure. He also coordinated each gown with his most beautifully worked pieces of jewelry.

"Where am I going to enjoy such finery? 'Tis against the law to dress above our station." Even though she would never have to thus humiliate herself, Margery could not resist needling Crull about such overreach. How inappropriate he was. How grasping and pretentious. Who did he and others like him think they were fooling by aping their betters?

"Now that I have been elected mayor, I am equal to any lord. And once knowledge of your heredity becomes known, your wardrobe will be in accordance with your position."

"You should not spin such grand tales around the two of us. You are bound to be disappointed."

"Did not John Montague, Earl of Salisbury, marry the daughter of a draper? I am richer than many nobleman, and as Mayor of London, more powerful. You will dress, act and do as I say without argument, and be grateful for my generosity."

Margery let most of his words flow around her without comment. What did they matter? Simon Crull could say what he wished. Soon Matthew would whisk her away from this grasping old fool. She clung to the promise in her lover's letter, that he would not fail her. Margery did not doubt. Nor did she fret the vows she'd exchanged with Crull or her bondwoman status. In all things, Matthew Hart would protect her.

When the wedding was less than a week away, Margery began to worry. So much could go wrong. He should have arrived on the heels of his letter. Where was he? "His Grace has not declared another war, has he?" she asked Simon during one of the few times she initiated conversation.

Simon's face rearranged itself in the particularly sour lines he reserved for children and idiots, and lately for her. "'Of course not. What are you talking about?"

Margery shrugged in response, though she was relieved she would not have to compete with a campaign. War might be the one thing that could prevent Matthew's return, but even then he would somehow make things right. He was fond of quoting, "Tout est perdu fors l'honneur"—All is lost, save honor—and while Margery would be forever skeptical of such a virtue among the upper classes, she knew her lover would not forsake her.

But he did.

Margery Watson was married on Lammas Day, just as Simon Crull had decreed, in a gold brocade gown with trailing sleeves lined in green sendal silk, with a golden circlet holding back her unbound hair, a sapphire necklace round her neck, and slippers threaded with gold upon her feet. All chosen by her bridegroom.

The ceremony contained only the necessary witnesses, also per Simon's wishes. A more elaborate celebration, he assured his bride, would be planned for their one year anniversary, which all of London, including King Edward and all his sons, would be eager to attend.

Throughout the walk to the church of St. John Zachary, Margery, clutching a sachet of potpourri, found herself looking around, half-expecting to see Matthew on horseback, clattering down the cobble-stoned streets in time to sweep her up and away. Even as she knew, aye, how well she knew, that Matthew Hart had indeed done the unthinkable; he had broken his word.

When they reached St. John Zachary's and a waiting Father Crispin, the reality of Margery's impending fate caused her knees to buckle. She grabbed the elderly priest's arm to keep from falling and raised one hand to her throat, as if that might aid her breathing.

"Are you sick, child?" Father Crispin asked. Having heard many of Margery's confessions and knowing of her previous adulterous relationship, Crispin wondered whether she might be with child. That would explain this admittedly rushed ceremony.

"Aye." Margery slumped down on the porch step and placed her head between her knees. No matter how she struggled, she felt as if she were strangling. What had happened to Matthew? Had he been waylaid by robbers? Summer flooding? Or had he been lying to her all along? She pressed the sachet to her nose, hoping its scent might revive her.

Simon said, "She'll be fine. 'Tis just the heat of the day. Let us be on with it."

Father Crispin frowned. "Her color is poor."

"Something to drink, Father," Margery said. "I feel faint."

The priest obliged. Aye, no doubt she was pregnant, though she was not the only bride to find herself in such a state.

Margery and Simon Crull's wedding ceremony was performed on the porch steps outside St. John Zachary. Margery barely heard the vows. Father Crispin's voice seemed little louder than whispers heard through a wall, and his bright vestments, his tonsured head and gilded book all appeared indistinct, as if viewed through a fog.

He had betrayed her...Matthew Hart had betrayed her...

Father Crispin framed the final question. "Do you both freely consent to this marriage?"

"Aye." Simon said.

The priest turned to Margery. She did not answer.

"And you, child," He prodded. "Do you consent?"

Margery licked her lips. If she did not, would Father Crispin declare the marriage invalid? Would she be able to walk away a free woman? She tried to reason it through, to grab onto the snatches of memories, questions, and impressions darting through her mind long enough to make sense of what was happening.

I cannot marry Simon Crull, she thought, *but 'tis too late*.

"Well?" Father Crispin glanced at the goldsmith, whose face had turned a mottled red. "Do you consent to this marriage?"

Margery suppressed the urge to look over her shoulder, as if Matthew might yet rescue her. "Father, I am confused."

"'Tis a simple enough question."

"Of course she consents," said Simon Crull.

"I do not. I need time to think."

"Pardon, Father." Simon gripped Margery's hand and pulled her away from the priest. "What is wrong with you? If you think to thwart me now, 'ere evening I will have you thrown in the Clink."

He led her back to Father Crispin. "Everything is fine. Continue."

Simon took Margery's right hand, as was customary, but squeezed it hard. She did not doubt that he would make good on his threat. She'd heard what happened in London's prisons, that the condemned were often lowered into deep, foul-smelling well-shaped holes, where rancid food and water were provided at their jailers' whim and where the unfortunates shared the eternal blackness with toads and snakes and other creeping things. Or would Simon forgo the agony of a slow death and simply have her hanged?

Unable to concentrate on anything beyond the reality of Matthew Hart's trickery, Margery mindlessly parroted her vows. Matt must never have intended to return for her, but how could that be? She thought back over his message, every word of which she'd memorized. 'I love thee…I'll not forsake thee…I will stop the wedding…'

What game were you playing? Why did you do this to me?

He'd seemed such an ardent suitor, so eager to have her as his leman. What had changed his mind?

No matter. The deed was done.

For when Margery left St. John Zachary, she was Dame Margery, wife to Simon Crull, master goldsmith and London's newly elected mayor.

AS SUNSET PAINTED the golden dome of St. Paul's Cathedral and London's other buildings an eerie red, Father Crispin arrived to bless the Crulls' chamber and their nuptial bed. Simon then ordered Margery to bathe.

"Call me when you are finished."

Sinking down on the sponges in the bottom of the wooden tub, Margery tried to sort through the day and a future course of action. She was attended by Orabel as her private maid, who while sympathetic, was also practical.

"He will die soon, dear heart," Orabel said, placing another kettle of water above the fire. "Then you'll be a rich widow and can do as you please. Count yourself lucky."

Margery nodded, though she had not been blessed with Orabel's practical nature. But she must learn if she were to survive—and survive she would. First of all, her marriage did make her a person of some consequence and she would use that power to the fullest. While she might be unable to outwardly rebel against her husband, didn't priests charge women with forever manipulating the opposite sex?

As the kettle heated, Orabel retrieved soap, a washing cloth and two jars containing herbs and flower petals for sweetening Margery's bath water, and arranged them on a tray beside the tub, which was tucked inside a tent of sheets.

"Do not look so sad. 'Twill soon be over." When Margery did not respond, she continued, "Beauty soon fades so use your looks to full advantage. Whether with the master or others, make the most of what you have. 'Tis all any of us can do."

Margery thought suddenly of her mother. *I will do as you did. But I will also use my wits. Since Simon considers me stupid, I will have the advantage. Somehow...*

Orabel sprinkled flower petals around her. Margery tried to relax but her mind soon leapt to visions of their marriage bed. Sitting forward in the tub, she brought her knees to her chest. "I cannot bear it," she whispered, her eyes filling with tears.

"He is not your knight," Orabel said gently, "but sometimes we must endure things we would rather not. And look what ye be gaining. I remember when you first came to London—"

"How can I ever lie quietly beneath *him* and allow him to befoul me with his seed? How could..." she wanted to ask how Matthew Hart could have so lied when he'd sworn in his letters he would arrive in time to stop the marriage, that nothing would deter him. But Orabel could not answer that or any other question regarding her perfidious lover.

"Lean back, dear heart, and I'll massage your scalp."

While Orabel's skilled fingers worked their magic, Margery closed her eyes and leaned into the soothing touch. She tried to keep her thoughts away from Matthew, but they had a way of tumbling back to him, to beds other than the one she would soon share with her odious groom, to his calloused hands and his soft lips and his muscular body fitting atop her, curve to curve...Aye, Matthew Hart was worse even than the serpent in paradise. He'd betrayed her as surely as the devil had betrayed Eve, whispering sweet words and promises that were naught but lies. Margery wished she were an actual witch so she could weave a dark enchantment causing her former lover to die a slow painful death.

But since that is not possible I will just pretend you are dead.

"More hot water?"

How could you have done this to me? I will never think of you again, NEVER. I will root you from my heart as if you were a noxious weed. Never. Never!

Orabel carefully poured the water so that she would not scald her new mistress. Margery leaned back, and gradually relaxed into the warmth, the rising steam. Her maid followed with a handful of herbs whose strong, pleasant aroma filled her nostrils. She found herself mentally sorting the identity of each individual herb, listing their properties and...

"Damme!" she whispered, sitting up straight. "I know what I am going to do." At least about Simon Crull.

"Pardon? Is something wrong?"

For the first time on her wedding day, Margery actually smiled.

AFTER DISMISSING Orabel and while keeping an ear attuned to the arrival of her bridegroom, Margery sprinkled hyssop, rue, centaury, and other herbs into a ewer of wine. For years, she had been charged with taking care of her master's personal needs. She'd (unsuccessfully) treated his baldness with peach tree kernels bruised and boiled in vinegar until they become a paste thick enough to apply to his pate, and daily concocted a brew of essence of balm mixed in ale, designed (also unsuccessfully) to preserve youth. Before retiring Crull routinely drank a cup of wine to aid his digestion. Oft times he would list his current complaints and Margery would add whatever herbs she thought might alleviate them. Tonight she devised a mixture that should loosen Crull's bowels and render him impotent. While she knew little enough about male sexual problems, she had enough experience helping other members of the household to improvise. As Margery added an extra pinch of dittany, she prayed she wouldn't miscalculate or combine herbs that might have the opposite effect intended.

After readying the potion, she pulled a small table close to the fire and positioned two stools—one directly in front of the fireplace, the other farther back and at an angle. Retrieving a finely worked ivory comb—another gift from the usually parsimonious Crull—she sat in the stool nearest the flames so that, in silhouette, her chemise would reveal enough to entice her spouse. Hopefully, he would be so distracted that, should the wine taste peculiar, he would not notice.

Margery carefully worked the comb through her waist-length tresses.

I cannot do this. I do not want to be beautiful for Simon Crull.

But was he really any worse than Matthew Hart? Hart had been comely to look upon, but his heart was every bit as black. Simon Crull or Matthew Hart, it made no difference. Two sides to the same coin. She loathed them both.

When Crull entered the solar, he found a provocative scene with the flickering firelight revealing enticing curves and causing Margery's tresses to shimmer like spun gold.

"Come sit and watch." Margery forced a smile while gesturing to a nearby stool. She had a sudden image of her mother, carefully combing her hair in the smoking cottage light, fanning between her fingers each strand, delicate as cobwebs spun upon forest bracken.

Why did you leave me? She was not sure whether she was addressing Alice or Matthew.

A clearly mesmerized Simon sank down on the stool across from Margery and silently accepted a goblet of wine.

"I've added some herbs for nerves," she said. "'Twill relax us both."

As if unaware of Crull's stare, Margery returned to her ministrations, pausing occasionally to pretend to drink from her goblet, though she merely wet her lips.

How can I be here when 'tis my lord Hart who should be sitting across from me, knee to knee, close enough to caress my cheek and brush his lips against mine and run his fingers through my hair?

She thought of other times when just gazing into her lover's eyes had caused her every fiber to ignite and her head to swim until it could contain no thought other than that she must possess and be possessed, when the hunger for his body, for his very essence was nearly beyond endurance. *My faithless lord...*

Long minutes passed. A log cracked, sending sparks dancing up the chimney. The great bell of St. Martin's le Grand rang curfew, reminding Londoners that it was time to settle in like nesting chickens for the night. Boats would be moored along the Thames, watchmen would patrol the streets and strangers would scurry for city exits rather than be thrown into prisons as nightwalkers. The Shop of the Unicorn, with its endless passageways, stairs, and warren-like rooms, seemed even quieter than usual, as if the entire household had fled, or the building itself was waiting, listening, invisibly observing this unfolding tableau.

From the corner of her eye, Margery noted each time Simon picked up his goblet, each time he drank. So engrossed was he she doubted he even noticed how many times she'd re-filled his cup.

I could learn to enjoy this power...

Margery had a sudden flash of her mother singing an innocuous ditty in her slightly off-key voice. What songs had Alice sung? Words from a more recent, far darker refrain popped into Margery's mind:

"A sickly season," the merchant said,
"The town I left was filled with dead,
And everywhere these queer red flies
Crawled upon the corpses' eyes..."

Simon rose from the stool. Removing the comb from Margery's hand, he said, "Stand."

Reluctantly, she obeyed. *Soon he will lead me to the marriage bed; soon I will have to...*

"Remove your chemise," Simon said.

"Sir?"

"Remove it and let me look at you. It has cost me dear to wed a woman without dowry. I want to see whether 'twas worth it."

Mother Mary protect me! Of course, 'twas natural enough for people to sleep naked, but not to parade around so beforehand. What was wrong with her potion; why had it failed her?

"Do not hesitate, wife. A disobedient bride bodes poorly for the rest of the marriage. Hurry. I am eager to see you."

"I am shy. I would rather remain clothed."

"I don't care what you would rather do. Undress and be quick about it."

"'Tis brazen. As if I were a stroller." Her throat felt curiously thick. "I am a modest woman. No man has ever seen me naked."

A necessary lie, for she assumed Simon believed her to be a virgin. Margery had a sudden mental image of Matthew coming to her, smiling as he freed her hair, of the admiration in his eyes as he viewed her body. She turned her head away, so Crull could not see the sudden tears.

I will not cry over you. I will not mourn.

Simon drew himself to his full height, which was barely on a level with her and glared, as if evidence of his displeasure could intimidate her to compliance. Margery felt her temper rising, felt venomous words roiling to the surface. Let him imprison her. She would tell him the truth about Matthew and that she wasn't pure and he, pompous little man that he was, would be universally mocked—

"There are a few things you and I must sort between us." Crull slapped Margery across the face. "'Tis against all laws for you to disobey me. Do you understand?"

"Nay, I do not." His slap enraged far more than it hurt. "'Tis not a husband's duty to humiliate his wife. Furthermore—"

Simon clipped her with a closed fist, causing her head to snap back. This time it hurt.

"If you fail to immediately comply, I will do far worse. 'Tis within my rights to beat you."

Margery knew this was true. Even someone so impossibly ancient could inflict damage. By the morrow, her jaw would bear proof of that.

Simon drew back his arm, as if to hit her again.

Margery jerked the chemise over her head to stand naked before him. "Is that more to your liking?"

Simon inhaled sharply. For a moment she thought the potion might have taken effect, but realized his reaction came from excitement rather than illness. Embarrassment immediately replaced anger, and Margery sought to shield herself by balling the discarded chemise against her breasts.

"Do not be shy. Let me look at you."

When Margery did not comply, he placed his hands over hers, forcing her arms down until she stood revealed. Crull's eyes perused her length, followed by his fingers. He lifted the mane of hair from her breasts, weighing its thickness, marveling at its shine.

"I have never seen anything so fine, finer even than my silver or gold thread. 'Tis a shame 'tis not blonde, which would make it beyond compare. Would you enjoy being a blonde? I think even King Edward himself would then envy me my perfect spouse."

It took all the restraint Margery possessed to keep from jerking away from the goldsmith's touch.

I should have poisoned you. Next time, I swear by all that's holy, I will.

Simon Crull examined her as minutely as he did his necklaces and finger rings, as if calculating her worth. He ran his hands along her shoulders, her arms, her torso and down her thighs to her ankles, judging the size of her waist and breasts, the flatness of her stomach. Margery forced her expression to remain impassive, but she could not still her mind. *This is the worst moment of my life.* She heard Crull's labored breathing above the crackling flames, beyond the listening walls.

"I picked well. Gisla had drooping breasts and a stomach bloated as the udder of a milk cow. I despised her body."

Beads of sweat had formed on Crull's forehead. From lust or had the potion finally taken effect? He reached out, seemingly to touch her breasts, but abruptly stepped back and collapsed on his stool. As if trying to rid himself of some invisible irritation, Simon passed his hand across his forehead.

Suddenly he bolted for the garderobe.

"Get in bed and wait for me," he ordered before pushing back the tapestry and disappearing inside.

Scooping up her goblet, Margery hurried to the open window and tossed its contents. If Crull later thought to question the potion's contents, she could counter that she had drunk hers without effect.

Then she approached the marriage bed.

Jesu! I canna do this.

Margery could not bear to reach out, to test the feather mattresses for softness, to scoop up the rose petals scattered between the finely fashioned linen sheets and tear them apart in order to release their fragrance.

"I hate you, Matthew Hart," she whispered.

How could he have so betrayed her? How could she endure another man's touch, another man's lips when she had so loved curling her fingers in the hair at the nape of his neck; loved trailing kisses along his chest, following the line of his stomach down to his groin, stroking and teasing him until he moaned with delight; loved Matthew's soft sigh each time he entered her, as if he'd finally come home and there was no place in the world he would ever find so welcoming...

Slipping into the impossibly narrow bed, Margery pulled the covers to her chin. Soon Simon Crull would settle beside her and there would be no way she could make herself small enough to keep her flesh from touching his.

If only I could fade away like the curfew bell until I am no more than an echo drifting through the darkness...

Her husband finally emerged from the privy chamber. Though his color was unnaturally pale, he appeared recovered.

Margery felt faint.

After undressing, Simon blew out the large candle beside the bed, replacing it with a small night light. Before turning away, she glimpsed his hairless chest and legs, sagging belly and buttocks and withered arms. Bile burned her throat.

Crull drew back the counterpane and top sheet so that her entire body lay exposed before him.

Margery kept her head turned.

I am going to be sick.

Another memory of Matthew, "My sweet Meg, let me love thee." Eyes dark with desire, that look that nearly drove her mad with her own answering lust; his hands cupping her breasts, that slight smile playing on his mouth as he leaned forward to kiss each nipple...

Simon stretched out, his weight sinking her toward him, causing their legs to touch. His skin was as smooth and soft as the scattered rose petals. Margery jerked away.

"Look at me," Crull commanded.

Margery shook her head. She could not bear his smell—of capon grease and rose soap; the iris of his perfume, the primrose he chewed to relieve the pain from his rotting teeth.

Crull grabbed her chin, jerking her face toward him.

"Listen, wife, and listen well. I mislike repeating myself. The purest love is that which is celibate, such as the Virgin Mother's and St. Joseph. The church teaches that."

Margery's eyes widened. "What are you saying? Do you think to have a chaste relationship?" Perhaps God had just granted her a boon. Some marriages were indeed kept physically pure. 'Twas not considered a shameful situation, but an honorable one.

"Just be still and listen. Gisla knew when to keep quiet. You will learn to do the same." Crull adjusted his nightcap, which had slipped back on his head. "'Tis known that some young women, if left unserviced, go mad from unfulfilled desire. 'Tis a female's greatest duty to be chaste, and if you are frustrated, you could turn to others, bringing shame upon my house."

"I would never be unfaithful. I am not interested in dalliances, I swear I am not, so—"

"Bah! Women never know their mind from one moment to the next." When she opened her mouth to deny it, he clamped his hand over it. "I will service you because it will forestall trouble. I assure you I would far rather look at you than indulge in the filthy act of copulation. But I will not neglect my duty. Understand you what I am saying?"

Margery prayed the potency part of the potion had taken effect.

"Understand, wife?"

Almost imperceptibly, she nodded.

Dispensing with foreplay, Crull climbed atop Margery. Several times he tried to penetrate her. She turned her face away, into the pillow, imagined yanking a dagger from a nearby chest and slicing off his private parts.

I would rather face execution than a lifetime of this.

Finally, without completing his mission, Simon rolled off her. "I never had this trouble with Gisla," he said in accusation.

Margery stared up at the canopy. She nearly smiled at his words. She nearly cried.

Abruptly, Crull turned to face her. "I know what is wrong."

Thinking he had figured out her ruse, Margery stiffened, awaiting a torrent of invective.

"It happens sometimes. A mature husband can be intimidated by youth and beauty and rendered incapable of performance. 'Tis a temporary condition and easily rectified."

"How so?" She could not resist adding, "Would you have me wear a mask to bed?"

"Your brain is as flawed as your body is perfect," Simon said irritably. "That would not help. I will just have to become accustomed to you. We will make another attempt later."

During the night, Simon tried several times—always in vain.

In the morning, he awakened in a foul mood. "I cannot have this. If word gets out, I will be a laughingstock."

"I would never tell."

"I couldn't trust you. Your sex never knows when to keep silent."

After performing his morning toilet, Simon ordered Margery to mix his usual potion. Sipping his drink, he studied her thoughtfully.

"I know what I am going to do," he finally said, tossing the leavings in the ashes of last night's fire. "I have not time to hope that matters improve. 'Tis imperative that I be a proper husband before your base urges drive you to others."

"I would not..."

"I am going to seek God's help in this matter," Simon said, cutting her off. "You and I, wife, are going on a pilgrimage."

CHAPTER 24

London

Matthew Hart guided his horse down Bread Street, toward the Shop of the Unicorn. In her letters, Margery had repeatedly reminded him to return at Michaelmas, but he was so eager to see her he had decided to arrive early. He was still unclear as to his beloved's reasoning. Upon his return she would be departing the goldsmith's service anyway so why would she care whether her master needed her for some wedding? But Matthew had wanted to please her.

I am as docile as any knight in a minstrel's tale, who, in order to win his lady's love, accedes to her every wish. No matter how ridiculous.

It happened so often in verse and so seldom in reality that Matthew had never even given lip service to the concept of courtly love. Yet here he was, acquiescing to Margery as if she were some exalted court lady and he her moonstruck suitor.

Truth to tell, life in Cumbria had made compliance easier. Matthew enjoyed the clean air and slower pace, the days spent hawking and hunting or just taking long rides with his father. Finally, however, not even Cumbria's charms could hold him. Once on the road, he had made the journey to London in a week's time. Now he was saddle-sore, in need of sleep, and filthy from the dust and grime of the byways, but he had not seen Margery in more than four months and that was enough. Until battle or duty called him, he would be content to live with her. Perhaps someday they could even retire to Cumbria.

Who would have believed I could so eagerly embrace domesticity, he thought, smiling to himself. But who would have thought the Black Prince, Christendom's greatest warrior, could be tamed by a twice-married cousin past her prime? *Yet 'tis so. Prince Edward's carefree days will soon be over, and he does not mind any more than I mind settling down with Meg.* They were are all growing older. War and a good woman, taken either in marriage or love, were enough for any man.

Two apprentices were working in the public area of the Shop of the Unicorn. One was seated at a table while a second, using a hammer and tongs, stretched and pulled a sheet of gold across an anvil. The shop's lone customer, an elderly matron, intently examined a display of pater-nosters.

Matthew beckoned to the apprentices.

Brian Goldman stepped forward. "Aye, my lord?"

"Would you inform Margery Watson that Lord Matthew Hart wishes to see her?"

Even without the introduction, Brian would have recognized Lord Hart from Lady Cecy's description. While she had told him to apprise her immediately of Matthew Hart's arrival, Lady Cecy had never instructed him on what to say should the knight ever actually address him. Brian nervously cleared his throat and wiped his slender fingers upon his apron. 'Twas not easy to relay bad news to such an intimi-dating figure.

"Margery…Watson is not here, sire." He glanced at Nicholas Norlong who remained bent over his painted table, copying a design of flowers. Nicholas, who normally had an easy way with customers, put down his chalk long enough to scrutinize Lord Hart.

"Where might she be?" asked the knight. "When will she be back?"

Stalling for time, Brian carefully placed the hammer and tongs beside the anvil. After swearing him to secrecy, Lady Cecy had paid him handsomely for his part in her deception. At first he had enjoyed acting as liaison. Not only was the money a godsend to an apprentice attached to a miserly master, but Brian had enjoyed causing Margery Watson mischief. She had always been an aloof one, as if she thought herself superior to the rest of the household. But now, Brian wondered whether participation in Lady Cecy's machinations may have involved more risk than he realized.

Brian cleared his throat. "I canna say, sire."

"You canna say what? Where she's gone or when she'll return?" Matthew leaned forward, unconsciously fingering the dagger at his belt. "I mislike wasting time, and you are wasting my time."

"She—"

Nicholas Norlong, mindful that the knight might make a scene and drive away business, spoke. "She and her husband went on pilgrimage, m'lord. Soon after their wedding."

Brian quickly stepped away from the bench, toward the stairway to the family quarters, in case Lord Hart thought to act out upon this news.

Matthew's eyes narrowed. "What wedding? What are you talking about?"

Ignorant of Brian's treachery or of impending danger, Nicholas Norlong continued, "She married Master Crull on Lammas Day. They have been gone on pilgrimage a month now."

Before Norlong realized what was happening, Matthew bolted through the entrance, jerked the rotund apprentice from his seat, and slammed him against a wall. The table crashed to the floor, scattering boxes, flasks, and pottery. The elderly matron screamed, dropped her paternosters and tottered out the door. Brian scurried for the stairway.

"What do you mean Margery Watson is married?" Matthew twisted Norlong's under shirt so tightly round his neck that the apprentice gasped for breath. "You'd best make sense now, or 'twill be your last moment on earth."

"'Tis so, sire. They were wed at St. John Zachary in a small ceremony, but all the banns were posted and 'twas legal. Please loosen your grip, I beg you, m'lord, for I can scarce breathe."

Matthew relaxed his hold. Slightly.

Norlong rushed on. "They left immediately on pilgrimage. Master Crull thought to go to Canterbury, but his...Dame...um...preferred visiting St. Swithin at Winchester and the holy thorn-tree at Glastonbury. What more can I say? They mean to return before All Hallow's Eve. I know naught else."

Matthew turned to Brian, cowering behind the stairway. "Is this true?"

Brian nodded. He prayed Lady Cecy never revealed their collusion or he would be a dead man.

Matthew continued to address Brian. "Who married them?"

"Father Crispin at St. John Zachary's," Brian squeaked, terrified. 'Twas easy to forget that, despite their polite manners and professed interest in the gentler arts, the sumptuously dressed knights who daily patronized the shop were trained killers.

Matthew released Nicholas Norlong so abruptly the apprentice fell to the floor. Spinning around, he strode from the shop, vaulted upon his horse, and jerked it around in the direction of St. John Zachary.

He found Father Crispin distributing alms to beggars in front of the church.

"A word with you, priest."

Although Father Crispin was in the middle of his task and already late for an appointment with his superior, the look on the knight's face brooked no argument.

Pulling him by the arm, Matthew led the priest away from the beggars. "Tell me what you know about the marriage of Margery Watson and Simon Crull."

MATTHEW RETREATED to Hart's Place in a daze. Nothing made sense. Margery married? She'd given no hint in the three letters she'd had sent. What sort of trickery was this? How could she be pregnant, as Father Crispin had intimated? If that were true, she would have had to be sleeping with Simon Crull on the heels of his departure. What game had she been playing?

Matthew tried to remember every detail of their last meeting, as if something in the conversation might explain the unexplainable. Margery had initially been reluctant to be his leman, but that was understandable. She had also mentioned the truth of her father.

Might Thomas Rendell have something to do with this?

But Thomas had been a subject soon passed over. What had happened then? He knew women did not always think logically, but what could have happened in Margery's mind to cause her to so betray him?

Matthew wished Harry were still in London, but he was with his lord, John of Gaunt, now Duke of Lancaster. Matt had no one to talk to, to help him understand what had happened.

But I must reason this out.

He dragged himself upstairs to the solar and eased his road-weary body down upon the seat in the bay window where he and Margery had shared their last moments.

Staring down at the garden, with its flowers fading into fall and its leaves carpeting the dying grass, he whispered, "How can this be? What have you done to us...to me?"

CHAPTER 25

London

On October 10, 1361, Edward of Woodstock, Prince of Wales, married Joan of Kent. The wedding ceremony took place at Windsor in the presence of the entire royal family, as well as members from England's noblest houses. Though gossips had long whispered that His Grace was unhappy with the prince's choice of bride, outwardly both King Edward and Queen Philippa appeared pleased. His Grace had already declared that he would make the Black Prince lord of Guienne and Gascony. Which meant Prince Edward and his household would soon be heading for Bordeaux, from whence the prince would govern the French provinces.

While Matthew participated in the wedding and all subsequent festivities, not even frantic activity could alleviate his unhappiness. He was relieved that they would soon set sail for Bordeaux. In a different environment, memories of Margery Watson would quickly fade. But first he had unfinished business with her. In anticipation of her return from pilgrimage, he had taken to watching the Shop of the Unicorn. As festivities intensified, his trips became less frequent, but he vowed that before leaving England he would have his say to Dame Margery. In his mind he re-enacted his revenge.

I will tell her I am glad she's married, that I never cared for her anyway. I will reduce her to weeping, if she possesses a heart, and then walk away and never give her another by-your-leave. He did not add what he'd silently vowed, that he would never again allow himself to be so vulnerable. EVER.

He even tried to convince himself 'twas a good thing, being free of one woman. He had already taken others to bed, in particular Desiderata Cecy. Easy enough to detach feeling from lovemaking; it was the difference between enjoying a banquet or settling for crumbs, but he'd never minded before. Sex was an act, a release, nothing more. He took little pleasure in it and even less in pleasing his partner. He would get over that hollowness inside, that feeling that something was missing no matter whether he was roughhousing with other members of Prince Edward's household or practicing his swordplay to pass the time, or having new armor fitted, or allowing Desiderata Cecy to service him. Life went on; he did not care.

Yet in Matthew's unguarded moments, he could not help but grieve for Margery. In the early hours when sleep remained impossible, he would think back to their first meeting, and run through his mind the subsequent years, trying to decipher what he had done to make her betray him.

I can have any woman. I do not need Dame Margery Watson, the mayor's wife. I will not waste one minute mourning her.

Yet he did. Every hour of every day, 'twas like a headache or toothache or a bruised rib that pained him each time he took a breath. A condition that the minstrels called…heartache.

Two weeks after the wedding a huge celebration was held at Edward's palace at Kennington, across the Thames from London. The banquet, as well as the wedding, was considered the year's social event. In addition to most of the royal family, all of London's dignitaries planned to attend.

Matthew entered Kennington's hall late. At sight of him, Desire disengaged from one of John of Gaunt's retainers, who had been trying to impress her with the antics of his trained monkey.

"I have been waiting for you, m'lord," Desire said, gliding up to him. "Will you sit with me tonight?"

Her gaze was as bold as any man's. No denying she was a provocative woman, and more willing in bed than most. But she had an irritating habit of wanting to talk about Margery Watson, and Matthew was not interested in her views on the subject. Particularly not tonight, when he and Harry, who had just returned to London, had had a hurried conversation about his brother's last meeting with Margery. Harry's recollection was vague, but Margery's demeanor seemed at odds with her subsequent letters. "She was in a blessed hurry for your return," Harry had said. "That much I do remember."

At that moment an obviously flustered Harry hurried up to Matthew and Desire. "This place is swarming with Londoners. Remember when Father tried to match me up with Henry Ypres' daughter, Rohesia?"

"Aye," Matt said. "Father found her wealth most attractive."

"Well, Rohesia is here tonight. She accosted me outside in the great garden and I swear she fancies she has found herself a husband. I will never forgive Father for mentioning marriage in front of her."

"What is wrong with that?" Desire slipped her arm possessively through Matthew's. "She would be a fine catch for a second son. Her family has amassed a fortune in wool."

"No wonder she so resembles a ewe," Harry muttered. Looking over his shoulder, he yelped, "Here she comes! Help! Someone! Hide me!"

Harry plunged into the crowd drifting to the benches in front of the dais where the royal family and London's most prominent citizens had already begun to take their seats.

When Rohesia Ypres charged past, Matthew commented, "Damme! She does resemble a ewe."

"What can you expect? Breeding will always tell."

"Not every woman need paint her face and dress like a stroller to be considered beautiful," Matthew countered, glancing at the dais, where Joan of Kent was already ensconced with her new husband. Matt would never understand what Edward saw in the lady Joan. While most rhapsodized her beauty—she was not called the Fair Maid of Kent for naught—Matthew considered her blonde hair unattractively brassy and her manner so studiedly coquettish as to be tiresome. Save for her wealth, he couldn't comprehend the prince's attraction to her.

Desire brushed against Matthew, and stroked his arm with her fingertips. "I know first-hand what a connoisseur of women you are. So tell me, how do you consider me, m'lord?"

"Do not hang on me so. I mislike it."

Desire smiled and obligingly removed her arm. Let Matthew Hart be irritable. In a few weeks' time she had advanced her cause further than she would have thought possible. And she expected to advance it still more before evening's end. Days ago, Brian Goldman had sent word from the Shop of the Unicorn of the Crulls' return, and of their attendance at tonight's banquet. Confronted by the reality of Margery's marriage, seeing husband and wife together on the dais should be an image Matthew would carry for years to come. And should he begin to forget, she would be at his side to remind him.

MARGERY HAD NEVER SEEN a hall so large or lovely as Kennington's. Nearly ninety feet long and fifty feet wide, it was faced with Reigate stone and decorated with brightly painted statues. A fireplace graced each wall and the floors were covered with glazed tiles, some fired with Prince Edward's arms. Several sets of the prince's tapestries, which he carried from household to household, covered the walls. Torches flickered in iron holders, in fiery wheels overhead. Laughter and conversation floated above the smoke, the sounds of lutes, flutes, and castanets, shawns and trumpets. 'Twas a dramatic change from these past two months on the road, sleeping in lice ridden beds or enduring countless hospitals where accommodations consisted of straw-covered pavement shared with dozens of unwashed pilgrims.

Margery and her husband had begun at Westminster Abbey, where

Crull had placed his waxen image before Edward the Confessor's shrine and implored the saint to cure his impotency. Then they'd left London for the hinterlands. Simon had prostrated himself before the bones of St. Swithun and Waltham's cross of black marble, and at Glastonbury, where Joseph of Arimathea had received the Holy Grail from an apparition of Jesus before travelling to Britain to found its church.

Margery no longer feared hell; these past months she'd experienced it. She had spent every hour of every day with her fussy, doddering, dithering husband and swarms of irritatingly pious pilgrims. How many times had she heard breathlessly recited tales of blind men whose sight had been restored and of withered limbs made whole; how pleas to Thomas Becket had cured one man's leprosy and how Richard, Bishop at Chichester, had enabled a mute man to speak. Margery didn't believe any of it. If praying really caused miracles, Simon Crull would have been dead their first day out.

The Crull pilgrimage had culminated at Walsingham, which boasted a bejeweled statue of the Virgin that leaked milk from its breast. Walsingham was second in popularity only to Canterbury where Thomas Becket had been murdered and where his burial chapel attracted pilgrims from Europe and beyond. In Walsingham's Virgin's Chapel, resplendent with its gold and precious stones, Simon had purchased a pardon that erased all his sins. Thus cleansed, he declared they could return to London.

Once home, Simon's virility remained an intermittent problem but Margery pretended all was well. If he could not perform his duties he might spirit her away on another pilgrimage, a terrifying prospect. She could be thankful for one change, however. At one of the cathedrals— Winchester, if memory served—a priest had helpfully suggested that instead of sleeping naked, Simon might wear a *chemise ca joule,* which was a nightshirt with a strategically placed hole designed to minimize pleasure during intercourse. While staring at Margery, the priest had speculated that perhaps Simon had angered God by taking too much pleasure in servicing his wife.

Of course Crull blamed Margery for his sexual shortcomings. After their presence had been requested at Prince Edward's Kennington Palace fête, he had said, "'Twill be our first official appearance as man and wife. I expect you to do me honor but with your common looks, 'twill be impossible."

So he'd hired a personal maid, Williamina, skilled in the art of cosmetics, to pluck Margery's eyebrows and hairline in order to widen her forehead—after the fashion of ladies—and apply charcoal to her eyes and cochineal paste to her lips. Simon instructed Williamina to dye his wife's hair a shade indistinguishable from that of a dandelion. Margery hated its color, as she hated the alien face that stared back at her when she could not ignore her reflection.

Tonight, as Margery took her place at the dais, she studied the dress of all the other ladies in the great hall and embarrassment further reddened her already artificially stained cheeks. From her gown's white marbled silk embroidered with scarlet roses to its enormously long train, Margery's clothing was forbidden to a woman of her station. Sumptuary laws, proclaimed by criers in county courts and public assemblies, detailed exact gradations of fabric, color, fur trimmings, ornaments and jewels for every rank and income level—and Margery broke them all. Only Joan of Kent was clothed more extravagantly; only Queen Philippa wore more jewels.

Wine was poured, grace said and, with a flurry of trumpets, the banquet began. Margery quickly scanned the U-shaped tables below the dais: lords and ladies more brilliant than the jewels in Simon Crull's locked box, liveried servants scurrying hither and yon. She began to relax. Among all these exalted personages, no one would give a thought to the mayor's wife, no matter what she wore.

Soon, Margery gave herself over to the meal, though she did not again let her gaze drift beyond the dais. For certes, there was enough right here to command her attention. She had never been so close to so many members of the royal family, who, according to mythology, were descended from Satan himself. Could that be true? Everyone knew the legend of the Plantagenets, of how the line's founder, Count Fulke the

Black, had returned to Anjou following a mysterious journey in which he'd found himself the world's most beautiful bride. In the fullness of time, his wife bore Fulke four perfect children. However, she had some peculiarities, chief among them being her refusal to attend mass. Which was hardly surprising. For when the count forced her to attend, the countess had screamed an unholy scream upon the priest's elevation of the host, flown into the air and disappeared out the chapel window, nevermore to be seen. Only then did Count Fulke realize that the mother of his children was not flesh and blood but Melusine, daughter of the devil.

Margery studied the king and his progeny for outward signs of evil, though she suspected the Plantagenet legend contained about as much truth as pilgrims' blatherings. Each of Edward's sons had been blessed with a comely countenance, though Prince Edward and John of Gaunt were by far the most striking. Of course, there was no mistaking England's king. Although Edward III was five decades old, 'twas obvious from his erect bearing and authoritative manner that he easily wore the cloak of power. Despite the fact that one eye had a tendency to droop and he insisted on an unfashionably long forked beard, His Grace possessed a winning smile and a charming way of cocking his head and gazing into his wife's eyes.

King Edward and Queen Philippa were seated beneath a velvet canopy. As they conversed, Philippa would sometimes reach out and pat her husband's arm in a motherly gesture. Were they commiserating on the loss of their two daughters in the latest plague? Even in the happiness of the moment, even in their obvious pleasure at Prince Edward's wedding, they must be mourning. Margery studied the queen more carefully, as if she could see her loss, but Philippa's strong pleasant face bore an unfailingly placid expression. In different circumstances Margery might have mistaken her for a burgher's wife, chatting with other matrons about the price of bread or the quality of the clothing available in Threadneedle Street.

Halfway through the first course, Margery counted fifteen dishes with more to come. Never had she seen so much food, though she found herself drinking far more than she ate. Repeatedly, her attention drifted to Edward of Woodstock and his bride. Some said that the Black Prince was thus named because of his ruthlessness toward his enemies, but seeing the soft looks he bestowed upon his bride, he looked more like a besotted teen.

A love match. Margery reached once more for the loving cup she shared with her husband. *Priests and bishops will be clucking their tongues over this one.*

From the way Edward and Joan conversed, their lingering touches, it was clear that for them the world beyond them did not exist.

'Tis the way it is with all lovers, she thought, willing herself not to remember...

A blast of trumpets announced the second course. Jongleurs wandered the hall singing or playing their instruments. Margery kept her eyes on the dais or on her folded hands.

Simon Crull leaned against her shoulder. "Eat your venison. Do not drink so much."

Margery shrugged him off. For the first time she allowed her gaze to scan the guests at the U-shaped tables on either side of the dais. How many dined in Kennington Hall? Hundreds surely, though, with their hair coverings and uniformly dazzling dress, it was hard to distinguish one from the other. But without a doubt, somewhere among the press, would be Matthew Hart. He would never miss the wedding celebration of his liege lord.

Margery's fingers grasped the stem of the loving cup so tightly her knuckles turned white. All this night she'd had to force herself to keep from searching for him. It wasn't drink that suddenly made her feel lightheaded.

Where are you? Will you be bedecked in rings and jewels and arrayed like a peacock? Who will be your dinner companion? The woman with whom you betrayed me?

Then she spotted him, as she knew she would. A pair of pages set a huge silver tray containing a roasted pig at one of the middle tables, before a lady with dark eyes and raven black hair—and Matthew Hart.

Unconsciously, Margery leaned forward. So long she had imagined this moment and how she would react. Now, she made no effort to keep from staring, as if careful scrutiny might reveal the reason for Matthew's treachery.

"If 'tis not love I feel, 'tis something fine," he had said. *He had promised he would not forsake me.*

Here amidst the noise and laughter and music, Margery felt such a sudden, aching loneliness. For once she wished she could be like her husband and revel in the outward trappings of success rather than be swallowed up by her own miseries.

The black-haired woman with the slanting eyes leaned against Matthew's shoulder and whispered in his ear. Margery saw Matt smile. It did not take a soothsayer to know they two were lovers.

So she is the one for whom you forsook me. But how had that happened, in a handful of days?

Matthew had seemed so sincere. But he'd not returned and he'd never sent one word of explanation or regret. What other conclusion could she draw but there was someone else—or that he'd simply been playing with her heart?

Margery mechanically tore a hunk of bread into smaller and smaller pieces, until they dropped like tiny blossoms into her soup. She imagined the woman's black tresses snaking across her ivory breasts as Matthew stood above her, admiring her nakedness. Conjuring a vision of their lovemaking—and she forced herself to imagine it all from beginning to end—an ache lodged in her throat until she could not swallow.

Did not I always say knights brought naught but pain? Why did I not listen to my head rather than my heart?

A ROUND of sweetened spice wine was served with wafers, fruit and cheese signaling the end of the banquet. Following a final grace and handwashing, guests awaited the removal of tables so that the formal entertainment could begin.

Desire turned to Matthew. "You must promise you'll dance with me, m'lord." She maneuvered him toward the minstrel's gallery where she'd seen Margery Watson standing with her husband.

"Ask Harry. You know I am the worst dancer at court. Lady Joan threatened to have me banished from the floor."

"Harry is as poor a dancer as you. Only he thinks he's good, which makes him even worse."

Matthew stopped to speak to another member of Prince Edward's retinue. Outwardly curbing her impatience, Desire waited. She could not believe her lover's obtuseness. Despite Margery Watson's changed appearance, Desire had recognized her hours ago. And the goldsmith's wife had certainly spotted *them*. If the creature's mouth had gaped open any wider she could have trapped a bird.

So, here they were, everyone together. Time to manipulate a meeting of the former sweethearts in order to facilitate a final confrontation.

"My lord, to whom is the Duke of Lancaster speaking? Over there." John of Gaunt was exchanging pleasantries with Crull and his wife.

Matthew glanced in the direction of Desire's pointing finger before shrugging and returning to his conversation.

It was a puzzle how someone so remarkably inattentive could even survive one pass in battle. Desire tugged at Matthew's arm, but quickly released her grip when he fixed her with a warning look. Not for the first time did Desire think that the phantom lover of her imaginings was falling far short in reality. For one thing, Matthew Hart had absolutely no fashion sense. While the other lords strutted about in tight fitting cotehardies and breeches, Matt wore a long, shapeless over gown which effectively hid the one thing that did surpass her fantasies —the finest body she'd ever bedded. And, not only was he sullen and morose, his lovemaking was half-hearted, as if he were somewhere else—or *wished* he were somewhere else.

At that moment, Harry Hart appeared. "There's a cockfight near the stables, brother. Would you like to attend?"

Desire had had enough. "Do you know that woman, m'lord?" she said, addressing Matthew. "She keeps staring at you."

Once Matthew recognized Margery—if he ever would—he would feel even more betrayed. A new appearance, a rich husband, an exalted position. Tonight might also be a propitious moment for Simon Crull to become cognizant of his wife's fornication. Immediately following the wedding Desire had planned to contact the goldsmith and give him all of Matthew's intercepted letters plus her version of events, but had been thwarted by the pilgrimage. Once Mayor Crull understood that he'd been cuckolded, he would keep the pair separated without help from her.

Following Desire's pointing finger, both Matthew and Harry studied Margery.

Matt shook his head. "Nay, I've never seen her."

Harry said, "She looks familiar though I can't place her."

Desire sighed inwardly. "Are you certain? Look closely. Please."

Matthew noted that the woman's clothes were of the finest quality, and fitted her form to perfection. The low cut bodice revealed enticing breasts. Her hair, caught on either side of her ears in a caul, was a brassy yellow; her face, 'neath artfully supplied makeup, was hauntingly seductive.

The woman raised her gaze to look directly into Matthew's eyes. Something clicked.

"God's blood!" he whispered. "Meg?"

Forgetting Desire and Harry, Mathew jostled aside several couples in order to reach her. Margery made no effort to move, but rather deliberately positioned herself so that her back was to him.

Matthew jerked her around. "What have you done to yourself? Look at you. Is that why you married that goldsmith? So you could look like a Flemish whore?" Mindful of others, of creating a scene, he kept his voice low.

"Get away from me." Seeing him with another woman, seeing the anger in his eyes—as if he dared!—Margery understood how easy it would be to commit the sin of murder.

Crull and another alderman had their heads bent in intense conversation, something about the price of wool, a safe distance away but Margery had enough presence of mind to refrain from creating a public disturbance. Rather she shook off Matthew's grip and strode away in the opposite direction, thinking to hide in one of the alcoves or plead sickness or commandeer a carriage to return her to the Shop.

"We are going to talk." Matthew said, catching up to her. "You *will* explain your treachery."

"You are a fine one to speak of treachery." Aye, if she had a dagger she'd bury it in Matthew Hart's gullet.

"'Twill be easier to forget you now. I remember a far different Margery Watson. But that was probably a chimera as well. 'Tis obvious I never knew you at all."

Margery's heart pounded so loudly in her ears she could scarce hear his traitorous words. "I trusted you. You promised you would not forsake me, but you did. 'Tis you who are to blame for my marriage, as you well know, so do not play the part of wounded lover with me."

Matthew was aware of a lull in surrounding conversation, of curious stares. He drew her to him as if they were sweethearts and said against her ear, "Why DID you wed him? Did you think to have me until his wife conveniently died and he offered you marriage? Did you have so little faith in me that you thought to grab a certainty rather than a promise? Or was it because you were sleeping with him all along, and were pregnant with his child?"

Margery's vision went dark. Mindless of impropriety, she tried to smash her fist against his chest, though he caught her arm in mid-air.

"How could you speak such blasphemy? Do you think I would willingly go to bed with Simon Crull? How could you have had so little faith in me?"

"Quiet, Meg, unless you seek to draw as much attention with your manners as your dress." He kept his hand around her wrist and pulled her as close as if they were indeed lovers, or he was about to draw her to the floor for dancing, which had begun.

"Where were you? Why did you not come? I prayed so hard you would…"

Around them couples were departing the sidelines for the middle of the hall where Prince Edward and his bride were leading the carol.

"I have loved all this past year

So that I may love no more," sang the dancers as they sedately circled.

"I still cannot believe you'd marry him." Matthew's breath was hot against her, maddening her in its dangerous softness. As if he were whispering endearments rather than words of betrayal. "I was so eager to care for you I couldn't wait to see you, and then I find out you're married and I'm left looking like some lovesick fool."

"Spare me your false indignation. You know the only reason I married Crull was because you did not return for me—"

"But I did. I followed your instructions even when I did not agree with them. You told me not to return until Michaelmas—"

"Liar! You promised you'd return immediately and I believed you. Up until the moment I said my vows. Is your dinner companion the reason you stayed in Cumbria? Do you desire her that much?"

"I have sighed many a sigh,

Beloved, for thy pity."

Matthew drew back. "What are you talking about? I was in Cumbria with my family. I waited to return just as you wrote me."

"While I cannot read and write I trust Lammas and Michaelmas do not look anything similar upon the parchment."

"Sweet loved-one, think on me

I have loved thee long."

Matthew frowned and Margery fancied she saw confusion in his expression. He was acting far more wronged than guilty, which merely proved he was an adept fabulist.

"I told you I would not forsake you and I did not," Matthew said. "You are the one—"

"What are you doing?" Simon Crull scurried up to them, trailed by Desire and Harry. "Who do you think you are?" he said, addressing Matthew. "Why are you speaking so intimately to my wife? Get away from her, or I will have you arrested."

Matthew stepped in Simon's path. "Really, goldsmith. You'd think to threaten me?"

Crull shrank back, his bravado deflated. "Do not address me so rudely. I am mayor—"

"Come away, brother." Harry put a restraining hand on Matthew's arm. "Do not publicly disrespect your prince."

Matthew's fists clenched as though he would hit Crull.

"You and I will talk this through in private," Harry soothed, with a glance at Desire, who was watching the unfolding events with an enigmatic smile. "Dame...Margery, 'tis a pleasure to see you again," he added, ever mindful of his manners. "Now come along, brother."

Finally, Matthew's stance relaxed and he nodded to Harry. "You are right, of course. I would not dishonor Prince Edward's evening or our family name by creating scandal."

Regaining a measure of courage, Simon called to Matthew's retreating back, "I am warning you. Leave my wife alone."

Matthew spun around so quickly that Crull jumped back and held his hands up as if fearing a blow.

Harry looped an arm around his brother's shoulder. "Remember," he whispered in Matthew's ear, pushing him toward one of the side doors.

With one last withering glance at Margery, who stood still as a statue in her ill-considered finery, Matthew addressed Crull. "Do not fear for your wife. I assure you I no longer want her."

"WHAT IS WRONG?" Margery asked her husband. After talking to the black-haired woman, Simon had sent her home from Kennington alone. How long had he been absent? Trying to decipher Matthew's words, sort through their conversation, Margery had been grateful for the solitude, where she could suffer in peace. But now, as Simon stood before her, 'twas apparent by his expression that he was rattled.

"Lord Hart did not do something else, did he?"

Simon's inhaled sharply, as if struggling for control. "There are two kinds of women," he finally said. "The one who is immaculate, like the Virgin Mary—sweet mother and wife. Or there is the other." A jaw muscle twitched. "Glittering mud, stinking rose, sweet venom," he hissed. "Adulteress, lustful and treacherous, like Eve. Is that what you are, Margery Watson?"

Margery removed her head covering and freed her hair. How late was it? She should have been in bed and asleep by now but she'd been so caught up in trying to puzzle through hers and Matthew's confrontation…Her wits were dulled so that she was slow in considering the implications behind Crull's question. Matthew must have informed his mistress about their affair, and she in turn had most likely passed that information along to Simon.

So be it. I won't condemn myself by admitting to anything.

"You and Lord Hart's mistress must have had a very interesting conversation. Is that what you discussed, the types of women? Did she tell you which category she falls into?"

Simon poured himself some wine and stared into it, as if uncertain what to do next.

"Aye, Lady Cecy and I…She confessed she wishes to wed Matthew Hart, but he is enamored of someone else." Simon's voice shook as he asked, "Do you know who that someone might be?"

"Nay, I do not."

It cannot be me. This makes no sense.

"I do not know what you and this Lady Cecy discussed, but I assure you, if she is accusing me of improper acts, I am innocent." Matthew had intimated that he wasn't in love with Lady Cecy, but Margery had noted the way she had looked at him. Might he have been telling the truth—about that at least? But how would Lady Cecy know so much about their relationship unless Matthew confided in her? The woman could be bluffing, which meant Simon knew nothing at all.

Simon finished his wine. "Thomas Aquinas said woman is defective and misbegotten. He is a saint. Think you he tells the truth?"

"Aquinas also said that a wife is to be submissive to her husband, which I am. What more do you require?"

Simon blurted, "You would not be so stupid as to cuckold me, would you?"

Margery's eyes widened. "What are you talking about? What did that creature tell you?"

Simon grabbed a handful of Margery's hair, forcing her to him. "Matthew Hart is everything I most despise. He thinks because he is attached to the prince, and young and pleasing to the eye, he can do exactly as he pleases. He may be descended from the Conqueror himself and hero of a thousand battles, but he has not the brains God gave a goose, or the talent to do anything save cause mischief." Simon thrust his face close to hers. "Do you understand what I am saying?"

"Nay. You speak in riddles."

Simon released her, and began pacing as he pondered his next move. Lady Cecy had taken him to her residence and shown him Hart's letters. He had been stunned. Margery had shown so little interest in men he had assumed her to be a virgin, despite no evidence on their marriage sheets. The contents of Matthew Hart's letters had revealed that not only was Margery experienced, but she had consented to be his leman. Hart had come to his shop months ago, asking for Margery, but Simon would never have imagined they were lovers. How could he have been so blind? How much did others know? Were they even now laughing behind their hands at that old fool, Simon Crull?

I will not allow it. I am smarter than the both of them. By the rood, Matthew Hart's destrier is smarter than the both of them.

Simon paused in front of Margery. "Listen, wife, and listen well. I know that you and that knight were lovers. The thought angers me so I canna think, and you will stay away from him, do you understand? 'Twould be an intolerable affront to my honor."

So Lady Cecy did know about their affair. How had she found out? Had Matthew confessed to her, or had she uncovered the truth some other way? How? Might Harry have told?

"I am not admitting to a relationship with Lord Hart," she responded carefully, "but I do understand what you are telling me."

"Matthew Hart is naught compared to me. He was born into wealth and privilege while I started out with nothing, and look at me now. I am the most important man in London! As far as I am concerned, he is less than the garbage I throw to my dogs." Satisfied that he had made his point, Crull removed his chaperon and boots and began readying for bed.

Margery rubbed the back of her neck which hurt from Simon's brutality, and raised her hands to her throbbing temples. Her headache had returned with such intensity even the firelight pained her eyes. She sank down on the stool, and leaned back so that she could rest against the wall.

Somehow, I will reason through tonight's events. Given enough time, I will make sense of both Simon's words and actions...and Matthew's.

CHAPTER 26

London, 1362

When was it that Thurold Watson returned to London? As her altercation with Matthew Hart receded and her duties as Dame Margery Watson occupied her waking hours, time had a way of slipping along like the Thames. All Hallow's Eve, Twelfth Night, St. Valentine's Day, all passed with the usual festivities and duties. It was nearing Easter when Thurold arrived at the Shop of the Unicorn, following a lucrative campaign of raiding and looting under the command of John Hawkwood and his multi-national White Company, so named because of the white cloaks they wore. Once France had been picked bare on the heels of Edward III's disastrous Rheims campaign, Thurold, who confessed he transferred his allegiance as easily as his wage bills, had become a mercenary. After saving enough coin to purchase a comfortable cottage, he had planned to fulfill his long-ago promise to Margery. They would settle down in some quiet village outside of London, at least until restlessness once more overtook him or John Ball beckoned. Regardless, Margery would be cared for.

Such was not to be. Never could Thurold have imagined Margery's change in circumstance. And he blamed himself.

"I may have kept me word, but 'twas too late, just like during the plague," he lamented. "It seems 'tis a bad 'abit I 'ave. Too little, too late."

"'Twas not your fault. Events just…I had no choice but to marry…" She fumbled to a stop before declaring with vehemence, "How I hate being married to him. I hate everything about our life together. I hate sharing a bed with him, and being mayor's wife and having to appear in public together. I hate dining with lords and ladies and watching Crull puff up like a toad over his position. He is beginning construction on a mansion that will rival the wealthiest lords', and spins grand tales of the noblemen and women we'll entertain and the lavish feasts we'll give. I despise the very thought of it."

"First, explain to me exactly how all this came to be. What did you mean when you said you had no choice but to marry Crull?"

Carefully choosing her words so as to circumvent any mention of Matthew Hart, she said, "Crull said I was not free. He said he would throw me in prison if I did not agree. He was an alderman at the time, and knows the law."

"What law? Ye be as free as he is. I know that truth better than any man. Aside from the issue of your parentage, anyone that lives undetected in London a year and a day be free. No exceptions."

"He showed me the paper." Margery's voice cracked.

"What paper? Did ye take it to someone to read?"

Margery shook her head. "Simon told me what it said."

"There be no such law!" Thurold grabbed her by the shoulders. "The whoreson tricked you, can't ye see? God's bones, but how could ye've been so gullible?"

Taking her by the arm, he steered her away from the Shop, into busy London streets. "Come along, Stick-legs. I know someone who can 'elp us sort through your mess."

JOHN BALL DOMINATED the common room in Blossom Inn, located in the Cheap near Bread Street, not only because of his great size, but because he was surrounded by empty benches. As usual, the inn's other customers shunned him, but Margery was so pleased to see him she injudiciously threw her arms around him. John responded with a delighted laugh and when his eyes swept her, she saw no disapproval at the inappropriate clothes, the dyed hair, the plucked forehead and makeup, for which she was grateful.

After Thurold explained the situation, John Ball sipped his ale and peered into the distance, as if her answers might be written there.

"Annulments are sometimes granted," he said slowly, "but 'tis rare. Bigamy must be proved, or consanguinity. Non-consummation after a reasonable period of time is sometimes accepted by the courts."

"Non-consummation?' Margery considered this.

"Aye. But both husband and wife must be examined. Seven honest women are appointed to confirm the wife's virginity and seven honest men to verify the husband's impotence. It can be a humiliating process."

And since I am not a virgin, 'twill not do.

She appreciated John's frankness, as well as his refusal to lecture her on the indissolubility of marriage, or her sinful nature for refusing to gracefully accept her plight. "Continue. How else might I be rid of him?"

"Separation is not a rare thing, by any means. Informal ones often occur without court ruling. But then your husband would have to consent to separation, and it does not seem that he would."

Margery shook her head.

"You could take your grievance to church court. They often arrange formal separations, short of divorce—separations from bed and board, they are called."

"On what grounds might a separation be granted?"

"Cruelty, adultery, impotence, even incompatibility." John smiled slightly. "Simon would not happen to be a heretic or a leper, would he?"

"Nay, but I can prove cruelty, and impotence, I believe. And we are most incompatible."

"What mean ye by cruelty?" Thurold asked, his voice sharp.

John shook his head in a warning fashion. "Tell me, Margery, exactly what you mean."

"He hits me often." Margery heard Thurold's sharp inhalation of breath.

"Has he ever beaten you senseless or raped you?"

"Nay."

"'Tis not good enough. The law is very specific. A husband is allowed to beat his wife, injure her, slash her body from head to foot, and warm his feet in her blood. If he succeeds in nursing her back to health afterward, he will still remain within the law."

Margery was beginning to understand that laws were not designed to favor women. But why should that be a surprise? "Mayhap 'twould be easier to prove impotency. I will have to give these matters some thought. Will you be in London awhile?"

"Aye. Just ask your brother." John Ball studied her with his keen brown eyes. She remembered that gaze, that kindness from so long ago, when they'd left Ravennesfield. If only she had been able to find John Ball before Simon had tricked her. He would have set her life to rights.

John reared back on the bench, studying her. "You have told us that being married makes you unhappy, daughter," he said. "Know you what would make you happy?"

Margery thought fleetingly of Matthew. She shrugged. "No one has ever said that life should be happy. 'Tis basically sad, filled with tears, betrayal and death."

"Death is not sadness, Margery. Jesus loves the poor and humble. He will welcome them into heaven."

"So you priests say, but I do not believe it. If He loves us why does He allow such suffering? Why did he send the Great Plague? Why did He destroy so many innocent people and leave so many evil ones to prosper?"

"But the first plague, at least, was not a time of sadness for us. God's hand was in it, for the good of His children. Until the lords and those in power undid His handiwork."

Margery knew all about that. Her mind drifted as John spoke—of how so many teachers who taught French had died and been replaced by those who spoke only the native tongue so that children were now taught in English, the language of the common folk. Since learned men had died, new colleges had been founded to train more scholars and some like John Ball questioned the rightness to certain matters. The shortages of labor had caused landlords to begin competing for tenants and laborers, so better terms were offered. Not only had she heard it from John and Thurold, but from her husband, though Simon spoke of such changes with contempt and even a measure of fear.

"We were hopeful for a time," said John Ball. "But increasingly the poor face destitution. Any money left over from their labors is spent as soon as it is received to pay for increasing rents or food to fill their children's bellies. After the plague there was hope. Now our king is growing old and indifferent. We are taxed to finance endless wars in foreign lands."

Margery remembered seeing Edward III at Kennington. He did not seem old; perhaps indifferent for what would he know of the plight of the poor other than occasional forays into London's streets or through towns and villages? And John's portrayal of the poor certainly did not match her husband's assessment. Crull declared that since the Death people had become lazy and would not work, that peasants demanded better food and dress than their masters. They had once been content with bread of corn or beans, but now they wanted wheaten. And where they'd considered cheese and milk a feast and their garments of hodden grey adequate, they now wandered the land, seeking mischief, preferring begging to working.

Margery massaged her temples. Her headache had returned. She needed help with her personal affairs, but she could not fault John Ball —or Thurold—for not conjuring a way out of her dilemma. With so much wrong in England what did her petty concerns matter?

"I fear 'twill always be the natural order of things," she said when the hedge priest fell silent. "And what can be done when no one wants to be reminded? 'Tis all so complicated..."

"'Tis as simple as the rising and setting of the sun," Thurold interrupted. "'Tis called injustice, and this country stinks of it. "

"And I am merely the sower," John Ball said, "casting his seeds upon the soil. Some will take hold and spring up."

"And if the ground is completely barren?" Margery asked.

John shrugged and smiled a smile of sadness. "I must try all the same."

CHAPTER 27

London

argery Watson lay in bed, her husband's snores disturbing the night's quiet. She ran over her conversation with John Ball and Thurold. She thought of her last puzzling conversation with the Traitor and his brother at Edward the Black Prince's wedding celebration. She remembered her marriage night. She contemplated her mother and Thomas Rendell and the sickening parallels between her and the Traitor, just as she'd always known.

She thought of a thousand and one different things.

I am a woman now. Margery stared into the darkness, softened only by the dying embers from the hearth fire. *I will put aside childish things.*

Never again would she think about *him.* Or mourn him.

God has given me this life, whether I wish it or no.

And I will make the best of it.

DESPITE THE LATE HOUR, Matthew Hart remained wide awake. Along with his prince he would soon be bound for Bordeaux. Who knew when he might return to England?

Never, I hope.

Beside him, Desiderata Cecy's breathing was deep and measured. She never seemed to have any trouble sleeping when long into the night Matthew's mind careened like a wayward horse. He would force his thoughts to pleasant matters—a conversation with his father or Harry; a particularly tricky bit of sword play; a satisfying workout with his favorite destrier; Prince Edward's face at Poitiers when he said, "Come, Matthew, you will be first,"; the beauty of the lightning storm during the Rheims campaign; his recent visit with his sister, Elizabeth, and her rambunctious brood of boys.

What he could not, would not think of was Margery Watson. Of her betrayal. Or of their last meeting. Or of anything else to do with her.

I do not care.

He would embrace his future. Surely, war in France would soon break out again. If not, perhaps Italy. Or there was always a crusade upon which he could embark. His king or prince or *someone* would be in need of a stout sword arm and proven martial skills, both of which he possessed in abundance.

Life, Matthew assured himself, *will be better than ever.*

Now that he was forever free of Dame Margery Watson, wife to Simon Crull.

The End

WITHIN A FOREST DARK

THE KNIGHTS OF ENGLAND SERIES,
BOOK THREE

Along with nearly six thousand men at arms, Matthew Hart entered the white walled outskirts of Bordeaux as part of Edward the Black Prince's conquering army. Matthew's father, William, rode beside him. Ahead, among the pennon of St. George and countless other standards, Matthew spotted their lord, Prince Edward, flanked by John Chandos, his ever present advisor. The prince's right hand was solemnly raised in acknowledgement of the cheers of the Bordelais, who thronged the narrow streets leading to the cathedral of St. Andre. Since his appointment as duke of Aquitaine, Edward of Woodstock had been a popular ruler, and was now returning from a successful campaign in which he had furthered the cause of Pedro the Cruel, the legitimate king of Castile. From balconies, voluptuous beauties showered petals onto their returning heroes. Others ran forward to kiss them and thrust flowers into their hands.

A particularly persistent maid clung to Matthew's stirrup, and he swept her up to plant a kiss on her lips.

Matthew caught his father's eye. William Hart, earl of Cumbria, grinned in response for he was enjoying himself as much as his son. Friendly faces and the adulation of pretty women went far to ease the unpleasantness of war.

"A year away does not seem to have diminished our popularity," Matthew observed. Though often a contrary, independent lot, the Gascon people were friendly as stray pups to their English rulers. Gascon wine, exported by the millions of liters to England, was exempt from taxes, thus greatly enriching local coffers. As duke of Aquitaine, a title dating back to the illustrious days of Eleanor of Aquitaine, Prince Edward also ruled his subjects with an easy hand, though many of the nobles, fearful of their feudal rights, were far more quarrelsome than ordinary citizens.

William successfully dodged a woman bent on wrestling him from his saddle. "Christ's Cross!" he laughed, shaking his head. "We were safer on the plains of Najera than facing such enthusiasm!"

The current campaign, which had begun in October of 1366, had taken the English over the Pyrenees. They had crossed the rugged Pass of Roncesvalles in the dead of winter. A treacherous tapestry of snow had covered the mountains, which also contained deep gorges and brutal winds capable of whipping up blinding snow. Beyond had been Navarre, an ungodly bleak country.

Near the town of Najera, the English had finally encountered their enemy, Henry of Trastamare, heading an army of thirty thousand. Prince Edward had sworn to champion Trastamare's rival, Pedro the Cruel—a diabolical man who had murdered Trastamare's mother. Though the Black Prince was personally repelled by him, Don Pedro was a lawful king, as well as the son of a king. If Trastamare's usurpation remained unrectified, Prince Edward believed the security of all rightful rulers would be jeopardized. Therefore, he had no choice but to champion the tyrant.

Edward and his troops had faced the greatly superior Spanish force and triumphed—just as they had in 1356 against the French at the fabled Battle of Poitiers. Used to fighting the undisciplined Moors, Henry Trastamare's men had been unnerved by the English, who would neither yield nor flee. Though the largely peasant force had used their slingshots to deadly effect, they had ultimately panicked. The English and their Black Prince had seemed to the Castilians not real flesh and blood, but creatures out of myth, like their el Cid.

Few desired to lose their lives to a legend.

The gilt spire of St. Andre glittered like an enormous topaz. Matthew wiped rivulets of sweat from his forehead. Even though it was September, the heat blasted him with the force of a blacksmith's bellows. The white buildings with their red roofs shimmered before his eyes, as did the garish greens, crimsons, and yellows of Bordeaux's abundant foliage. Trapped inside his armor, Matt felt like a scalded lobster. Saints be praised he'd not been knocked low by the epidemics which had debilitated so many, or he'd not have the strength to complete the ride. Dysentery, along with malaria, had greatly dissipated the English ranks throughout the campaign's final stages.

Prince Edward had been among those bothered by the sickness, but Matthew was certain he'd been more stricken by the treachery of Don Pedro, who had proven an unreliable friend, just as Edward and his advisors had feared. Though Prince Edward had regained Pedro the Cruel his throne, Don Pedro had reneged on his promise to pay certain lands and treasure, as well as three million gold florins to Edward's army. In response the Black Prince had allowed his soldiers to extract their wages from the countryside, but the pickings had proven desultory.

"I understand the sword," Prince Edward had lamented at the time. "Victory belongs to him who is strongest and most skilled. In war I can look my enemy in the eye, and victory or defeat will be clean and immediate. But this political intrigue mystifies me. 'Tis for clerks and prelates and Spaniards and devious Frenchmen who exercise naught but their minds."

WITHIN A FOREST DARK
Available in eBook and Paperback

ALSO BY MARY ELLEN JOHNSON

The Knights of England Series

The Lion and the Leopard

A Knight There Was

Within A Forest Dark

A Child Upon the Throne

Lords Among the Ruins

ABOUT THE AUTHOR

Mary Ellen Johnson's writing career was sparked by her passion for Medieval England. Her first novel, *The Lion and the Leopard*, which took place during the doomed reign of Edward II, was followed by *The Landlord's Black-Eyed Daughter*, a historical novel based on the Alfred Noyes poem, "The Highwayman." (Published under the pseudonym, Mary Ellen Dennis.) *Landlord* was chosen as one of the top 100 historical romances of 2013.

In 1992, Mary Ellen's life took a 20 year detour when she became involved in a local murder. Later she championed the fifteen-year-old, Jacob Ind, who killed his abusive parents and chronicled that event in *The Murder of Jacob*. As the Executive Director of the Pendulum Foundation, a non-profit that serves kids serving life in prison, she has been featured in *Rolling Stone*, on the documentaries, PBS Frontline's *When Kids Get Life* and *Lost for Life*, as well as countless radio, TV and print outlets around the world.

As Mary Ellen's goal of sentencing reform nears its successful completion, she has happily returned her attention to her first love, novel writing, and her favorite time period. Her five book series, *Knights of England*, will follow the fortunes of the characters (and their progeny) introduced in *The Lion and the Leopard* through the

Black Death, the reign of that most gloriously medieval of monarchs, Edward III, the Peasants Revolt of 1381 (with issues of class and inequality that remain relevant) and ending with the tragic death—or was it murder??—of Richard II. A tumultuous and exciting century as seen through the eyes of characters, both historical and fictional, who Mary Ellen hopes you will find as engaging, frustrating, complex and unforgettable as she does!

www.MaryEllenJohnsonAuthor.com

 facebook.com/mejauthor